HEART OF A COWBOY

BY

SUSAN PAGE DAVIS
MIRALEE FERRELL
YVONNE LEHMAN
VICKIE McDONOUGH

Heart of a Cowboy
Published by Mountain Brook Ink
White Salmon, WA U.S.A.

ISBN 978-1-943959-02-0

The Team: Miralee Ferrell, Susan Marlow, Cindy Jackson, and various proofreaders
Cover Design: Vickie McDonough

Mountain Brook Ink is an inspirational publisher offering fiction you can believe in.

Printed in the U.S.A. 2016

CONTENTS

HEARTS IN PURSUIT

BY SUSAN PAGE DAVIS

Susan Page Davis

CHAPTER ONE

Southern Texas, August, 1880

"I THINK PABLO'S SCARED."

"Hold still." Abigail Bunter ran her hand through her younger brother's shaggy, pale locks and measured their length between her fingers. She clipped off an inch and scooped up another handful of hair. Charlie's hair grew so fast, it was all she and her mother could do to keep it shorn to an acceptable length. Next thing you knew, he'd look like one of the old-time buffalo hunters Papa told about.

"What are you talking about, anyway?" she asked as tufts of blond hair fell to the floor.

Charlie was only seven, and Pablo Hardy, the son of rancher Ike Hardy to the north of them, was a friend he saw only now and then, when the ranchers had cause to gather. What on earth would Charlie know about Pablo's fears?

"Last Sunday, he told me his Grandfather Hernandez wants him to go live with him in Mexico."

"And Pablo doesn't want to go?"

Charlie shook his head vigorously.

"Hold still. You don't want me to stab you by accident, do you?"

Charlie froze on the stool. She began clipping again, and he shivered as one scissor blade rested for a moment on his skull.

"Don't hurt me, Abby."

"I won't, if you'll quit wiggling."

Twelve-year-old Cynthia, who was peeling potatoes at the table, said matter-of-factly, "Boys always wiggle."

"I'm sure Pablo's pa will keep him here," Abby said to her little brother. Pablo was the only boy close to Charlie's age living within ten miles of their ranch. She could understand Charlie not wanting to lose his friend. "Mr. Hardy loves Pablo very much, and he wouldn't want him to go live in Mexico."

"I hope he stays." Charlie still sounded fretful.

From outside, Abby heard a shout. She thought it was her father's voice, but she wasn't certain. Then hoofbeats drummed swiftly closer, and her mother replied, louder, "What is it? What's happened?"

Abby and Cynthia stared at each other, and Charlie squirmed around to look up at Abby, his mouth hanging open in surprise.

"You two stay here." Abby plunked the scissors on the table and dashed out the door.

Her mother stood at the clothesline with a dry petticoat she had taken down flapping in her hands as she gazed toward the approaching horse. Papa's bay mare galloped toward them, with him leaning low over the saddle.

The mare stopped abruptly just before the doorstep, and Papa slewed to the off side and slid out of the saddle, landing sprawled in the dirt. Ma let out a little cry and ran toward him, still carrying the petticoat. The mare shied and sidestepped, then stood snorting, her sides heaving.

Abby reached Papa first. She went to her knees on the path and touched his shoulder. He moaned and looked up at her, clutching a hand to his side. Beneath his fingers, blood soaked his shirt.

"Papa! What happened?"

"Shot." He grimaced.

Ma plummeted down on his other side "Charles! Dear Lord, save us all!"

"He says he's shot," Abby said.

Ma crumpled her best petticoat and pushed it against the bloody shirt.

"Charles! Who did this?"

"Ellen. They've got Ellen."

Abby and Ma stared at him in shocked silence for an instant.

"Ellen?" Ma said. "No! Where is she?"

"Gone." Papa closed his eyes.

"Ma . . ." Abby's stomach churned. Ellen was only fourteen,

five years younger than Abby. What horror was she going through?

Her ears registered more hoofbeats, and she stood and looked northward. A haze of dust rose where the road disappeared over a rise in the prairie. "Riders, Ma. A lot of them."

"Get the rifle off his horse." Ma looked toward the door, where Charlie and Cynthia stood gaping down at Papa's prone form. "Cynthia, come help me. We need to get him inside."

Abby lifted her skirts and sprinted to her father's horse. The mare gave a little squeal and sidled away. Abby stopped. She knew better than to rush up to a horse like that.

"Easy, Minnie. It's all right, girl." She took baby steps, and the mare let her approach and grab the trailing reins. Abby pulled her around and yanked Papa's rifle up and out of his saddle scabbard.

The hoofbeats grew louder. She pivoted, bringing the rifle up as she moved. As soon as she dropped the reins, Minnie backed away from her, bumping into the corral fence. Abby stood her ground, aiming the rifle at the approaching band of riders, wondering if the weapon was loaded. Probably not. If someone had attacked Ellen, Papa would have emptied it at them.

As the riders in broad-brimmed hats swarmed into the dooryard, she was aware of Ma and Cynthia half dragging Papa inside the house. It struck Abby that she would be left all alone out here. Before she could move toward the doorstep, one of the men shouted. It was their neighbor, Mr. Hardy. She lowered the heavy rifle. Her head swam, but she fought the sensation. This was not the time to swoon.

She made herself look at the other riders as the door to the house closed firmly. There were five of them in all. Mr. Hardy had his elder son, Sam, with him. Sam was twenty, or maybe a bit older. The other three men riding with them were Mr. Hardy's ranch hands, no doubt. They looked familiar in their plaid cotton shirts, with bright neckerchiefs and tooled saddles, but Abby couldn't put names to them.

Mr. Hardy slowed his mount to a trot and brought the pinto up close to her. "Miss Bunter, have you seen any strangers?"

Abby pulled in a deep breath and gazed up into Ike Hardy's weathered face. "Someone shot my pa, and he said they've got Ellen."

"That your sister?"

Abby nodded. "She was out with him, helping bring in some cows from the east range. Papa's hurt bad. He just rode in, but he couldn't talk much."

"Can I see him?"

"I guess so. Ma's got him inside."

Mr. Hardy swung down off his horse and let the reins trail. He walked quickly to the door and gave a peremptory knock. After a moment, Cynthia let him in. The other men let their horses graze while they waited. Sam got down and walked over to Abby. Her heartbeat had begun to slow, but it quickened again as Sam approached. He always had that effect on her lately.

"I'm sorry they got your sister. They've got Pablo, too." Sam's mouth set in a grim line.

"Why?" Abby asked. "Who was it? Surely not Indians."

"Naw, they're long gone in these parts. It's Hernandez's men. About a dozen of 'em."

"Don Hernandez?" Abby frowned at him. "Your grandfather?"

Sam's gray eyes flickered, as though she had said something painful. "Not mine. Pablo's grandfather."

"Of course. I'm sorry." Sam's real mother had died ages ago. Abby couldn't even remember her. His father had married the beautiful Mexican woman, Luisa Hernandez, when Sam was about ten. So far as Abby knew, Sam had loved his stepmother and always honored her. But she was dead now, and apparently what Charlie had said was true. Don Hernandez wanted his grandson.

"But why would they take Ellen too?"

"I expect they grabbed whatever came in their path."

"Whatever they thought they could sell, you mean," one of the cowpokes said.

"Hush," Sam said sharply, but it was too late.

"You think they'll *sell* my sister?" Horror washed over Abby. She had heard of such things, south of the border, but their home was far enough away from the Rio Grande that she hadn't supposed they needed to worry about it. "Not Ellen!"

"We're going to get Pablo back, and we'll get her too," Sam said.

Abby looked numbly at their horses. Five ranchmen against a dozen ruthless caballeros?

"We hoped your pa could ride with us," Sam added.

"He can't. He's hurt too bad."

"Do you have any men working now?"

She shook her head. "Papa said he didn't need to hire anyone until roundup." They scraped by, with Ma and the girls helping whenever he needed them. Their profit on steers last year hadn't been enough to justify hiring hands. If they had a few men, Mr. Hardy's chances of getting Ellen back would be greater.

Poor Ellen. Even if they managed a rescue, she would be terrified. Abby's sisters didn't know Mr. Hardy and Sam very well. They saw them every couple of months when the preacher came around for a church gathering. Papa saw them more often, for roundups and other ranch work where the men traded labor. Abby and Sam knew each other well enough to talk, but Ellen wouldn't feel comfortable with him. He was so much older, and she was timid around people outside the family. At least she would recognize them. But she would be all alone with these men, and she was no doubt terrorized already. She needed family close by when they rescued her. And a woman.

Abby thrust the rifle into Sam's hands. "Put that back on my pa's saddle, will you? And check his canteen." She ran into the house.

Behind her, Sam said, "What are you doing?"

Abby didn't stop to answer.

Mr. Hardy was standing near the kitchen table with Ma.

"We'll do whatever we can, ma'am. I'm sorry I can't promise anything."

"Ma," Abby cried, "get me the rest of Papa's cartridges."

"Why? What is it? Are they coming here?"

She had alarmed her mother again, and Abby said quickly, "No. Papa can't ride with Mr. Hardy, but I can. I'll be there for Ellen."

"No! You can't."

Ma's stricken face didn't stop her. Abby hurried to the small room she shared with Ellen and Cynthia and pulled an extra petticoat and a pair of stockings from the wooden crate where she kept her clothes. From the pegs on the wall, she grabbed an extra dress of Ellen's and the woolen cloak she wore in winter. It could serve her as a blanket. No time to make a bedroll, but Abby hoped they wouldn't be gone that long. She shoved the clothes into a pillowcase and pinned it shut, then hurried back to the kitchen. Mr. Hardy had gone out, leaving the door open.

Abby expected her mother to protest, but instead, she held out a box of rifle cartridges and a cloth bag.

"There's food in here for a couple of days, and extra coffee. Mr. Hardy said they didn't stop to pack."

Abby took the things. Ma held out her arms, and Abby hugged her fiercely.

"I shouldn't let you go," Ma's broken words were low in Abby's ear. Over her mother's shoulder, she saw Charlie, huddled near the cookstove, staring at her.

"I have to," Abby said. "Just like you have to stay here."

"Guess I don't need to tell you to be careful."

Abby almost laughed. "I won't take any unnecessary risks."

"Go, then. Mr. Hardy said he won't wait."

Cynthia came from her parents' bedroom and held out her father's sheathed hunting knife. "Papa says to take this and his rifle. And to come back."

Abby took it. "I will." Without another word, she strode to the door. Mr. Hardy was already in the saddle. Sam stood by Papa's mare, holding her reins.

"I filled your canteen and reloaded the rifle."

"Thanks," Abby said. She was surprised none of the men argued with her about going. Maybe they realized how important every gun was when they were so few. Quickly, she stowed her things with Sam's help.

"You keep up," Mr. Hardy said, wheeling his horse.

"Yes, sir." Abby stepped in Sam's cupped hands and threw herself onto the mare's back. If she'd had ten minutes, she could have changed into trousers. She had worn some of Papa's cut-down pants before, when he desperately needed her help on the range, but not where other men could see her. Her skirts would give away her gender from a long distance. That might be unhelpful in this pursuit. She also wished Minnie had gotten more time to rest after Papa's wild ride, but the mare seemed ready to go with the other five mounts. The family had no other riding horse except the one Ellen had ridden out on that morning, and that little chestnut was probably with Hernandez's men now.

Sam jumped onto his dun and set him into a lope, following his pa's pinto and the other three horses. They were already halfway to the dirt road. Abby gathered her reins and put her heels to Minnie's sides.

Sam kept his dun gelding up to the pace his father was setting, but he rode last in line except for Abby. He didn't want his pa or the men to think he was soft on her, but somebody had to look out for her. Why had Pa let her come, anyway? Sam could barely believe it.

When his father had come out of the small ranch house at the Bunters', Abby was still inside.

"The girl's coming with us," he'd said.

"They're lettin' her?" Franco asked, his eyes wide. Pa had hired the big, dark-haired man a year ago. He was strong, which was good when you needed extra muscle, but he wasn't an easy keeper. He ate twice what some of the men did.

"We'll have a better chance with more guns," Pa had replied. "Her father says she's a dead shot."

Sam hadn't hesitated then. He'd rummaged through Mr. Bunter's saddlebags and found half a box of cartridges for the rifle. Charles Bunter had a nice Spencer repeating rifle—if he was fit to ride, he'd be a good addition to their band. But Abby? Sam wasn't so sure. He'd never had occasion to see the girl shoot.

He reloaded the rifle as fast as he could and filled the heavy canvas water bag from the trough at the pump. The moisture would slowly seep through the canvas and evaporate, keeping the water cooler than a metal canteen would. He also found a small tinderbox in the saddlebag, and a handful of jerky. Those might come in handy for Abby too, before they were done. He made his best guess at adjusting the stirrups.

She came out of the house carrying a plump pillowcase, a hunting knife, another box of cartridges, and a small canvas bag.

Sam reached for the pillowcase. "Clothes?"

"Just a couple of things for me and Ellen." She had stashed the cartridges in the saddlebag. Sam was glad she'd brought extra ammunition. He mashed the pillowcase flatter and tied it behind her saddle. Meanwhile, she found a place somewhere in her clothing for the knife and hooked the strap of the small cloth bag over the saddle's pommel.

By the time Sam had Abby in the saddle, his pa was heading south. He jumped on Stubby and took off after him. Abby would have to keep up, because Ike Hardy wasn't one to wait around while a woman adjusted her skirts.

They stuck to the road for about seven miles. They would be within sight of the outlying buildings of Harrisville soon. Sam wondered if Don Hernandez's men had ridden boldly through town with their captives, but Pierce, who was one of their best cow punchers and a phenomenal tracker, halted them. They bunched up together near him, and Pierce pointed to the flattened dry grass off the trail.

"They left the road here. Avoiding the town, most likely." Pierce lifted his hat for a moment, letting air under it, and settled it again on his thinning brown hair. He glanced at Abby and quickly looked away, which made Sam look at Abby.

She sure had grown up. Over the past couple of years, he'd only seen her at church and his stepmother's funeral last February. Sporadic as services were, he and his father had made only three since Luisa's death. Sam hadn't paid much attention to Abby Bunter for most of his life, but he couldn't help noticing her now.

She rode astride on her pa's saddle. Her sturdy leather shoes and a few inches of gray stocking showed beneath the hem of her plaid dress on this side. The dress was faded and plain, but it was still a shade darker than her blue eyes. He recalled her hair being nearly white when she was little—like her brother Charlie's was now. Abby's tresses had mellowed into a deep, burnished gold, and they were braided and pinned up today. She wore a battered felt hat atop the braids, probably an old one of her father's. For some reason, it didn't look silly on her. It said something about her personality. She carried herself with a feminine air, and yet she was ready to ride out on a difficult errand at a moment's notice. She hadn't fussed or cried or fainted. She had grabbed a few essentials and mounted up. A Texas-bred girl. He liked that. In fact, for the past six months, he'd toyed with the thought of calling on her. That thought came again, stronger, but he pushed it away.

Pablo and Ellen first. He could think about courting later.

For the next two hours, they cut across range, mostly

jogging, skirting bunches of grazing cattle. Abby kept up, though when his pa signaled for another halt, her horse seemed to be flagging a little.

"We'll rest here a few minutes," Pa said.

A small house was visible in the fold of a hill three quarters of a mile away, with a sluggish plume of smoke rising from its chimney.

"That's the Martins' place," Pierce said. "Should we go ask if they saw anyone?"

"It would only waste time and energy," Pa said. "We know they came by here."

They dismounted and let the horses browse on the sparse vegetation. Abby didn't have hobbles for her horse, but the mare seemed content to graze near Stubby and the others. Sam took his canteen from his saddle and sauntered over to where Abby had sat down on the ground. He crouched beside her and held out the canteen.

"Thanks." She opened it and took one mouthful and handed it back.

Sam drank and stoppered the canteen. "How are you doing?"

"I'm afraid Minnie's tiring," Abby said.

Sam smiled. She hadn't answered the question, but he guessed that was like her—to think of the horse's condition more than her own.

"You didn't have a fresh horse, I guess."

"No. Ellen was riding our only other horse." She looked up at him from under the brim of her hat. "Sam, do you think they'll hurt her?"

Sam didn't like to think about it, but he put the best face on it he could. "Not yet. They're too busy getting over the border before anyone catches them."

Abby let out a ragged sigh. "But they will. Sam, she's fourteen."

"Yeah." He grimaced and looked up at the sky. The sun was high now. An hour 'til noon, maybe. "What was she doing out this morning?"

"Helping my father bring in some cows. Ellen and I both help him with things like that. This morning, she went. I didn't have time to get the whole story, but I'm guessing she and Papa were separated a little. The outlaws must have come on her alone at first and thought they had easy pickings." She scrunched up her face. "Sorry. I mean, Pablo's grandfather's men."

"No, you're right. They *are* outlaws. They became that when they crossed the river to steal my brother. And even if you call that a family squabble, snatching Ellen is definitely a crime—a serious one. They can hang for this."

Abby's lips twitched. "They could hang just for taking her horse."

"Yeah, well, we're gonna get the horse back too."

"I hope so."

She was right to be skeptical. Sam oughtn't to be promising things he couldn't guarantee. If those caballeros got over the border and into a Mexican town, they could sell Ellen within minutes. A pretty, young, blond girl—someone would give a lot for her. They'd take her to Rio Bravo, or all the way to Monterrey. Maybe even farther, so she wouldn't be easily found. And Ellen would be lost to a life of slavery and debauchery. Sam clenched his teeth. They couldn't let that happen.

At least Pablo would be treated well. Don Hernandez would kill the men if anything happened to the little boy. But Ellen Bunter? Unfortunately, Sam doubted his grandfather would care what happened to her.

CHAPTER TWO

"SO HOW DID THEY GET PABLO?" Abby asked.

Sam pulled in a deep breath, not looking at her.

"He was playing around the front of the house. Pa and I were still drinking our coffee in the kitchen. We were heading out to the range with the men as soon as we finished. Pablo was going to stay behind with Frannie. She's our housekeeper."

Abby nodded. She knew who Mrs. Pierce was, from church. By now she had figured out that the lean, fortyish man who did the tracking was her husband.

"Hernandez's men came charging in and opened fire on our hands. They dove into the barn. Franco peeked out, and he saw one of them scoop up Pablo. By then, of course Pa and I had heard the gunfire. We rushed outside, but they were already riding away."

"Were any of your men hurt?" Abby asked.

"A kid called Denny. Got him in the arm. We left him with Frannie and saddled up as quick as we could. We figured they went right by your place. That's why we stopped."

"I'm glad you did. Very glad."

Mr. Hardy, who had been reclining, pushed himself to his feet.

"Let's ride. Those Mexes don't have fresh horses either. This is our best chance to catch 'em."

Sam stood and held out a hand to help Abby up. "If we ride near a ranch or a town, Pa will try to get some fresh mounts, but he doesn't want to veer too far off the trail to do it. If Hernandez's men make a beeline for the border, so do we."

They rode for hours. Abby was used to hard work, and

some days she sat in a saddle for long periods of time, but nothing like this. One of her legs began to chafe against the stirrup leather, but she didn't dare say anything. There wasn't much she could do about it, and she didn't want to cause Mr. Hardy to regret letting her join them. Besides, as Ma had told her innumerable times, a lady should never indicate in mixed company that she had limbs beneath her skirt.

When they stopped again for a short rest, she managed to tuck one of the extra stockings she had brought between her calf and the leather. That helped some.

The sun was lowering when Franco's horse stumbled. After that he limped, and before long the big, bearded man dismounted and walked, leading the horse. Mr. Hardy's scowl deepened. Abby wondered if he would leave Franco behind, but he needed every man, and, if the truth were told, all of their horses were tired. Their coats were dark with sweat, and some had lathered around their girth straps. The poor animals were probably glad for the slower pace they adopted.

After half a mile or so at a walk, Pierce pulled up and consulted with the boss. Mr. Hardy then turned his pinto and addressed them all.

"There's a hamlet ahead—Ripton. It's not much, but Pierce says there's a saloon and a trader and a few other businesses. We might be able to get fresh mounts there." The men smiled and nodded, until Mr. Hardy continued, "That's the good part. The bad part is, Don Hernandez's men appear to be heading straight for it. Franco, I thought maybe we'd ride on ahead and see if we can make arrangements. You come in as quick as you can."

"But what if the banditos are there, boss?" Franco asked.

"We'll have to size up the situation before we show ourselves." Mr. Hardy looked at Abby. "Your mare's winded. Why don't you stay with Franco and keep pace with him? That way, if we can't get new mounts, yours will at least be taking it easy a tad longer. And if there's trouble … well, two of you together is better than one."

Abby looked at Franco, and the big man nodded. "We'll keep each other company, missy."

"A-all right." She would have to trust Mr. Hardy on this one. He must have faith in Franco, or surely he wouldn't leave his neighbor's daughter alone with him. She looked at Sam, and he gave her a quick half smile. She took that as encouragement and assurance that Franco would watch out for her.

After a few more instructions, Mr. Hardy, Sam, and the other two men loped off, leaving her alone with her mare, the big cowboy, and his limping gray. Abby hesitated and then slid to the ground.

"Might as well walk with you." She fell into step beside him, and Franco switched his reins to his other hand, so that he and Abby walked between the two horses' heads. Minnie would get the maximum rest this way, Abby told herself, in case they had to ride on without getting different horses.

Their shadows lengthened, and the heat of the day eased. The night should stay warm, since it was only the middle of August. The dust raised by the departing horses began to settle as they plodded along.

"So, your pa is bad hurt?" Franco asked.

"Yeah. I don't know how bad, but he talked to Mr. Hardy, so maybe he'll get better."

"I hope so."

They walked on in silence for about ten minutes, and Abby felt she should say something, if only for courtesy's sake.

"So, how long have you been working for the Hardys, Mr. Franco?"

His chuckle almost boomed out, and she flinched.

"Just Franco," he said. "My name is Alain Cartier."

"Oh." Abby frowned. She didn't want to be rude, so she didn't ask the question that rose immediately in her mind. The big, bearded man seemed to read her thoughts.

"My grandfather was a Frenchman," he said. "In Louisiana. So the men, they call me Franco."

"It's a nickname?"

"That's right. I like to think, a friendly one."

Abby nodded.

"I've been here a year last spring. I like it."

"Good. That's good."

After a moment, he said, "You like it here?"

"Sure. It's the only place I ever lived, though. My grandparents came here thirty years ago. From Kentucky."

"That's a good place," Franco said.

They walked along in pleasant conversation as they approached the town. Franco told Abby about his childhood in Louisiana, and she was beginning to like him, despite his looks.

His dark beard and shaggy, unruly hair, coupled with his size, made him seem like a bear. He may not be a gentle one, but at least he had a tame side. He would never be anyone's pet, Abby thought, but he was not so bad a companion.

A cloud of dust rose in the distance, and soon they could make out three riders loping toward them.

"Maybe Mr. Hardy found some good horses," Abby said.

Franco stopped walking and squinted into the distance. The dying sun tinged the clouds purple and pink, and the horses appeared to be charging out of them in a magnificent blaze.

"That's not the boss."

Franco shoved her behind him, between the two horses, and drew his sidearm. In seconds, the three horses pulled up a few yards before them. All three riders held guns aimed at them, and the leader leveled a pistol at Franco's chest.

"State yer business."

Sam saw the riders ahead of him and kicked his new horse's ribs. The leggy bay gelding rewarded him with an impressive burst of speed. Even so, the three townsmen beat him to where Franco and Abby were walking. By the time Sam galloped up, Franco had his hands in the air, and Abby stood behind him, not cowering exactly, but definitely sheltering behind Franco's bulk.

"What's going on?" Sam demanded. One of the strangers pointed his rifle in Sam's direction.

"They're from the town," Franco said. "Making sure we're not with the banditos, I reckon."

"A little late." Sam turned to the leader. "My father's leading the posse that's chasing those outlaws, and these two are with us. I came to get them and tell them we've got fresh mounts for them."

The leader grunted and lowered his pistol.

Sam looked the bunch over and made a quick decision.

"Abby, why don't you climb up here with me? Franco can ride your mare and lead his horse in. We'll make better time that way."

Abby shoved her reins into Franco's hand and ducked past him to the near side of Sam's bay. Sam took his left foot out of the stirrup. Abby was quick, and she didn't seem to have any trouble getting her foot up there. He grabbed her wrist and pulled her up, swinging her around behind his saddle. She landed with a pouf of skirts and quickly smoothed them down. The three men from Ripton watched every move. Franco was already in Minnie's saddle, his feet hanging low below the stirrups, and had his own gray in hand for leading.

"Let's ride," Sam said.

Abby held on to him, her arms squeezing around his waist. He liked having her there, though their closeness made him sweat. She never said a word, and he didn't either, but he knew he would think about this later. They reached the little town swiftly, and he was almost reluctant to have it end. He let Abby slide down the horse's flank in front of the blacksmith's shop, where his father and the others were waiting.

Ripton consisted of half a dozen small adobes and a couple of hovels made mostly out of junk. The saloon, or cantina, was the largest of the adobes. Pa, Wally, and Pierce stood outside it, surrounded by a cluster of men. A dark-haired man of about fifty, wearing a stained apron, stood among them. The bartender, Sam guessed.

"They took our Sally." The bartender's eyes smoldered. "I can't go off and leave my business unprotected. What am I supposed to do?"

"I'd think a lady's life was more important than a saloon," Pa said, but the bartender just scowled at him. Pa looked around at them. He spotted Sam, Abby, and Franco and nodded at them. "Look, three or four more guns might make the difference. You all want this Sally back, don't you?"

"Sure," one of the townsmen said. "We all like Sally."

Several others murmured in agreement.

"You go, Harry," a white-bearded man said to the bartender. "I'll watch your place."

Harry frowned at him. "What could you do against a bunch like that, Joe?"

"That bunch isn't coming back here," Pa said firmly. "They've got what they want, and they're headed for the border. Once they cross into Chihuahua, their prisoners are lost."

"I didn't see any prisoners," Joe said. "Well, not if you don't count Sally."

"What about the children?" Pa asked.

"I didn't see any kids," said Harry, the bartender.

"They had a boy and a girl with 'em when they came here," the blacksmith offered. "I seen 'em. Little boy, looked like a Mex, and a girl a bit older. Pretty thing. Blond, like this one." He nodded at Abby.

"She's my sister," Abby said. "They stole her and Pablo Hardy."

"My son," Pa added. "We're going after them, and if we can get your Sally back too, we will. We appreciate your willingness to trade what horses you have left, but we need men." He looked at Harry. "Can we get food at your place?"

"If you got money," Harry said.

"I'll pay. There's six of us. Me, my son, this young lady, and my three hands."

Harry nodded. "I'll give you what I've got."

"Shouldn't we get right on their tails?" asked Wally, the youngest of the Hardy hands in the group.

"How far behind them are we?" Pa asked.

"You came in about half an hour after they left," the blacksmith said, scratching his chin. "But you been jawin' and tradin' for another half hour."

"Right. Let's make it quick, men. Abby."

They left their spent horses and the four new ones and two mules they had traded for in the care of the blacksmith and hurried into the cantina. Sam could tell from the way Abby slumped down onto a bench that she was bone tired. They all were, but the men were used to it. This was a rough day for a young woman like her. He wouldn't exactly call her delicate or pampered—Abby had shown she could ride hard, and he was sure she worked hard at home, too. But he doubted she was used to a full day of unrelenting effort, made heavier by the knowledge that her sister was in peril and her father lay badly wounded at home, perhaps dying. Abby had taken hope from the fact that her pa was talking when they left, but Sam knew all too well that infection could set in and claim the patient quickly. Men with much less serious wounds died out here.

Harry and the old man, Joe, brought them stew and coffee, and beer for the hands. Abby waited, watching Sam's father. When all the men dove into their food without prelude, she lowered her head for a moment, eyes closed. Sam was sure she was asking a blessing. His father offered prayer at home, at the family table, but not when he was out with the men. Slightly shamed, Sam closed his eyes.

Lord, thank you for bringing us this far, and for this food. Let me not forget You're there. Help us get Pablo and Ellen back. Please.

He opened his eyes. Abby was eating. He picked up his spoon.

Abby seemed to perk up with the first bite of stew. She looked around the dim room with interest, her gaze lingering on the lurid painting behind the bar, the keg resting on it, and the sparse row of bottles that caught the light from the lanterns Harry had lit.

Sam could tell the exact moment she realized he was watching her. She jumped a little, then smiled.

"I've never been in a saloon."

"Is it like you expected?"

She shook her head. "I'm not sure what I expected. It's smaller, and darker, and not as noisy. I guess I thought there'd be music and gamblers and dancing girls."

"That'd be a big, fancy one, I guess. We're far out from any of the big towns, and we're near the border."

"It must be hard for Harry to keep his place well stocked," she mused.

"Yeah, not to mention their Sally was stolen. She probably livens the place up when she's here." She didn't smile, and Sam realized it was a poor joke. "Sorry."

"It's probably true," Abby said, "and that makes me sad."

They ate quickly. Pierce left the cantina before the rest of them, and Sam was sure Pa had sent him to make sure all their mounts were ready. When they got to the blacksmith's pen, their saddles were on the new horses. Franco got a big mule that looked like it could go all day, but maybe not too swiftly. They had to take what was left after the outlaws took the pick of the town's horseflesh.

Sam's bay would be serviceable. He'd shown that on the short ride back to bring Abby and Franco in. Abby had fallen heir to a nondescript chestnut gelding. The horses the Mexicans had traded and left in the corral looked much better, but they'd been pushed to their limits all day, so Pa had settled for fresher, if poorer, animals.

Ellen stared at the spent horses. She glanced over at Sam. "That's our horse—the one Ellen was riding. The little mare." She nodded toward a small chestnut that stood with its head down against the far fence of the corral, nibbling at a wisp of hay.

"When we come back, we'll get her," Sam said.

Without a lot of fuss, they mounted up and left the town. Sam was surprised when three other men rode out to join them as they passed the last of the adobes—Harry the bartender and a couple of ranchers who introduced themselves as Mac Macklin and Tracy Smith.

Sam loped along beside Abby, hearing only snatches of the conversation the ranchers carried on with his pa.

"If we have to cross the river ..."

"Can't catch them by full dark."

The sun had slipped below the horizon, and the dusk had deepened. From things his pa let drop, Sam gathered they would keep on for a while—maybe several hours. Pa still hoped to catch up with the outlaws tonight. The horses jogged along at a steady, unrelenting pace, but Sam still wished the bandits hadn't beat them to the little town and gotten the pick of the available horses.

"You ever been to Mexico before?" he asked Abby.

"No. You?"

"Once. When Pa married Luisa. We visited Don Hernandez's rancho."

"What's it like?"

Sam's memories of the place were vague, but some things stood out. "It's big. Fancy stuff in the house. Silver doodads and china from Mexico City. Rugs everywhere. But it's all adobe. The land—well, he owns a lot of it, but it's dry. Real dry in some years, I guess. He can't run as many cattle as we do per acre. They have a lot of horses, and he has lots of caballeros. I'm not sure how he supports them all. But it's like a little village, where they live. His men have their wives and children living there, on the rancho land."

"So, he's rich," Abby said slowly.

"I think so. By some standards, anyway."

"Richer than your pa?"

Sam laughed. "We're not rich."

Abby frowned. "You have a big house, and it's painted white. You run a lot of cattle—more than anyone else for miles around."

Sam shrugged. "I guess everything's relative. Do you think we're rich?"

"Compared to us, yeah."

Sam didn't think he liked that assessment. "Your pa's a good rancher. A lot of people gave up and left after the last drought. Not your pa."

"He's still scraping by."

Of course, her father didn't have any sons big enough to help him with the work yet, and he had Abby's mother and four children to support. Pa had only Sam for many years, and he was nearly full grown when Pa remarried and Pablo came along. Pa also found the means to hire some cowpunchers early on. He must have started out with more resources than Mr. Bunter, and he'd stayed ahead over the decades they'd ranched near each other. And Abby had said they only had two saddle horses now. That was a sure sign that the Bunters were on hard times.

Sam's legs ached from riding so long. The bay horse didn't trot as smooth as his usual mount. He shifted his weight in the saddle, stretching what muscles he could.

"You all right?" Abby asked.

"Yeah."

"Thinking about Pablo?"

It irked Sam that he hadn't been.

"No, but ... thanks. When I do think of him, it makes me forget about how much I want to sleep."

"He and Ellen must be horrified," Abby said.

"Yeah, but as long as they keep moving ..." He broke off, wishing he hadn't voiced the thought.

"You mean, they can't abuse the children while they're on the run?"

"Something like that. This is hard on the kids, but it could be worse. And now they've got Sally with them."

Ahead of them, the column stopped and bunched up. Sam and Abby jogged their horses up where they could hear. His father spoke quietly.

"We're coming to a hilly stretch, and I'm sending Pierce ahead to scout. If they don't know we're behind them, they may have stopped. Sam, you go with Pierce. The rest of us will go on, slow and quiet."

Sam was shocked that his father had chosen him, and a

little pleased, though his apprehension rose. Abby's warm hand patted his sleeve, and he looked over at her.

"I'll pray," she whispered.

Sam nodded and moved over to join Pierce on the edge of the group.

"Let's go," Pierce said softly. He set out at a jog, and Sam's horse followed without urging.

CHAPTER THREE

WHEN SAM AND PIERCE LEFT THE party and rode ahead in the darkness, Abby's senses sharpened. Every noise their horses made seemed louder, every glint of moonlight on metal sharper, the smells of horseflesh and leather and dust more potent. She shivered, feeling alone for the first time.

She reminded herself that Sam was not her only friend on the trip. Mr. Hardy and his men had welcomed her into their company too, but all the others were older than Abby. Wally, the red-haired cowboy, looked closest in age to Sam, but he hadn't spoken one word to her since they had left her house. He was probably shy—or had Sam's friendliness to her warned him off? In any case, all were strangers to her, except Sam's father, and she wouldn't claim she knew him well. She had probably talked to Franco more on their walk into Ripton than she ever had to Mr. Hardy.

Her thoughts turned to her younger sister. She couldn't imagine how isolated Ellen would feel if she were the only girl in this bunch, let alone with the ruthless caballeros.

Of course, Sally was with them now. However hardened she was, Sally might be a buffer between the men and the children. If the caballeros were bent on mischief, she might save Ellen from their abuse. On the other hand, she might encourage them to place Ellen in a brothel or a cantina. The saloon girl was an unknown quantity that could save Ellen or do her irreparable harm.

Abby sent up another prayer—one of many she had formed silently that day. *Comfort Ellen, Father. Keep her safe!* She would ask neither for herself, provided Ellen arrived home unmolested. That was her greatest fear. Saddle sores and even a beating or a wound, Ellen could survive, but if she was violated, Abby knew her little sister would never recover. She added another prayer. *Thank you for Sally. Use her, Father. Let her be a blessing to Ellen.*

She had heard stories—they all had—whispered among the women when they visited, discussed more frankly by the men when they thought the women and children were out of earshot. Raids by the Indian tribes had been the worst, but they were past now. The Comanche, the Apache, the Kiowa, all the native tribes were confined to reservations now. For the last five years, even the last of the renegade Comanche had disappeared from Texas. They were gone, like the buffalo.

But the people remembered. As a girl, Abby had overhead shreds of conversation about the raids. She had nightmares for weeks afterward. She didn't want to know about that. But she did know. Some of the people captured by Comanche, especially women and children, had been sold and enslaved. She had heard about the Valley of Tears, where the captives were kept until the traders came to take them to Mexico. Children were stripped of their clothing as soon as they were captured, to remove all ties to their homes. Later, they were given Comanche dress, but the humiliation and isolation had done their work. Women were sometimes assaulted and then killed or sold into slavery. Some children were absorbed into the tribe.

Ellen's captors wouldn't do that. They were Don Hernandez's men, not Indians or Comanchero traders. Surely they would treat Ellen better than the savages would have.

Somehow she couldn't convince herself, and she sent up another flurry of prayers.

No one spoke as they moved stealthily over the undulating land. Mr. Hardy stayed in the lead with one of the ranchers they'd picked up at Ripton. The others strung out behind them.

Mac Macklin claimed he knew this area fairly well and said there was a stream not far ahead. Abby wondered why Mr. Hardy hadn't sent him with Pierce, the tracker, instead of Sam. Maybe he wanted Sam to feel he'd done something important in the quest for his little brother.

They stopped again. Pierce and Sam loped toward them in the moonlight, and Mr. Hardy waited for them.

"It's a good mile," Pierce said. "They've camped by the river."

"Did they see you?" Mr. Hardy asked.

"They did not, sir."

"Sam?"

"We left our horses back, Pa, and slipped in close. They didn't see or hear us. And we saw Pablo."

"Is he all right?" Mr. Hardy asked.

"Seemed to be. I think he was sleeping. They had him tied to a man by his ankle, but he looked all right. We couldn't get real close."

"What about the Bunter girl?"

Sam and Pierce glanced at each other.

"Didn't see her," Sam said.

Abby's heart sank. She pushed her horse forward, until Sam looked at her. "What do you mean? Where was she?"

"I don't know," Sam said with a grimace. "We stayed hidden for a long time, watching. They had a guard sitting on the other side of the fire from where we were, but back away from the fire. The fire had died down, and he didn't add to it."

Mr. Hardy said, "They mustn't think anyone's following them, if they had a fire."

"They seem pretty confident," Pierce said. "Only one sentry, and he wasn't patrolling or anything like that."

Mr. Hardy grunted.

"But where is Ellen?" Abby insisted. "Wasn't she in their camp? The blacksmith said he saw her when they were trading with him."

"And Sally," Harry added. "Did you see our Sal?"

"They must be there somewheres," Pierce said, "but out of sight from where we were. Like maybe over on the other side, where the sentry was at. The camp was quiet. We dasn't go any closer."

"And Pablo looked all right?" Mr. Hardy asked.

"Yes, sir," Pierce said, with a glance at Sam.

"I saw him roll over, Pa. I think he was asleep, but maybe not. He's probably scared silly if he's awake."

"Kids sleep when they need it." Mr. Hardy's face looked wrinkled and old. Abby wondered if the moonlight had that effect on all of them, or if his worry for the little boy caused it. She'd always heard moonlight was flattering, but maybe it wasn't true. "Can we get Pablo out without a gunfight?" he asked.

"Doubtful," Pierce said.

"They've got him right there in the middle of their camp." Sam shook his head. "If we try to sneak in there to free him, the sentry will see us."

"Maybe we can distract him." Mr. Hardy looked up at the sky. "The moon will be down in two hours. I think we should sleep while we can. When the moon sets, we'll creep in close." He looked at Abby. "You stay back with the horses, Miss Bunter."

"I want to be there for Ellen."

"If we find her, we'll bring her to you directly."

Abby didn't like that plan, but she supposed Mr. Hardy felt he had to look out for her. He couldn't go back and tell her parents he'd lost their eldest daughter too.

She nodded, and he turned away from her.

"Pierce, you know how to move quiet. Go in and get as close as you can. If they see you and raise an alarm, we'll open fire. You grab Pablo and get out."

"Let me go in," Sam said.

His father frowned at him.

"If Pablo sees me, he'll know we've come for him," Sam said earnestly. "He won't question it. But he might not recognize Pierce in the dark."

Mr. Hardy started to shake his head, but Sam spoke again, firmly.

"Pa, he's my brother. Pierce has done a great job of tracking them, but we can't ask him to walk into their camp for our kin. That's my job."

"Or mine," his father said grudgingly.

"No offense, but I can move faster than you." Sam held his father's gaze until Mr. Hardy let out a breath.

"All right. The rest of us will cover you. What is there for cover near the camp?"

Abby huddled in the saddle, suddenly cold. She wished she had taken her cloak out of her pillowcase. Maybe once the men left to penetrate the outlaws' camp, she would do that. For now she kept silent, listening to their plans. They tried to anticipate everything that could go wrong as they discussed rescuing Pablo, but not once did they mention her sister.

Sam moved slowly, stealthily. He could see the faint glow of the dying campfire now. All it would take was one misplaced step, and their surprise attack would be ruined. His father, Pierce, Franco, and the others were back there, watching the quiet camp. The light from the embers didn't reveal much, but starlight showed him the clearing. A few boulders were strewn across the dry ground, and some scrub bushes tried to get a foothold in the barren land.

He could hear their horses champing and snorting now and then, off to his left, where Pierce and Wally had taken up their positions. They had thought that the caballeros might sprint for their horses if they were alarmed, and that made sense. Without them, Don Hernandez's thugs could not get back to the rancho in Mexico.

Sam could not have told where Pablo lay if he hadn't reconnoitered earlier with Pierce. The lump beside the large, snoring man to one side of the fire ring must be his brother. Could he get to Pablo and cut the rope that bound him to his captor without awakening the others? Sam was not at all confident that he could.

Even worse, he couldn't see the sentry now. He stayed motionless in the shadow of a rock for several minutes, trying not to let his breathing make even the tiniest sound. His eyes darted about, probing, seeking. Several men lay in slumber. Had the sentry gone to check on the horses, or had he gone back to sleep?

It occurred to Sam that the bandits had probably changed sentries since his earlier visit to the camp. They had all taken his father's advice and rested for two hours, until the moon was down. Sam had dozed fitfully, but he kept waking and thinking about Pablo. How would he feel if he were the one who was snatched and hauled off toward the border?

Pablo had met his grandfather only once in his young life. Don Hernandez always presented a booming, imperious, persona. The two times Sam had met him—once in Mexico, once at the Hardys' ranch—he had felt intimidated and small. How must Pablo feel? Being ripped away from his loving father and big brother and the only home he knew must be terrifying, even with his grandfather at the other end of the journey—a grandfather who scared everyone.

Still he saw no movement in the camp. The only sounds

were the fluttering of leaves, the horses' muffled champing, and crickets chirping away at the stars. Where were Ellen and Sally? Perhaps they had allowed the women to sleep apart from the others, for privacy. He hoped that was the reason he couldn't see them.

Sam eased his knife from the sheath on his belt. He had to keep Pablo from crying out somehow when he reached him. He was about to move forward when Pablo sat up and peered around him, squinting into the darkness. Sam drew back, but none of the men stirred.

Sam held his breath a moment longer. Pablo began working at the rope tied around his ankle. Surely if the boy wriggled too much, the caballero tied to him would rouse. Sam left his hiding place and inched forward, wary but determined. Where was the sentry? There had to be one somewhere.

Pablo looked up suddenly, staring straight at him, his features frozen in terror.

Sam lifted a finger to his lips. Would Pablo recognize him in the darkness? Just for a moment, Sam lifted his hat, so it wouldn't shadow his face. Maybe his hair, several shades lighter than the Mexicans', would help identify him too.

Pablo gasped and then jerked his head around. He was looking for the sentry too, Sam realized. He made himself stay still for several seconds, then moved stealthily closer to his brother, hunched over, his knife in his hand. Was he sealing his death, and Pablo's too?

The boy leaped up and hurled himself toward Sam. With only enough time to balance himself and catch the boy in his arms, Sam couldn't help letting out a puff of air. Pablo had untied the rope and hurtled into his arms.

The man who had lain beside Pablo stirred, and off to Sam's right, another caballero sat up, rubbing his eyes.

No time for stealth now. Sam whirled and ran.

The first bullet struck the rock where he had sheltered moments ago as Sam sprinted past it. He clutched Pablo against his chest, which made it impossible to crouch down. The boy's arms clenched around his neck, pulling his head down and making it hard for Sam to fill his lungs with air.

Ahead of them, a rifle barrel flared and the sound of the shot boomed. Pa and Franco were shooting. Gunfire erupted around them, and Sam kept running. He had to get Pablo away from the skirmish, away from the flying lead.

By the time he topped the rise and ran down the other side to where Abby waited with the horses, he was panting. Their mounts, alarmed by the not-too-distant gunfire, were lunging and squealing, but all had been hobbled or picketed. Abby walked along the picket line, speaking softly.

Sam slowed his steps so he wouldn't disturb the animals further.

"Abby," he called.

She spun toward him, her chestnut's reins in her hands. Sam could barely make out her features in the starlight, but her hair fluffed out around her face as airy as spun sugar.

"Sam?"

"I've got Pablo. Get on your horse and take him away from here. Ride back along the trail at least a mile and take cover. Wait for us there."

"What about you?"

"I've got to go back and help Pa."

Sam stepped up to the chestnut's side and flung Pablo into the saddle.

"You stay with Miss Abby," he said sternly. "Understand?"

Pablo nodded. "Where's Papa?"

"Back there. I'll bring him to you."

Before Sam could even think of giving Abby a boost, she had her foot in the stirrup and swung up behind Pablo in a flurry of petticoats.

"We'll find you," he said. "Don't show yourselves until you're certain it's us."

"I understand," Abby said.

Sam turned and darted back toward the caballeros' camp. The gunfire was now sporadic and scattered. He would have to approach with caution until he could assess the situation.

Behind him, Abby called, "Get Ellen, Sam. You must get Ellen."

CHAPTER FOUR

RELUCTANTLY, ABBY TURNED THE HORSE'S HEAD and urged it to walk away from the other mounts. They had calmed, now that the gunfire had nearly stopped.

Everything inside her rebelled. She was moving away from Ellen, getting farther from her sister with every step.

But Sam was right. She had to get Pablo away from the outlaws' camp. If any of Hernandez's men survived the attack, they would come looking for the boy. They could not return to Don Hernandez empty-handed.

She squeezed the horse's ribs, and it broke into a jog. A mile, Sam had said. That was too far. She wanted to be within sound of the gunshots and easy for Mr. Hardy and his men to find. But if they stayed close and the Mexicans prevailed, she and Pablo might be captured.

She forced herself to keep going. All sounds of the fray faded. She wasn't sure if that was because the skirmish had ended, or because of the distance she was putting between them. She could barely make out the trail in the darkness, and she gave the horse more rein. He probably wanted to return to Ripton. So long as he didn't turn back toward the other mounts, she would let him pick his own way.

Had they gone a mile? She didn't think so. She tried to turn in the saddle and look back, but Pablo's body, pressed against her stomach, made it hard to move much.

"Is my papa all right?" he asked.

"I think so. I don't know." A few trees loomed beside the trail. Abby slowed the horse to a walk and took stock. As best as she could tell, the ground wasn't too uneven beneath them. They probably wouldn't find better cover. "We're getting off the trail," she said. "Hang on to the horn."

The chestnut stepped gingerly off the rough road into the dry weeds and plodded at Abby's guidance to the shelter of the nearest cottonwood. In its shadow, she halted and turned the horse to face the road. She got her right leg over its rump and slid to the ground.

"Stay up there," she told Pablo.

She held the reins, not daring to chance ground-tying the strange horse. She walked around to the other side and tried to pull her father's rifle up and out of the scabbard, but it was too heavy for her to manage while standing on the ground.

Pablo's warm hands touched hers on the rifle stock.

"I will help you."

Pablo was small, but with his help, Abby was able to get the rifle out and lower it safely.

She stood beside the horse, waiting.

After about five minutes, Pablo said, "Who are you?"

"I'm sorry," she said. "I'm Abby Bunter, Charlie's big sister."

"Oh. I know you."

"Yes. It's dark, and I should have told you right away. I came with Sam and your father to get you and my sister Ellen back."

"Where is Papa?" Pablo asked.

Abby pulled in a shaky breath. "He's back there. With Sam and some of your ranch hands. A few men from the town where you changed horses are helping them too."

Pablo was silent for a few minutes, and Abby wondered what he was thinking.

"Ellen was with you, right?" she asked.

"Yes. They took her after they got me."

Abby noticed how precise his speech was. She recalled hearing her father say that even though his wife spoke Spanish, Ike Hardy had insisted the boy speak English. He didn't have much of an accent.

"Do you know why they took her?" she asked. "Did they say anything about her?"

"Oh, yes," Pablo said. "They want to sell her to a man they know in Monterrey. They said they can get money for her and the extra horse, and that she will bring more than the horse because she has fair hair."

Abby's stomach clenched, noting that the boy must be

fluent in his mother's language, because the caballeros certainly wouldn't discuss their dealings in English.

"What about a woman named Sally?" she asked. "The men where we traded horses said they came there and stole her. Was she with you after the town?"

"I don't know her name, but yes. There was a new lady after we got the new horses. She rode with them, but she didn't talk to me."

"Sam and Pierce went to the camp while you and the men were sleeping," she said. "They wanted to find out where you were and how many men they had to fight to get you back."

"I saw Sam come to get me," Pablo said. "I untied the rope."

"That's good," Abby said. "But that was his second time at the camp. The first time, they just went to look. And they didn't see Ellen. Do you know where she is now?"

"Yes."

Abby waited, but the boy said no more.

"Can you tell me?" she asked at last.

"She is gone."

Abby stared up at him and tried to see his face, but the tree shadowed him too well.

"What do you mean, gone?"

"We did not know Sam was coming. Or Papa, or you. We saw Ellen's pa get shot. We thought we would have to escape by ourselves."

Abby's heart beat slowly, methodically, as she took that in. "You had an escape plan?"

"Yes. But ... they would not let us talk much, you know."

"They kept you separate?"

"Yes. One of the men carried me on his horse at first. They led Ellen on her chestnut, but they did not let us talk. She cried at first, and one of the caballeros slapped her."

Abby caught her breath. "He hit her?"

"Yes, and she was quiet after that. But I saw her tears."

"So ... how did you make your plan together?"

"After a long time, they stopped to trade horses. The men at the village did not want to trade, but Cinco made them."

"Who is Cinco?" Abby asked. "And how did he make them trade?"

"He is one of Grandfather's men, and he is the boss of the men who came to the ranch. There was a livery stable at the village."

"We saw it," Abby said.

"Cinco told the man if he did not give them good horses, they would kill him and take the horses anyway. So he traded. And they got a gray pony for me to ride, but the caballero kept it on a rope, so that I could not ride away from him."

"I see."

"While they changed the horses, that is when Ellen and I talked. One man kept us outside to wait while they put all the saddles and stuff on the new horses. Ellen said her papa was shot, and she didn't think anyone would know she was captured. How did you know?"

"My pa made it back to the house and told us," Abby said. "He's hurt bad, but he's not dead. And your father and the others came and told us those men had come from Don Hernandez's rancho, and that they were taking you back to live with him in Mexico."

"That is what I thought." Pablo let out a plaintive sigh. "I do not think my grandfather is as nice as my papa. And I would not want to leave Sam."

"Is he a good brother to you?" Abby asked.

"Yes." He said it so softly, Abby barely heard him.

She wondered if Pablo was crying now, and she didn't want to upset him further, but she needed to find out all she could about Ellen. She touched his hands, where they clutched the saddle horn. "Can you tell me about the plan you and Ellen made?"

Pablo sniffed. "She said they would have to sleep sometime, because it was a long way to my grandfather's, and when they did we would run away, she and I. And if one of us was caught, the other would run for help. That was very important. 'Do not stop for me. Run to the nearest house or village,' she said."

"Is that what happened?"

"I think so. After they got the new horses, and after we rode for a while longer, they did make camp. But they set a guard. And they wouldn't let us lie down near each other. They took Ellen and the new lady farther from the fire and gave them blankets. I tried to sneak away, to where Ellen was, but Cinco caught me. He tied me to his leg with a rope. Then he lay down to sleep, while one of the men kept watch."

Abby nodded. This agreed with what Sam and Pierce had

seen on their first foray.

"And then what happened?"

"I fell asleep, but the ground, it was hard. After a while, I woke up. I sat up and saw that the men were mostly sleeping. The one called Jose was on watch, but he wasn't looking, so I started trying to undo the rope. And then I saw Ellen. She was looking at me from behind a rock. I knew she was waiting for me."

"What happened?" Abby asked.

"It was time to change the guard. Jose kicked another man and told him, your turn. So they switched, and Jose got his bedroll. But the other man, he sat down by the fire, where he could see me all the time. I didn't even dare to look at Ellen. But after a while, the man went to get something out of his pack. I tried to get the rope off, and he came over and held his knife near my face. He said, *'Ir a dormir, muchacho.'* And so I lay down. The next time I looked at the rock, Ellen was there, and she kind of—well, I could tell by her face, she wanted me to come. But I couldn't, so I shook my head, no. And she ... she waved, and then she was gone."

"Did they find out she was gone?"

"I don't think so. They would have yelled and woken Cinco. But after a while the guard walked around. I thought he went to check on the horses. So I started on the knots again. That's when Sam came for me."

Abby patted his knee. "You were very brave, Pablo."

How different things would have been if Luisa Hardy had lived. The whole Bunter family had attended Pablo's mother's funeral in February. Abby remembered Pablo's puffy little face, and the way he had clung to his father at the graveside service. Don Hernandez had not attended, since there was not time to inform him of his daughter's death before the burial, but until that time, while his daughter remained alive and happy, he had not tried to remove Pablo from the Hardy ranch.

Now everything had changed. Mrs. Hardy had died.

Five years ago, Papa had brought word that the last of the renegade Apache and Comanche bands had been forced onto reservations. Ma had said, "Texas is safe for our children now." Her daughters could grow up to be ladies in an atmosphere of peace. Everyone had breathed a little easier. And now, evil men had snatched Ellen away.

The sound of many hoofbeats approaching from the site of

the skirmish chilled Abby's blood. She raised the rifle and pointed it toward the road. She didn't need to tell Pablo to be still. She wouldn't give away their presence until she was certain they were not Don Hernandez's men. If only the horse would remain quiet, the riders might go right past and leave them undetected.

A half dozen horses pelted toward them, suddenly close, tearing up the powdery trail. Abby held her breath, her heart tripping. They galloped past, but one horse slowed and turned back. The rider steered toward the trees and stopped, eyeing the dense patch of shadow.

"Abby?"

Relief washed over her.

"Sam!" Pablo kicked the horse and rode out of the tree's shelter. Abby lowered the rifle and walked behind him.

The other horses had stopped, and it was quiet for a moment. Sam leaped to the ground and ran to embrace his little brother. When Abby reached them, he pulled her into the hug, too. She felt warm and safe with his arm around her. After a moment, she pulled away, wanting to laugh, but not with everything so uncertain. Not with Ellen still out there.

"How did you know we were there?" Pablo asked.

Sam chuckled. "It looked like a place Abby might pick."

A confused sound of men's voices and hoofbeats came from down the trail. Mr. Hardy and the others were coming back.

"What happened?" Abby asked Sam.

"We routed them. They're headed for the border. But, Abby—I'm sorry. We couldn't find your sister. They must still have her. It was dark, and we couldn't tell for sure. None of us actually laid eyes on her or Sally."

"No, Sam," Pablo cried. "Ellen, she escaped. She wanted me to go with her, but I couldn't get away. She ran to get help. I hoped she would find you."

Sam shook his head. "She didn't. Where do you think she went?"

"I don't know," Pablo said mournfully. "I thought she would come to the road and head back home. But maybe the guard was between her and the trail. What will we do?"

Sam ruffled his hair. "It's all right. We'll find her. Maybe she went out away from the camp to circle around."

The other horses were close now. Sam turned to meet his father and the others and apprise them of this development.

Abby worked the rifle back into its scabbard and waited with Pablo and their horse. The men's voices were gruff as they talked. One man's sharp comment reached her clearly through the darkness.

"Well, Tracy's hurt bad. We got to get him home."

Abby hadn't realized one of the ranchers who had joined them had been wounded. She led the horse a few steps closer.

"I appreciate that," Ike Hardy said, "and I want to get my son home and out of danger, too. But there's a young girl out there alone now. We can't just abandon her."

No, Abby's heart screamed, though she kept her lips pressed tightly together. You can't leave Ellen! How could those men even think of such a thing? Sam had promised. She wanted to shout at the men and tell them not to waver.

"Where's Pablo?" Ike asked.

Sam pointed to where Abby waited with the boy.

"Son, come here."

Pablo ran to Mr. Hardy's horse, and his father pulled him up onto the saddle and hugged him. "Did they hurt you, son?"

"No, not much," Pablo said. "I heard them talking. They said Grandfather Hernandez would be angry if they brought me to him with a scratch on me."

"They were right about that," Ike said. "But what about the Bunter girl? Did they say anything about her?"

Pablo hesitated.

"It's all right," Ike said. "Tell me everything you remember."

"They...they wanted to sell her, Papa." Pablo hid his face in the front of his father's vest.

"Where? To whom?" Ike asked, stroking his back. "Did they say?"

"They knew someone in Monterrey. I didn't hear the name, but it was someone who would buy girls from them." Pablo raised his head and looked gravely up at his father's face. "I didn't tell Ellen, Papa. She was already scared."

Ike's somber gaze met Abby's. "We'll have to look for her, but I don't want to take Pablo back into danger. Will you take him back to Ripton and wait for us there?"

Abby's throat felt tight, and she put a hand to her collar. "I can't. My sister is out there alone. The more of us looking for her, the better our chance of finding her."

Harry, the bartender, cleared his throat. "Me and Mac are

going home. We've got to get Tracy to a doctor. If you want, we'll take the boy with us. You can pick him up when you come back through town."

"No, Papa!" Pablo burrowed his head into Ike's chest. "I want to stay with you!"

Ike held him for a moment, as if considering. His eyes met Sam's, and he patted Pablo's back. "Don't worry, little one. You will stay with me. Go to Sam now."

Sam stepped forward and lifted his little brother gently down from the saddle. "You ride with me now, pal."

Mr. Hardy turned to the men, who had gathered around him, waiting for his orders.

"Harry, Mac, take your friend home. Thank you for helping us, and I'm sorry he's hurt."

Harry nodded. "I think he'll make it, but he needs help. We'll watch for the girl along the way."

"Thank you. Her name is Ellen Bunter."

Harry nodded.

The sound of approaching hoofbeats reached them, and everyone looked back along the trail, toward the outlaws' camp.

"One horse," Pierce said.

They all waited. The rider would see them grouped together in the starlight.

A feminine voice cried, "Whoa!" The horse pulled up short, ten yards away.

"Sally?" Harry called, his voice cracking slightly.

"Who's there?" the woman asked.

"It's me, Harry. We were trying to find you."

Harry and Macklin rode forward.

"Sal, how'd you get away?" Harry asked.

"Harry Goss! I've never been so glad to see anyone in my life!"

The two men rode back toward the group, accompanied by a woman in a low-cut dress. Abby couldn't tell its color in the twilight, but it shimmered in the faint starlight.

"Sally, this is Mr. Hardy and his men, and Miss Bunter. They've been looking for the kids those raiders stole." Harry nodded to them.

"And we've been looking for you, Sal," said Mac.

"Well, thanks, boys. I dunno about the kids—"

"We've got the boy," Harry said. "Do you know where the

girl got to? Is she still with them outlaws?"

"I don't think so. She fidgeted around for a while, then she took off into the dark. I ain't seen her since. I decided if she could get away, I could too, so I sneaked over near the horses. They had a feller watchin' 'em, so I wasn't sure I'd be able to get one. But then shootin' broke out, so I nabbed the closest one and lit out. Took me a while to find my way back to the road, and I'm not sure even now I'm headed for Ripton."

"You are," Mac said. "We was just going to turn back, on account of Tracy being shot."

"Tracy Smith?" Sally asked, her voice sharp.

"Yep, he's hurt bad, and we're taking him home," Harry replied. "We'll send someone to get the doc from the next town."

"Those no-good Mexicans! You're lucky you got the little boy back. Who is he, anyhow?" Sally asked.

"He's my son," Mr. Hardy said. "You'd best go back with these men, ma'am, but can you give us any clues as to where Ellen Bunter headed?"

"They had us a little ways off from where the men bedded down—for which I was thankful." Sally shook her head. "I told that Cinco if he so much as laid a finger on me or that girl, I'd kill him."

Abby would have laughed if the situation weren't so dire. How could this woman hope to fight off a band of armed men?

Harry turned in his saddle. "Mr. Bunter, we'll be heading out."

"Go," Ike said. "I hope we'll be back soon and pick up our horses."

Harry and Mac Macklin headed off down the trail, with Mac leading Tracy Smith's horse and Sally riding between them. Smith slumped in the saddle, and Abby wondered if he would make it back to town without pitching off the horse.

Mr. Hardy surveyed the men that were left. Franco, Pierce, and Wally.

"If any of you boys want to head back, now's the time."

Franco spit off to one side. "No use quittin' now, boss."

"We're in it to bring the girl home," Pierce said.

Wally nodded. "Me, too."

"All right, then," Ike said. "Sam, you keep back with Pablo. Miss Bunter..."

"Call me Abby."

"All right. Stay alert and don't take any chances. Let's ride. Pierce, you lead."

Abby mounted her horse. By the time she was up, Sam was settled in his saddle with Pablo behind him, hanging on tight around his big brother's waist.

"All set?" Sam asked.

"Yeah," Pablo said.

They struck out with Pierce before them, trotting quickly toward the scene of the fray. Sam stayed more or less next to Abby, near the back of the party. She was glad for his presence, but she knew his focus was on protecting Pablo now.

They came to the outlaws' abandoned camp and rode through the middle of it. Pierce slowed his horse to a walk, peering about in the faint glow from what remained of the fire.

"How long do you think before dawn?" Abby whispered to Sam.

"Two or three hours, at least."

She nodded. It seemed years since they had halted to wait for the moon to set.

Mr. Hardy turned in his saddle and called softly, "Sam, bring Pablo up here."

Sam guided his horse past Franco's.

"Where was Miss Ellen?" Ike asked the boy.

Pablo pointed to a cluster of rocks east of the fire's embers. "I last saw her there. I think they gave her and the lady a spot over there to sleep, but I'm not sure."

Pierce came toward them through the darkness, walking and leading his mount. "Found this, boss." He held up a thin strip of cloth that fluttered in the faint breeze.

Mr. Hardy took it and rode over to Abby. "This looks like a hair ribbon."

Abby wasn't prepared for the hot tears that filled her eyes or the painful lump in her throat. She reached out and took the foot-long strand. In the starlight it looked almost black, but she knew it was a bright, shimmering red.

She stared at the bit of ribbon, the tears blurring her vision. "It's Ellen's. I tied it on her braid this morning. Or yesterday . . ."

CHAPTER FIVE

"LOOK FOR HER FOOTPRINTS," MR. HARDY told Pierce.

"Pablo, you get in the saddle," Sam said. He swung his right leg over the pommel and slid down, then made sure his little brother had control of the horse before he joined Pierce, out beyond the edge of the camp, to look for more evidence of Ellen's passing.

They all waited in silence until Sam came back to his father's side. "We need light, Pa. Can we light a torch?"

Mr. Hardy looked around. "We don't know where those caballeros are. I doubt they crossed the river."

"You think they'll come back and try to snatch Pablo again?" Sam asked.

His father nodded. "I do. Especially if we make it easy for them to see we haven't headed home yet."

"They've got a couple of wounded men," Sam said.

"That won't stop 'em."

Pierce walked back to them. "Sorry, boss. If there's anything there—any prints or anything like that, we might trample them in the dark."

"You think we should wait?" Mr. Hardy eyed him critically.

Pierce nodded. "I do. Unless you want to split up and have us all ride around and yell her name."

"The Mexicans would hear us if they're close by," Franco said.

Mr. Hardy sighed. "Get a torch. Just one. We'll follow a little ways back. Send Sam to tell us if you find anything. And don't get too far from us. I don't want you ambushed."

Pierce worked in circles, outward from the campsite. He located the hoofprints of Sally's horse as she fled from the picket line, leading off at an angle roughly north. The other horses had gone south. Pierce continued to look for signs of Ellen.

An hour later, he had found nothing new, and they had made little progress from the camp. On one of Sam's reports, Mr. Hardy told him to bring Pierce in.

"Only an hour 'til daybreak. We might as well rest," he told Sam.

"Do you want a fire, boss?" Wally asked.

"No. I'm not convinced those caballeros have given up. They probably know exactly where we are by now, but I don't want to give them any assistance in kidnapping my son again."

Abby got out the food bag her mother had passed her that morning, realizing how hungry she was. None of them had eaten since lunch in Ripton, and she was sure all of the men's bellies were as empty as hers.

She found a packet of cornbread, wrapped in newspaper, and a dozen biscuits, half a dozen apples, several strips of dried beef, and another newspaper bundle. Unwrapped, it revealed a dozen oatmeal cookies, crumbled into small pieces.

She walked over to Sam's father, who had hobbled his horse and was removing its bridle. "Mr. Hardy? My mother gave me what food she had on hand this morning. It's not much, but I'm happy to share it with you."

"Why, thank you, Abby. I'm sure we'll appreciate it."

She smoothed out the newspapers on a rock and laid the food offering on top. They would hardly be able to see what they were eating, but they ought to appreciate Ma's cooking.

"Everybody eat up," she said.

Franco, Wally, and Pierce sidled closer.

"Thanks, Miss Abby," Franco said, "but make sure you save something for your sister. She'll be hungry when we find her."

Tears sprang into Abby's eyes. "Thank you." Her voice broke. She had been able to keep her anxiety for Ellen at bay while they rode and listened and watched, but the rough man's thoughtfulness broke open the reservoir of pain inside her. She tucked an apple and a biscuit back into the bag and looked up at the men. "Please, help yourselves."

They all took an item or two, and Mr. Hardy placed a piece of meat and a slab of cornbread in Pablo's hand. Quite a bit was left when they all had something to chew, and Abby suspected they were holding back, to make sure she got something herself. That was all right. What she couldn't eat would serve as a meager meal later.

"You all rest now." Mr. Hardy picked up his rifle and started to walk away.

Abby hurried after him. "Mr. Hardy, wait. I've had more rest than any of the men. Let me stand watch."

"Can't let you do that, ma'am."

She sighed. "I won't be able to sleep, with my sister out there."

He frowned at her. "All right. Get your weapon and find yourself a spot over that way. Stay within sight of our horses. I'll be within calling distance. Can you whistle?"

"Yes, sir."

"Give one little chirp if it's quiet, but you think something's going on. If they come in loud, I'll hear 'em."

She nodded and dashed to her horse to get Papa's rifle. Sam was settling down next to Pablo, and the three cowpunchers tossed their bedrolls on the ground and lay down, wriggling to find a comfortable spot. She found a slight knoll about twenty yards away, where she could sit with her back to the rise and not make a silhouette against the sky, but still see the dark blotches of the grazing horses. A sweeping gaze let her see both east and south, but it was too dark to glimpse anything more than a few yards away.

She sat in silence and prayed for Ellen. *Lord, let us find her. Keep her safe now. Calm her fears and help her to think clearly. Let us find her.*

The stars seemed less brilliant than before, but still she saw no sign of dawn.

Soft footsteps from behind made her swivel, her heart accelerating.

"It's me." Sam dropped down beside her. "Pablo's sleeping, but I couldn't. Why don't I take over for you?"

"I know I can't sleep. My mind keeps racing." Abby looked up at him. She could see the outline of his face, and a glimmer of starlight in each eye. "Sam, what will I do if we don't find her?"

He let out a long sigh. "It's possible the Mexicans might find her before we do. If they do, we'll have to go after them."

"Will your father want to do that?"

"I don't know. He wants to get Pablo home safe. That's the main thing on his mind right now. If we stay out here, we're easy targets. He knows Don Hernandez won't give up if he thinks there's a chance of getting Pablo."

"But Ellen," Abby said. "What if they don't find her either? What if she just wanders away, or holes up someplace, and we miss her?"

Sam was silent for a moment, then said, "Maybe we could get more men from Ripton. Once they know the outlaws are gone, more of them might be willing to come out here and search. Or we could go home and leave Pablo with somebody and get some men from Harrisville."

Abby tried to swallow down the lump in her throat. "I can't go back without her, Sam." As she said the words, she knew they were true. Her father had nearly lost his life defending Ellen. Even now, he might be dying. This wasn't the first time he had risked his life for his children, either.

"Do you remember when our house burned?" she whispered.

"Yeah."

"My pa almost died then, too, getting me out. I have to do this for him."

Abby vividly remembered her terror when she woke to find the walls in flames around her. Ellen was an infant, and she'd been in the big bed with her mother. They got out first, but her father had lingered to get Abby out. They'd made it, barely, and her family had not been able to salvage a single thing from their home. Sam's father and other ranchers had come to help them rebuild the house a few weeks later, when her father's burns were healing.

"I won't go back and face him without Ellen," she said fiercely.

"It's dangerous, Abby," Sam said gently. "Maybe Pa would take you back and leave Pablo with you and your folks—"

"No! I can't."

As they gazed off into the east, not looking at each other, it seemed to Abby the sky was lighter, more gray than black, and the stars were fading. Soon Pierce would be able to track again, and they would set out. If Mr. Hardy let them, that is. If he didn't insist they take Pablo to safety before they resumed the search for Ellen.

At last Sam stirred. He reached over and took her hand in his. Startled, Abby realized how cold her fingers were, and how warm Sam's hand was in comparison. She looked into his eyes.

She could tell they were brown, like coffee, but richer, and alive. It was surely getting lighter, and it was getting harder for her to breathe.

"All right," Sam said. "If Pa wants to take him home, I'll stay here with you. We won't give up until we find her."

Pierce went out again, making an arc fifty feet out from where they had rested. Sam walked inside the arc, about three yards from Pierce. The others stayed with their horses, watching in silence.

Pierce chirped, and Sam ran to him. The tracker said nothing, but pointed to a small shod hoof print in the dry ground.

"A donkey?" Sam hazarded.

"Too round for a donkey. It's that pony they had for your brother. It must have got loose last night, when they ran for their horses."

"Do you think Ellen could have caught it?"

Pierce shook his head. "I think she was long gone when we attacked. It's probably off somewhere grazing."

Pa rode up and stopped his horse a few yards away. "Find something, Pierce?"

"Pony tracks is all. If we're lucky, we might find the little one Pablo rode."

Pa looked around for a moment, then nodded. "We'll be watching." He rode back to where Abby and the others waited. He spoke to them in low tones, and Sam heard Pablo's joyous cry.

"My pony?" Pablo grinned. "I like that pony."

Pierce and Sam resumed their search. They crested a knoll and worked their way down the other side. Pierce let out a whoop, and Sam trotted to his side. In a low place between two small ridges, the ground was softer. Pierce knelt beside several partial footprints, smaller than Sam's boots would make, heading almost due east.

"It's got to be her," Sam said, "but she's heading away from the road."

"Yup. She's going toward those hills yonder." Pierce pointed with his chin.

Sam sighed. "She struck out in the dark, not knowing which way to go, but hoping she'd find a farmstead or a town."

"She'll go a ways without finding one, if she keeps on that way." Pierce stood. "Get your pa. I'll try to find more sign."

Sam hurried back to the others.

"He found some footprints. Most places they don't show, but Pierce has got her path for sure, and the direction she was heading last night."

"On foot, not on the pony?" Abby asked.

"On foot."

Her gaze fell, and he realized she'd had hopes her sister had caught the pony and was riding.

"I'm sorry, Abby. But we'll find her."

Sam took the reins of Pierce's horse from Wally and swung into the saddle. They rode out to the spot where the footprints showed, and he dismounted. Pierce was walking bent over, a few yards up the next rise in the ground, casting back and forth for another find.

Pa and Abby dismounted and joined Sam to look at the tracks.

"It's not much," Pa said, crouching beside the telltale marks.

"No, but Pierce will find her," Sam said. "Wait and see."

Abby's eyes misted as she stared at the evidence of her sister's passing. "It's got to be Ellen."

"Who else could it be?" Sam asked. He touched her shoulder for a moment, and they all stood.

Pa looked around. "We're getting into brushy country. It might be harder to follow her now."

"It might mean we're close to water," Sam suggested. "If she found a place to get a drink, Pierce will find more sign."

"Should we brush out her footprints?" Abby looked up at Sam, and his heart lurched. She was counting on him. Him and Pa and the others, but mostly him, because he'd promised to stick it out.

"Why would you do that?" Wally asked, edging his horse closer.

"In case the caballeros follow us," Sam said. "We wouldn't want them to know we'd found something."

"You think they're still out there?" Wally swiveled in his

saddle and looked back, but the small hill they had descended blocked their view of the back trail.

"I'll go take a look," Franco said. He turned his mule and trotted off up the hill.

They waited. Sam could see Abby's chest jump with each anxious breath. He wished he could comfort her and assure her this would end well. While they talked before dawn, he had wanted more than anything to hold her in his arms. But that wouldn't find Ellen, even if he dared. Bringing back her sister was the one thing that would satisfy Abby.

Franco came back a couple of minutes later. "I didn't see anything. Maybe they gave up."

Pa said nothing, but Sam could tell he didn't think his father-in-law's men had turned homeward.

Sam left them and rejoined Pierce. The tracker pointed to his left. "You look over there. I'll follow the straight line, but the ground's a little easier that way. She may have veered northeast."

The task was tiring and discouraging. As the sun rose higher, so did the temperature. Sweat trickled down Sam's back and soaked his shirt. He took off his hat, wiped his brow with his sleeve, and put the hat on again. He looked around in a wide sweep. The withering grass didn't show any signs of disturbance. He followed a fold in the land downward. Pierce was ten yards off to his right now.

Ahead, the brush thickened. Sam studied the line of bushes before him. Farther to his left, it almost looked as though something—or someone—had pushed through. He walked to the spot and studied the shrubs. Something had been here all right. A few leaves had torn off and fluttered to the ground. He spotted a broken twig.

Hauling in a deep breath, Sam parted the bushes and took a cautious step. All he needed was to wake up a snake.

He took two more steps, watching the ground closely, and stopped. A small, almost square depression in the ground could have been made by a boot heel. One of the same boots that had made the tracks they'd seen earlier. Through the brush ahead, a gleam caught his eye. Was that water? A lazy stream, maybe, or a water hole?

Sam whistled. "Over here."

CHAPTER SIX

ABBY PUSHED HER HORSE FORWARD. THE chestnut was reluctant to shove its way through the brush, but with Mr. Hardy's mount leading the way, she was able to persuade him to follow. Sam and Pierce stood three feet from the edge of a shallow stream that trickled through a ravine. The water appeared to barely move. With a few more dry, hot days, it would probably disappear.

But the rivulet provided enough water to draw wildlife and to soften the ground so that it showed footprints.

Pierce held up a hand, indicating that they should keep the horses back. "She crossed here."

"How long ago?" Mr. Hardy asked.

Pierce shook his head. "I'm not sure. Hours, I'm guessing. She was still moving fast—I'd say she didn't stop to drink."

"We're not all that far from where they camped," Sam said.

Abby looked back. She couldn't see over the last rise they had descended. Pablo, Franco, and Wally were coming through the brush with their horses.

"Sam, you go across here," Pierce said. "See if you can tell if she kept on straight."

"What will you do?" Sam asked.

"I want to check along the stream for a bit."

What was he looking for? Abby watched the weather-beaten cowboy hunch over and resume his scouting, this time northward, toward the source of the brook.

Sam waded across, careful not to disturb Ellen's clear footprints at the water's edge, and picked up her trail on the other side.

Mr. Hardy turned as the other horses came up to them.

"They found more sign. We'll give them a few minutes. Don't want to cross over and mess up the ground before they get a good look."

Pablo, riding Sam's borrowed bay, edged up beside his father.

"Is Ellen all right, Papa?"

"Seems like she was when she went over the stream. That's all we can tell for sure."

Pierce had ranged fifteen yards upstream, and he gave a little cry and plunged into the shallow water. He stopped short of climbing out on the other side, but bent over, his hands braced on his knees, studying the ground as the sluggish water flowed around his boots.

"What is it?" Mr. Hardy moved his horse along the bank toward him. Abby squeezed her horse's sides and put him in line to follow.

Pierce didn't speak until they were even with him. He turned his head and met the boss's gaze. "Cat tracks."

Abby's chest tightened. Wild cats didn't show themselves often, but several types were known in this territory. They weren't timid, exactly, her father had said once. More like sneaky.

"What kind of cat?" Wally asked.

"A big one."

"Bobcat?" Mr. Hardy asked, glancing toward Pablo.

"Bigger."

Pierce walked a few steps in the water and then climbed out on the far side. He bent over the grass and then looked toward the brush ahead of him. He straightened.

"Keep back a ways. And maybe you'd better tell Sam."

Abby looked downstream to where Sam had crossed, following Ellen's trail, but he was out of sight.

"I'll tell him." She looked to Mr. Hardy for approval.

"Go," he said, sliding his rifle from its scabbard. "Pablo, you stick close to me."

She turned her horse and rode along the stream until she came to where they had seen Ellen's footprints. She urged the gelding into the water and splashed across it. He bounded up the bank on the other side. The brush was not so thick here, and she could see over most of it. Sam was working on foot, about fifty yards out.

She trotted her horse closer, and Sam turned and saw her.

He stood still until she came up to him.

"Pierce found big cat tracks upstream from where Ellen crossed."

"That's not good." Sam frowned and looked at the ground. "I'm not sure, but I think she may have come through here. I haven't found any more prints, but some of the grass catches the light, where it's been bent over or stepped on. At least, I think that's what it is."

"Want me to get Pierce?"

Sam looked back toward the stream. "What's he doing now?"

"Following the cat's trail, I guess."

"He probably wants to make sure it doesn't cross Ellen's."

Abby clenched her teeth. She didn't want to think about that possibility. "Any sign of that pony?" she asked after a moment.

"No. I think he's long gone. Probably ran all the way back to Ripton last night."

She nodded and looked out over the rolling land. The sun was well above the horizon now, and the bunchgrass and mesquite looked dusty and tired.

"Do you think it's wise to be out here alone on foot? You can't see the others from here."

"I've got my sidearm." Sam patted the revolver on his hip. "Besides, I need to keep going as long as I've got this trail to follow. Pa will catch up soon."

Her horse's ears twitched, and he gave a low nicker. Abby patted his neck, looking out over the brown land smeared with green where prickly pear or a hardy clump of mesquite or blackbrush thrived.

"Did Pierce say what kind of cat?" Sam asked.

"Bigger than a bobcat. That's all I heard." She shivered. The horse snorted and shifted his feet, his ears folding back against his skull.

"A puma, you think?" Sam asked. "Or one of those jungle cats? They come up here from Mexico once in a while."

Abby caught sight of something in the brush twenty yards away. She could barely make out a head, and the body was shielded by low, spreading mesquite, but the eyes peered back at her from between the branches. Her heart jumped.

"It's one of them," she said softly. "A jaguar."

"Are you sure? Because I don't know as you could tell the

difference from the tracks."

"I'm sure," Abby said. "I can see it. Turn around, Sam. Nice and easy."

Sam's spine went rigid, and he looked into her eyes, his lips slightly parted. She gave a tiny nod and looked back to where she had seen the animal. At first she thought it was gone, but when she concentrated on the mesquite bush and carefully inspected every branch, she found it again.

Sam turned slowly and stared in the direction she was looking. After a moment, he whispered, "Where? I don't see anything."

"It's behind that big clump of mesquite. To the right of center. Look for his eyes."

She sat in the saddle, not moving but staring at the cat. Sometimes she lost focus on it, but then her gaze riveted on its face once more. She ought to pull the rifle, but she didn't want to scare it off. Sam stood beside the horse, silent for more than a minute. The horse fidgeted, but Abby didn't look away. She caught a flicker of movement behind the leaves.

"There! Its tail just moved."

"I think I see it," Sam said.

"What should we do?"

"Get Pierce, maybe?"

Abby considered that for a moment. If her horse made much of a disturbance, the cat would slink off into the brush.

"I don't think it's following Ellen," she said.

"Why not?"

"Because she's been out here twelve hours. It wouldn't take him that long to find her."

"Maybe he just found her scent," Sam said softly. "Maybe she's close by."

The back of Abby's neck prickled. What if Ellen had fallen asleep in the brush, and the cat was waiting for the moment to pounce?

The horse snorted and began to paw.

"Whoa," Abby said, tightening the reins.

"Look!" Sam pulled his revolver and pointed it toward where she had seen the cat.

The spotted figure oozed from behind the bush, visible only for a moment before it flowed behind a cluster of blackbrush and became part of the mottled landscape once more. Abby was left with an impression of savage beauty and muscles, fluid beneath the gold and black hide.

The gelding fought her for his head and backed up several steps, trembling.

Sam grabbed the cheek strap. "Whoa!" The horse stood still, and Sam looked up at Abby. "He was too quick. I couldn't get a shot off. Go get Pierce. I'll see if I can follow the cat. We don't want to lose track of it with Ellen out there."

"On foot? You take the horse."

Sam shook his head. "He won't want to get any closer to it."

"Then take my rifle." Abby reached for it.

"Thanks." Sam holstered the revolver and took the rifle from her. "Go." He walked toward the spot where they had seen the jaguar disappear.

The big cat probably weighed more than Abby, certainly more than Ellen. Appalled at the thought but uncertain as to what was best, Abby wheeled the horse. He willingly stepped out along the back trail. In the distance, she saw Pierce, walking along, watching the ground. Behind him by about fifty feet, Mr. Hardy, Pablo, Franco, and Wally, who was leading Pierce's mount, followed him slowly, holding back so they wouldn't destroy any sign.

Abby put her heels to the gelding's sides and loped toward Pierce. He looked up and watched her approach. She reined in when she reached him.

"We saw the cat."

Pierce's eyebrows shot up. "Where?"

She pointed back toward where she had left Sam. "Sam's going after it on foot. He wants you to come."

Pierce raised his arm and beckoned to Mr. Hardy and the others. They trotted their horses over and stopped.

"What is it?" Mr. Hardy asked. "Where's Sam?"

"Following the cat."

"You found more tracks?"

"They saw the creature," Pierce said.

"It's a jaguar," Abby added.

Pierce frowned up at her. "You sure? I've never seen one myself."

She nodded. "Spotted all over. Beautiful. But . . . kind of scary, too."

"What about Ellen?" Pablo asked.

Abby inhaled deeply. "I don't know. Sam was trying to

follow her trail when I caught up to him. Then we saw the cat. It was hiding in the brush. I'm not sure he was ... stalking anything." She saw the fear in Pablo's eyes, even though she had tried to choose her words carefully.

By this time, Pierce had mounted his horse and pulled out his rifle.

"My horse didn't like it," Abby said. "None of us will be able to ride up close to it. Be careful."

"I will. If I need to go on foot, pick up my horse."

"We will," Mr. Hardy said, "but if it gets wind of that cat, it might bolt."

Pierce shrugged and looked at Abby. "Show me where you last saw it?"

She turned her chestnut gelding and loped back over the ground she had covered. The trail she had left through the bunch grass seemed obvious. Why couldn't Ellen leave as plain a path?

She came to the spot where she had sat on the horse, talking to Sam. He was out of sight. She walked the horse toward the blackbrush, where the cat had gone. The horse began to dance and snort, and she turned to look at Pierce.

"I saw him right there, behind that mesquite, and then he went into the brush." She pointed, then urged the horse on. They pushed through a stand of bushes and down a knoll. Sam was ahead of her by two hundred yards, moving fairly fast along an open hillside. He must have seen the cat again. Beyond him, a higher hill rose, with rocks and brush dotting the slopes.

Pierce brought his horse up beside hers. "He's quite a ways up there. Maybe I should take Sam's horse and ride to where he is and see what's happening. You wait here."

He rode back to take Sam's horse's reins from Wally and then loped up the hillside. Mr. Hardy and the others gathered in a cluster around Abby.

"We saw someone coming on behind us," Mr. Hardy said, looking around.

"Don Hernandez's men?" she asked.

He nodded. "Once they top that last rise, they might see us. There's no decent cover between here and the hill."

"We'd better move on," Franco said. "Those rocks would be better protection than the brush down here."

Mr. Hardy nodded. "Pablo, you stick with me, son. You too,

Abby. Wally, keep an eye out behind. We'll ride up the slope to where there's more cover and then go along the hillside to intercept Sam and Pierce, if they don't get away from us."

"They must be chasing the cat," Franco muttered, drawing his rifle. "You go, boss."

"Come on, son." Mr. Hardy and Pablo took off toward the slope, and Abby followed, pushing her horse to keep up. They tore across the brushy plain at a dead run and began to climb the hillside. The horse stumbled once, but recovered quickly and pressed onward.

Abby's heart pounded. Their breakneck pace was enough to worry her, but people she'd grown to care about were in danger. Ellen was ahead somewhere, alone and frightened. And Sam—had he and Pierce forgotten Ellen and veered from their purpose to chase down the jungle cat?

Mr. Hardy reached the first of the scattered boulders and turned toward where Sam and Pierce had last been seen. Abby followed as they rounded the side of the hill.

Ahead of them, a rifle shot split the air.

CHAPTER SEVEN

SAM ROUNDED A LARGE BOULDER, HIS bay nearly slamming into the back end of Pierce's horse as the tracker's rifle discharged. The bay squealed and reared, pivoting away from the other horse. It happened so fast that Sam barely caught a glimpse of tawny fur above them. They had closed on the jaguar, and Pierce had let off a shot.

Sam brought his horse under control. Pierce had already dismounted with his rifle in hand. He hooked his reins over a juniper branch and strode toward the large rocks.

Sam pulled his rifle, hopped down, and hurried to Pierce's side.

"Missed," Pierce said grimly. "He's headed for Mexico now. We'll never catch him."

"Too bad," Sam said.

"That would have been something to tell on a winter night, huh?"

Sam shrugged. "You've still got the story."

"Yeah, but I was picturing that pelt hanging on the bunkhouse wall."

Sam smiled, seeing it in his mind, too. "We've got to think of Ellen Bunter now."

"You're right. She might have heard the shot and think the banditos are out here." Pierce let out a sigh. "I s'pose we'd better go back to where you saw the cat and see if we can pick up her trail."

"I think she's up here somewhere," Sam said. "Abby saw the cat in the first place because I was following her sign."

"You found more tracks?"

"No, but a grass trail. You know how the sun reflects

different when the grass has been mashed?"

Pierce nodded. "Where was the last that you noticed it?"

"Come on." Sam led him between the rocks, back toward where they had left their horses. He stopped and grabbed Pierce's arm. "Look. Pa and the rest are taking the horses into the rocks."

Pierce's eyes narrowed. "Hurry."

The ground up here was rockier, and the brush more sparse.

"Pa?" Sam called as they drew near.

His father looked up. "They're behind us. We need cover."

"It'd be better further on," Pierce said. "The terrain's rougher around the side of the hill. Hard going, but easier to stay out of sight."

"I heard you fire a shot," Pa said.

"Yeah. Clean missed that cat." Pierce shook his head.

"He headed for the river." Sam glanced back, wishing he'd had a chance at the jaguar.

Pierce said, "He's long gone now. I could track him, but we've got to find the girl."

Abby moved her horse forward. "Mr. Hardy, if we hole up now, we may never find Ellen."

"If we don't, we might not live to find her." Pa's lips twisted in a grim line.

"They might pass us and find her first," Wally said.

Pa let out a sigh. "We've got Pablo and Abby with us. We can't stay out in the open. If they want to fight, we'll have to make a stand. There's no better place we can get to in a hurry."

Sam caught Abby's gaze. She looked worried, but her blue eyes held a stubborn determination.

"I could go on with Sam and Pierce," she said. "We can try to find her."

She was clinging to hope, he could tell—but afraid the search for her sister was about to crumble. She knew it wouldn't do any good to find Ellen if the caballeros killed them all, or if they overpowered them and snatched Ellen again, along with Pablo.

"I haven't seen her trail since back where we spotted the cat," Sam said. The sun was high now. The dew was long gone, and grasses that had been stepped on were getting their shape back to normal.

"So the cat wasn't after her?" Abby looked almost

desperately at him, then Pierce.

"I don't know for sure," Pierce said. "I didn't see any sign of the girl up here."

"Would she come up the hill?" Pa asked. "Don't lost people usually go downhill, taking the easiest way?"

None of them had an answer.

Wally had climbed to the top of a large rock. Now he hopped down. "They're coming. Get ready." He checked his rifle load.

Pa looked hard at Sam. "All right, go with Abby. Take Pablo. Leave your horses with us. Find a place to hide him. The rest of us will stay here and make a stand. You got plenty of ammo?"

"I have more in my saddlebag," Abby said.

"Get it."

She hopped off her horse and opened the saddlebag. Pa touched Pablo's shoulder. "Hide him good, Sam."

Pablo looked up at his father uncertainly.

"It's your best chance," Pa said. "Just … keep your head down."

Abby was back, stuffing extra cartridges into her pocket. She handed a full box to Sam.

"Our guns take the same rounds."

Sam nodded and pocketed the box. Franco and Pierce were leading the horses along the hill, seeking a sheltered place for them. Sam grabbed Pablo's hand and hurried back toward where Pierce had taken his shot at the cat.

Abby stumbled along behind them, carrying her father's rifle. They were soon out of sight of the rest of their party, and Sam was glad. Maybe Don Hernandez's men wouldn't figure out for a while that they had split off.

"You okay?" he asked Abby.

"Yeah." She was puffing, though, carrying the rifle over the rough ground. "Do you think it was wise to leave our horses?"

Sam eyed the steep hillside. He understood her uneasiness at not having the option of trying to outride Don Hernandez's men. "I doubt we'd get them up here without being seen. We couldn't hide them up here, either. But there are lots of rock and hollows where we three can get out of sight. Come on. We need a place where we can see them without them seeing us."

"You think they'll get past your father and the others?" she asked as they labored up the incline.

Sam shrugged. "They're outnumbered."

"You could leave me and Pablo here and go help them."

"No. Pa said to stay with him. I need to do that." He studied each rock, bush, and stunted tree. "Looks like a good place up there. Come on."

They sat with their backs to a big rock, with Pablo nestled between him and Abby. The hill rose behind them, not too steep, but protective. A thicket of mesquite grew before them.

"This is how the jaguar hid," Abby said. "He watched us from behind the leaves."

Pablo shivered. "I would like to see him, but I don't want to meet up with him. Not close, anyway."

Abby smiled. "I know what you mean. I'm sort of glad he got away. He was very beautiful."

Sam studied her face. Talking about the cat, she seemed less worried than she had been since they'd left her home, and yet the danger was greater than ever before. He hoped he could get them home safe—not just the children, but Abby. He couldn't imagine how he could go on if anything happened to her.

In the distance, gunfire erupted, muffled by the hill between them and Pa.

Pablo's body went rigid and he burrowed his head against Sam's arm. Sam wanted to hold him and comfort him, but he needed to keep his rifle ready. He reached over and patted Pablo's head.

"We're all right."

Abby met his gaze over the boy's curled form. "So far," her eyes seemed to say. She took her half box of extra cartridges out and set it on the ground before her.

"Full load?" Sam asked.

She nodded. "I hope we don't need more, but ..."

"Right."

More gunshots sounded. Pablo sucked in a deep breath and shoved his head under Sam's arm.

Abby whipped her head around, just as Sam caught a sound out of place. A couple of small rocks rolled down the hill past him. He looked at Abby, but she was staring up the hillside behind them.

"Someone's up there," she hissed.

Sam's pulse stopped for a moment and then raced. He couldn't see anything, but there were rocks above them, and more brush. In his mind he saw the cat, crouched behind a low bush, ready to spring.

Abby tightened her grip on her rifle's stock and pointed the barrel at a boulder ten yards up the hill, though she couldn't see any movement near it. Whatever had dislodged the pebbles must be close.

The only sounds she heard were the pops of guns in the distance and Pablo's ragged breathing. He clung to Sam's shirttail now, because Sam was kneeling, facing up the hill like she was, his rifle pointed up the slope.

"The cat?" she whispered.

"Maybe. It doesn't seem right for a jungle cat, though. They like to stay near water."

Abby's upper lip trembled, and she bit it, scanning the terrain. "There has to be something." And if that something or someone was above them, it could probably see them. She looked back and forth, from one possible place of concealment to another. Her arms were tired. How long could she hold the rifle up?

A scrabbling sound came from the direction of the boulder she had focused on, and a moment later, Sam yelled, "Hey!"

Abby's heart lurched. "What?"

"I think it's Ellen. She ran."

Abby dropped the rifle and stood. "Ellen!" She scrambled up the hillside, pushing through the long grass and low bushes without thought of snakes or what sort of target she made against the drab hillside. "Ellen!"

Somewhere ahead, someone screamed. The sound was short, but high-pitched enough to be a girl. Or a wild cat.

Abby ran, panting as she fought her long skirts. She barreled over a rise and stopped abruptly, facing a drop-off of about ten feet.

"Ellen?"

After a moment's silence, her sister's quavering voice said, "Miss Sally?"

Relief washed over Abby. She felt squeezed out like a wet

dishcloth. "It's me—Abby. Ellen, where are you?"

"A-abby?"

"Yes. Honey, we're here to take you home. Where are you?"

"I fell. I heard shooting and voices, and I thought the bad men were coming. I ran, and I fell off the rock."

The shaky voice came from below Abby, and she leaned out over the precipice. Below, in a thicket of blackbrush, she saw Ellen's worn boots and the lower legs of the tan cut-down trousers she wore when helping Papa with the ranch work.

"I see you," she called. "Are you hurt?"

"My arm hurts, and I twisted my ankle last night in the dark. Is Papa here?"

"No, but Sam is. We're going to take you home. Stay right where you are. I'll get Sam."

Abby turned back toward where she had left him. Sam was lumbering toward her, carrying both their rifles, and Pablo trotted along beside him, puffing.

"I found her. She's hurt, but not bad. We need to get down below this rock ledge." She led Sam to the rim, where he could see Ellen's position.

Sam surveyed the situation and then looked back down the slope. Abby followed his gaze. No riders were in sight.

"Stay up here with Pablo," Sam said. "I'll go down and bring her up." He laid down the guns and hurried off to the side, seeking a path down the hillside.

Pablo crept close to the edge and peered down. "I see you, Ellen!"

Abby pulled him back. "Careful!"

Ellen cried, "Pablo? Is that you?"

"It's me," Pablo replied.

Abby leaned over once more. "Sam is coming down to get you. Hold on, honey."

"I will."

Abby looked down at Pablo's flushed face. He looked so delighted that she pulled him into her arms.

"We found her," he said in wonder.

"Yes, we did." She could still hear sporadic gunfire, and she wondered how long the fight had been going on. Was anyone hurt? Ellen's plight had driven all thoughts of the ranchmen out of her mind.

She sat down with Pablo on the rock and held on to him,

her eyes closed.

"Are you praying, Miss Abby?" Pablo asked.

She looked at him and smiled. "Yes. We still have much to do."

He nodded soberly. "We have to get home. I don't hear the guns anymore."

Abby swallowed hard. That could mean many things. She raised her head and listened. The only sounds she heard were Sam's thrashings in the brush below.

"I will pray too." Pablo bowed his head and squeezed his eyes shut tight.

Abby's eyes stung with tears. She stroked the little boy's shoulder. *Lord, thank You for letting us find them. Now help us get them home!*

Scuffling among the rocks jerked her back to reality. Sam was climbing up a steep incline, supporting Ellen, whose fair hair hung loose about her dirty face, tangled and matted, giving her a wild, unkempt air. Her plaid shirt had a torn sleeve, and her loose trousers were filthy.

Abby stood and waited with her hands clenched until they were level with her and Pablo, then she moved forward and took her sister in her arms.

"Ellen, dear! Are you all right?"

"I think so, except for my ankle."

"What about your arm?" Abby asked, pushing her away and eyeing her critically.

"I think it will be fine. Do you have anything to eat?"

"Yes, in my saddlebag."

"Where are the horses?" Ellen asked.

"They're—" Abby broke off and looked at Sam. What had happened to the others and the horses? Her legs began to tremble.

"We left them down with Pa and the other ranch hands," Sam said.

"Is Pa all right?" Pablo looked up into Sam's face.

Sam hesitated. "He may need help. I think I can go over the top of the hill and get to him—maybe be in a better position than if I went back the way we came." He looked hard at Abby. "Keep them here. Stay with them, won't you?"

Abby nodded. Mr. Hardy had told Sam to stay with her and Pablo, but what if he and his men were in desperate need? What if one more rifle made the difference for them all? She couldn't think of a better plan.

Sam hefted his long gun and sprinted up the hill away from them. Abby turned her attention to Ellen, who lay sprawled on the ground.

"How far are we from home?" Ellen asked.

"A long ways."

"I thought if I could get away, I could find the road, but I couldn't. I must have gone the wrong direction."

"Yeah, that's what happened," Abby said. "Sam and one of Mr. Hardy's men found your trail. But why did you come up here?"

"I was afraid." Ellen sniffed. "I thought they were chasing me, and I was looking for a place to hide. I guess I heard you, but I thought it was them. The Mexicans. Why did they want me?"

"They're Pablo's grandfather's men," Abby said. "They were taking Pablo to him." She hoped Ellen wouldn't press her about her own capture.

"They shot Papa."

Abby nodded. "He's hurt. But he made it home. Ma's taking care of him."

Ellen met her gaze for a moment. "I thought he was dead."

"No, he was talking to Mr. Hardy before we left." Abby looked up the hill, where Sam had gone. "If we get back to the horses, I've got one of your dresses and my cloak, if you want it."

"A dress? Why did you bring a dress?"

Abby opened her mouth and closed it. She wouldn't tell Ellen she had feared her clothing had been torn from her.

Pablo had listened avidly as they talked, and now he crept forward and knelt at Ellen's side. He touched her arm and peered into her eyes.

"I tried to get away, Ellen."

"I know you did. I waited, but I knew that sooner or later they'd see I wasn't where I was supposed to be. I figured it was better if I went back to that town where they changed horses and got someone to help than to hang around where they were and get caught again."

"You did just right," Abby said. She put one arm around Pablo and rested her other hand on Ellen's shoulder, trying to think what she could do now to ensure their safety. What if Mr. Hardy and the others had been overcome? How could she ensure that Pablo and Ellen would get home again? They had no horses now, and they were separated from the only people out here who would help them. Maybe they should have left Ellen below the ridge and climbed down there to hide with her.

"Did you see the cat?" Pablo asked.

"What cat?" Ellen blinked at him and stared up at Abby. "What's he talking about?"

"Sam and I saw a wild cat, that's all. We thought at first he might be following you, but Sam scared him off."

"A cat was chasing me?" Ellen struggled to sit up. "Was he going to kill me?"

"No, no, honey." Abby pulled her close and held her on one side and Pablo on the other.

In the distance, an outbreak of gunfire made her catch her breath. She raised her head to listen. The reports seemed closer than before.

Ellen grabbed Abby's arm and dug her fingernails into her wrist.

"Don't let them take me again!"

"I won't." Gently, Abby pried off her fingers and stood. She had left her rifle a few steps away. As she bent to retrieve it, she heard someone below, scrabbling on the path. She ducked low behind the brush that was her only cover. Three swarthy men were climbing the hillside with pistols in their hands.

She crawled back to Ellen and Pablo, dragging the rifle.

"Quick! We have to hide."

Ellen's eyes widened. "Where?"

Abby looked around. There was no time to take Sam's treacherous trail down to the thicket where Ellen had lain. Only one rock was close enough, and it wouldn't hide all of them. She shoved Ellen toward it.

"Get behind there. Take Pablo." She turned to the boy. He was standing and staring the way they had come.

"Get down!" Abby pulled him off his feet.

"It's Cinco," Pablo whispered, his eyes round.

"Did he see you?"

"I don't think so."

"Get behind the rock with Ellen." Abby gave him a shove. Ellen was already crawling toward the boulder.

Abby turned and checked the rifle. She saw movement on the path, and the big man's head appeared beyond the mesquite bushes, only yards away.

"Don't come any closer." She spoke as firmly as she could and trained the rifle on his face.

The man halted and stared at her. A slow smile crept over his face. "Well, well. Where did you come from?"

"Tell your men to stay back."

"You can't shoot us all," Cinco said.

"Can't I? I'm very good," Abby said.

He laughed. "Where is Pablito?"

She raised her chin a fraction of an inch. "If you make it back to the rancho, tell Don Hernandez that Pablo will not come. He is staying with his father."

"You can tell him yourself, when we get there." Cinco took a step forward. She could see his torso now, and she adjusted her aim toward his heart.

"I'm not going anywhere with you."

"No?"

He took another step. Two more, and his long arms would be able to grasp the gun barrel. He could throw off her aim and wrench the rifle away from her. A story Papa had told her flashed through her mind in an instant. His older brother had faced down a Yankee on the battlefield, and the Yankee got too close. Uncle Jay was out of ammo, but he lunged toward the enemy soldier and grabbed the rifle from his hands. He shot that Yankee with his own gun.

Abby swallowed hard. Could she really pull the trigger? In an instant, the alternative flashed before her. She would be in Cinco's power, and so would Ellen, if she failed. Pablo would be transported to Don Hernandez. She and her sister would be sold into evil.

Cinco moved one foot forward and then caught his breath. She heard a sound behind her at the same moment she pulled the trigger. The big man flew backward, his arms flailing as he plummeted down the hillside. The two men below ran to him, then looked up at her. She saw confusion and fear in their eyes.

"Take him back to Don Hernandez!"

She jumped at Sam's voice, so close beside her, and turned to stare at him.

"I came over the hill again."

"Your father?"

"He's winged, and Franco took a bullet in his leg."

Below them, the two caballeros were half carrying, half

dragging Cinco's body. In the distance, she saw three horses ground tied.

"How many outlaws are left?"

"This is it."

Her jaw dropped. "You're joking."

Sam shook his head, still watching the men below. "Pa and the men had picked off four of them by the time I got to the top of the hill. I was able to hit two more from up there. Three of the cowards rode off, heading for the river." He glanced down at her. "You all right?"

"Yes. Did I shoot him, or did you?"

"Maybe both. You did well, Abby. I guess you didn't really need me."

"I was shaking," she admitted. "I probably missed him clean."

"Maybe so," Sam said, but Abby doubted she had missed him at that range. Sam smiled. "Come on, let's get the kids."

Abby sacrificed the extra petticoat she'd brought to make bandages for Mr. Hardy and Franco. Both insisted they could ride home that day, but Sam made them stop in Ripton. The doctor who had come to tend Tracy changed Mr. Hardy's dressing for a proper bandage and took the bullet out of Franco's leg.

They had arrived with all of their horses except Wally's, which had been caught in the crossfire during the gun battle, but they had also rounded up four of the Mexicans' mounts.

"I probably will never see the others they took again," the blacksmith said, "but that's all right. I figured I got the best end of the trade with them in the first place."

"You'd better keep the extras to make up for the ones you won't get back," Mr. Hardy said.

He shook his head. "Too many. I think you've earned a couple of them. You must need extra horses on your ranch."

Mr. Hardy seemed to be deep in thought for a moment. "Well, keep one to replace the chestnut Miss Ellen rode in on when the banditos had her. She'll be riding him home. I'll take one of the extras. And one should go to Miss Abby."

"Me?" Abby stared at him.

"Sam tells me you shot Cinco," Mr. Hardy said. "And you kept Pablo safe. You earned it."

The blacksmith smiled at her. "Take one of those fancy saddles, too, miss. If you don't like it, you can sell it for a pretty penny."

"The saddles are worth five times what the horses are," Pierce confirmed.

The men continued to discuss the horses. In the end, they rode out on their original mounts except for Wally, who rode Mr. Hardy's new horse, a choice one he picked from among those the Mexicans had left with the blacksmith. Sam and Abby had Stubby and Minnie back, and Sam offered to lead Abby's new horse, a sturdy brown gelding, for her. Franco proved his mettle when he got into the saddle with a little help from Pierce.

At the last minute, the blacksmith snapped his fingers. "I almost forgot. Do you want the pony?"

"What pony?" Mr. Hardy asked.

"The little gray one they took for the kid. They paid me for him."

"My pony?" Pablo cried, his eyes bright. Clearly the pony was the one pleasant thing about the adventure for Pablo.

"He came tearing back in the middle of the night, trailing a picket line," the blacksmith said. "I reckon he belongs to the boy."

The little gray nickered when it saw Pablo, and he ran to it and threw his arms around its neck. "Papa, can I ride him home?"

Mr. Hardy cracked a smile. "I was hoping you'd ride with me, son."

"I will ride beside you."

"All right, I reckon you're big enough to handle him."

Sam caught Abby's gaze and smiled at her. "You ready to go home?"

"Past ready," she said. "Let's go."

CHAPTER EIGHT

AS THE SUN WAS SETTING, A horse approached the house. Abby looked out the window and quickly removed her apron. There was no time to brush her hair before a knock came on the door.

"Sam."

He smiled. "Hi."

He looked good, Abby thought. Rested. Content.

"Come on in." She held the door wide. Cynthia and Ellen, who were doing the supper dishes, turned toward them.

"Hello, Sam," Ellen said.

Cynthia gave him a shy smile and ducked her head.

"Hello, girls." Sam turned his attention back to Abby. "How's your pa?"

"Better. Still has a lot of pain." Ten days had passed since he was wounded, and the doctor from town said it would take him several months to heal. "Ma's with him now."

Sam nodded. "I'm going into town tomorrow for supplies, and I wondered if you folks needed anything."

"That would help us a lot," Abby said. "I'll get Ma's list."

She hurried into her parents' room, where Ma sat on the edge of the bed beside Papa, and Charlie played quietly on the rug with the toy animals Pa had carved for him last Christmas.

"Sam's here. He'll pick up supplies for us tomorrow if we want."

"That's nice of him." Ma got up and went to fetch the list.

"Tell him thank you," Pa said softly.

"I will."

Pa grimaced and put his hand over the spot where his abdomen was bandaged. "Sam's a good man."

Abby took the list from her mother's hand and carried the

scrap of paper to the front room.

"Aw, that old cat wouldn't want to eat you," Sam was saying with a grin at Ellen. "He'd see in one glance that you were too scrawny. Now, a coyote, maybe. He might think you were the right size for dinner."

Ellen laughed, and even Cynthia cracked a smile. Abby was glad to see Ellen able to take a joke about her ordeal.

"Here you go." She held out the paper.

"Good." Sam took it and met her gaze with sober gray eyes. "Could I talk to you for a minute?" His gaze slid toward the door.

Abby's heart tripped. She was surprised at his request, but she wasn't about to say no.

"Sure." She pulled ma's shawl from a hook by the doorjamb. "I'll be back in a minute, Ellen."

Before her sisters could respond, she ducked outside, and Sam followed her, shutting the door softly. She walked down off the porch and a few steps into the yard before she turned to face him.

"What is it? Is Pablo all right?"

"He's fine. Pa's keeping him close, though."

"That's understandable."

Sam nodded. "I wondered . . . well, I'd like to call on you."

Abby blinked. "You mean . . ."

"I mean . . . well, if you're of a mind to." Sam shook his head. "When we were on the trail, going after the kids, I realized I like you a lot. And after we got home, I kept thinking about you."

Abby pulled in a slow breath. "I've been thinking about you too, Sam." If he knew how much, they would probably both be embarrassed.

"So . . . could I come over to see you again?"

"There's preaching next week. Come for dinner after?"

She hadn't realized how tense he was until Sam relaxed his shoulders.

"That'd be fine. Do you need to ask your folks?"

"I don't think so. They like you. I'll look forward to it."

Sam smiled back at her, and her stomach lurched.

"Papa says thank you," she blurted, to break the silence. "For getting the groceries, I mean. Or maybe for what you did for Ellen and me. I'm not sure, really, but—"

Sam pulled her toward him, startling her into silence.

"I wanted to kiss you when we were out there," Sam whispered. "But then I thought it was just because of everything that was happening, and we were scared, and maybe I wouldn't ever get another chance. But after we got home, I still wished it."

Abby gazed up into his eyes. Sam was holding his breath.

"This might be another chance," she managed.

Sam Hardy was not a man to make the same mistake twice.

April, 1881

When the Bunter family's wagon pulled up before the little church in Harrisville, Abby's eyes went straight to Sam. He was waiting, with his father and Pablo, near the steps. All of them wore their Sunday best.

Mr. Hardy came over to help Ma down, and Sam gave Abby his hand. Then he offered a hand to Ellen and Cynthia, while his father watched Papa climb slowly down from the wagon as though expecting him to fall.

"Let me help you unhitch the team," Mr. Hardy said.

"I can do it, but I won't say no to a hand," Papa said. He walked around to the horses' heads with a slight hitch to his gait.

"You getting along all right?" Mr. Hardy asked.

"Did fine this week. I'll need some help at branding time."

Papa had made a slow recovery over the winter, and he still moved slowly, but the doctor said his lung had healed where the bullet had nicked it.

Abby turned her attention to Sam.

"Ready?" she asked.

"I admit I'm a little nervous."

"You look nice," she said.

Sam grinned. "You look wonderful yourself."

Abby smiled and wished she wasn't blushing. Ma had worked on the new dress with her for weeks. Her light blue wedding dress had yards of lace that she could remove later to make the dress more suitable for her usual pursuits. It would be her best Sunday dress from now on, and she would add the lace to a petticoat and the linen pillowcases she had stitched for her hope chest.

Pablo tugged at Sam's sleeve. "Lots of people are going in."

Sam looked toward the church, where two local families were climbing the steps.

"I guess word about the wedding got out," Sam said, glancing at Abby. "Hope you don't mind."

"Guess not," she said. "Ma made a really big cake."

"Frannie made six pies," Pablo said.

"Then we should have plenty."

Ma stepped up beside her. "You menfolk should go in. Sam, don't you know the groom's not supposed to see the bride before the ceremony?"

Sam shrugged. "Sounds like superstition to me. But come on, Pablo. Charlie, you might as well come with us."

Mr. Hardy and Papa finished with the team and laid the harness in the wagon bed. They all walked over to the church steps. Ma turned and pulled Abby into her arms.

"Bless you, child. I think you'll be happy with Sam."

"I think so, too," Abby whispered.

Mr. Hardy and Ma hustled the girls inside, and Abby looked up at her father.

"You doing all right, Papa?"

"I think I'll make it down the aisle." He smiled at her. "Abigail, you're a fine young woman. I hate to let you go, but Sam's a good man."

"Thank you, Papa."

He nodded soberly. "I don't know if I ever said it, but if you hadn't gone after Ellen ..."

"It's all right. We got her back." Abby wondered if Mr. Hardy would have kept looking for her sister if she hadn't been along, but she never told her parents about that. Sam was the one who had made sure the other men didn't turn back. He was her hero, and she would never forget his loyalty in her time of need.

Her father leaned down and kissed her cheek. "You are a picture. Like your Ma was."

Abby smiled. "That means a lot, Papa. Thank you."

"You won't be a stranger?"

"You know Sam's coming over on Monday to help you sort

the calves. And I'm coming too."

"That's all right, then," he said with evident satisfaction.

The church door opened, and Ellen peeked out, her eyes sparkling.

"It's time."

Abby looked up at her father, suddenly a little giddy. He crooked his arm.

"Shall we?"

"Yes," she said firmly.

They walked into the church together. Sam stood at the front with the minister. Abby was surprised to see about forty people in the pews, including all of the Hardys' ranch hands. Pablo and Charlie knelt backward on the front pew, peering at her down the length of the church. But she didn't think about them for long. Sam studied her gravely. When she met his gaze, he smiled with such promise that Abby knew her new life was going to be good, the future she'd dreamed of, and the settled happiness she had longed for.

The End

If you'd like to learn more about Susan Page Davis or sign up for her newsletter, please visit her website: www.susanpagedavis.com

HEARTS REUNITED

BY MIRALEE FERRELL

CHAPTER ONE

Tucson, Arizona, 1880s

JESSE TOWNSEND SCOWLED, HOPING HE HADN'T heard Warren, his ranch foreman, correctly. "Where is Twilight now, and how did she get hurt? That mare's been watched closely since she's due to foal in a few weeks."

Warren shook his head. "She's in the barn. We moved her out of the corral. Dunno for sure how she got hurt, boss. Maybe Johnny was asleep on the job again, but I don't think so. The kid learned his lesson after I tossed water in his face the last time. He was plumb embarrassed. Guess Twilight must have got bored and kicked the pen, then backed up and rubbed against a broken board to scratch herself. It's all I can figure. She's got a nasty cut that's gonna need doctorin'."

"Let's take a look. I need to see what we're up against. I've doctored plenty of cows on the trail, as well as horses here on the ranch. I'm guessing I can take care of whatever it is." Jesse stepped off the front porch of the single-story, sprawling ranch house he'd been raised in and headed toward the barn. He swung open the barn door and let Jesse pass through then followed.

Jesse stopped in front of the first stall and peered over the half door at the mare standing three-legged inside. He unlatched the gate and stepped in, talking in a low voice to the snorting mare. "Easy, girl. Let me take a look at you." He stooped and ran his hand over her hip. She flinched and moved away. "Warren, slip a halter on her and lead her into the alleyway near the outside doors where we have better light."

He waited for his foreman to move the mare then took

another look and groaned. A long, jagged gash ran from a point half-way down her hip to within inches of the top of her hock. "Looks bad. Did you clean it yet?"

"Yep. Washed it with clean water first, then doused it with whiskey. Thought she'd kick my head in when I done it. Maybe it will help. All I knew to do."

Jesse blew out a long breath. "Right. I've never tackled anything this deep. Sure hate the thought of my best mare not healing properly."

"I could send for the gal who works on horses from time to time."

"Gal?" Jesse didn't slow his stride as he glanced at his foreman. "I know I've been gone a few years, but don't tell me Dad used a woman to tend to his stock? I don't believe it."

Warren shrugged. "You know your pa. He did things his own self, and he did a right decent job of it too, so he didn't need anyone else. 'Sides, doubtful he would'a used this gal, anyway." He shot a sideways look at Jesse. "You might not either, but she's good. I can attest to that. We used her a couple times after your pa died and before you got word to come home. Didn't have much choice. I'm not a good hand at dealin' with sick horses, and with this blooded stock, I didn't want to lose any before you got home. I'd recommend you give her a chance."

"So who is this woman? I can't believe we don't have a male veterinarian in this area, with all the ranches around Tucson."

"We do, kind of—Doc Hadley—so he's called. He don't have any formal trainin', although he gets the job done most of the time. But he lives clean on the other side of town and out a ways. He mostly tends his own stock and a few close friends. He might come if we sent someone over there, but this gal is close by and willin'."

A sense of foreboding colored the thoughts churning in Jesse's mind. "Close? Exactly who is this 'gal' you keep referring to, and why haven't you mentioned her name? Is she new to town?"

Warren didn't meet his gaze. "Uh—no. She's been around these parts all her life. I expect you know her, boss, since she's a neighbor—Mercedes Taylor."

Jesse's eyes widened. "Mercedes Taylor, as in Joshua Taylor's daughter?"

"That would be her, boss." Warren scuffed his boot against the dirt floor of the alleyway. "Want I should put Twilight back in her stall?"

Jesse shook his head to clear it. "Yeah. Sure. Thanks." Mercedes Taylor, his childhood friend whom he hadn't seen much of for years. He hadn't spent time with Mercedes since she was fourteen and barely out of short skirts and pigtails, and hadn't seen her since she turned sixteen. He still hurt when he thought of what he'd lost with Mercedes—the daughter of his father's one-time friend who had been the cause of them losing a number of their best horses. "Warren, send someone pronto over to Doc Hadley's place and see if he'll come."

Warren narrowed his eyes for a brief moment then nodded. "Will do. I'll send Johnny and tell him to hurry. This mare needs tendin' sooner rather than later." He swung away, although Jesse didn't miss the glimmer of disapproval in the older man's eyes.

Well, so be it. Warren could disapprove all he wanted to. Jesse wasn't putting the welfare of one of his prize mares in the hands of the very girl who was riding the horse that caused his favorite gelding to die. Not now, and not ever, no matter how close a friendship or how smitten he'd been when he was sixteen.

He paced the area in front of the barn for over a half hour, waiting for Johnny to return. He'd ridden their fastest gelding with instructions to tell Doc Hadley there was urgent need of his services. Where was the man? He pulled out his pocket watch again, but only two minutes had passed since he'd last checked.

Hoofbeats thundered on the lane leading to the house, and Jesse strode toward the corner of the barn. Sure didn't sound like two horses. Maybe the doc had hurried ahead and Johnny was giving his horse a rest. He shaded his eyes against the harsh glare of the June sun and groaned as his cowboy pulled his lathered horse to a sliding stop, sending dust spraying in all directions.

Jesse stepped forward. "Where's the doc?"

Johnny took off his hat and swiped at the sweat trickling down his forehead. "Said he couldn't come. One of his cows is giving birth, and it's breach. Said when he's done tendin' it, he's got another one that needs doctoring. Told me he might be able to come later tonight if you still need him, but you probably better get someone else to sew up Twilight. He was real sorry, said you could dump carbolic on it and let it heal if you don't care about a nasty scar."

Jesse gave a curt nod. "Thanks for trying, Johnny. Go unsaddle that horse and cool him off."

"How about Twilight? You think about fetching Miss Taylor? She's good with horses—she has a way with 'em." He blushed. "Plus she's mighty pretty, if you don't mind me saying so."

Jesse's head jerked up. "Why would I mind? I haven't seen her in years." He waved the cowboy away. He wasn't going to ask Mercedes to tend to one of his horses.

Someone cleared his throat behind him, and Jesse pivoted.

Warren gave a short nod. "No Doc Hadley, huh? Pretty much what I figured. You gonna ride over to Miss Taylor's now? That mare's not gettin' any better standin' in that stall."

Jesse closed his eyes for a brief moment then opened them. "How about you ride over and ask her?"

Warren shook his head. "No, sir, boss. If I were to ask, she wouldn't come. Sorry, but everyone in Tucson knows about the fallin' out her pa and yours had years ago. She came while you were gone, after your pa died, 'cause she cares about horses. She may not even come if you ask her, but if you aim to get Twilight proper care then it's worth a shot."

Jesse swung around without speaking and headed into the barn, more irritated than he'd been for a long time. Visions of the dark-haired Mercedes flashed through his memory as he'd seen her that last day they'd spent together. Happy and carefree as they'd raced their horses neck-and-neck across the flat, sparsely grassed land on the edge of the ranch. Then she'd pulled to a sudden stop when her horse started wheezing, Mercedes' face a mask of concern. He shook the image away, refusing to dwell on the pain he'd seen reflected there. He didn't want to see her again, and he certainly didn't want to ask for her help, but it appeared he had no choice.

CHAPTER TWO

MERCEDES GRUNTED AS SHE SAT ON the prone horse's neck and wove the bandana under the rope halter, praying she'd get the angry young stallion's eyes covered before he gathered his strength for another lunge to his feet. She'd been tossed hard once already while trying to get this job done and didn't relish additional bruises on top of those. Good thing she had changed out of the skirt she used for riding and put on a pair of men's trousers, as even her split skirt would've been mangled or torn in the melee that ensued while throwing this horse.

"Need any help, Mercedes?" A man's slow drawl from the far side of the corral fence drifted easily to her ears.

She would know that voice anywhere—even if she hadn't heard it in years. It was all she could do not to jump off the horse and fly over to the fence to greet her old friend, but she clamped down on the desire and killed it. Jesse had deserted her when she'd needed him the most. "No thanks, Jesse. You haven't been around to help me for years, why should I want you now? Besides, I can't believe you came back to Tucson or showed up here." She cast a quick glance at the man who'd been her best friend when they were young—until the war between their fathers got in the way.

He shrugged a broad shoulder and stepped onto the split rail fence. "My pa died four months ago and someone needed to run the ranch. I always planned to return someday."

A flutter of hope rose in her chest, but she pushed it aside. "Five years is a long time to be gone playing cowboy when you were needed at home. Now quit bothering me. I've got to deal with this horse."

Her father had barely been in the ground for two years, and he'd be angrier than this quivery stallion if he knew she was talking to a Townsend. She opened her lips to ask Jesse to leave when the horse beneath her lashed out his hind legs, almost unseating her. A quick twist and she finished knotting the bandana around the halter. Now to get off and clear of those thrashing hooves. Where was Martin when she needed him? "Martin! What's taking you so long?"

No thump of footfalls sounded in the distance.

The stallion thrashed again, and Mercedes let go, rolling to the side and pushing to her feet. The animal was mad clear through, and she couldn't blame him. If she'd tolerated the kind of pain he'd been in the past twelve hours with a sharp rock wedged in his hoof, she would want to kick somebody too.

Jesse vaulted the fence and ran toward her. "Get away from there! What are you thinking? He's going to run you over or kick your head in." He slid to a stop beside her and grabbed her arm, pulling her to the side of the corral.

A sharp shock ran through Mercedes where Jesse's hand lay, but she shook him off. This was her first real look at Jesse Townsend in five years. She'd seen him around from time to time after their families parted ways, then he'd left the area two years later to hit the trail as a cowhand.

He'd grown up a lot—become a man. He'd been skinny as a boy, but his shoulders had filled out, probably from wrestling calves, chopping wood, and all the other chores that came with trail driving big herds of cattle. His eyes were still the same deep blue, his blond hair had darkened to a light brown, and he'd shot past her by several inches. She didn't remember having to look up so far when he was sixteen.

She pointed at the stallion standing frozen in the middle of the corral. "Does he look like he's going to run over anyone? Sure he kicked out. You would too if you were in pain. But he's not going to run over anyone. He can barely walk. Besides, you're the one who spooked him by running in here yelling. Where's Martin, anyway?"

Jesse took off his cowboy hat and slapped it against his pant leg, sending dust flying. "I haven't seen your ranch hand." He gestured toward the horse. "That's not what it looked like to me—when he got to his feet he lashed out with both back hooves. If you hadn't gotten clear he'd have broken your leg." He rammed the hat back on his unruly hair in bad need of a trim. "Why is he blindfolded if he's not dangerous?"

She shook her head. "Mind getting on the other side of the fence? I haven't had him long, and he doesn't trust men. At all. I think someone beat him pretty bad while trying to break him. I got a halter on him, but when I tried to slip the bandana over his eyes, he reared then fell on his side. Lucky I sat on his neck before he got up, or I'd still be trying to catch him." She didn't bother to tell him about having to throw the horse again after he'd unseated her and sent her rolling.

"Lucky, or stupid." Jesse's barely discernable words reached her ears as he climbed up and perched on the top rail.

"I heard that." She glared at him. "Now leave me alone while I get this rock out of his hoof before it permanently lames him."

"Let Martin do that. Why do you keep the man around if he's not here when you need him?"

"Like I said. This horse doesn't trust men. Martin is good with horses, but he'd never get close to this one." She edged forward, dropping her voice to a low croon. "Come on, beautiful. You know I'm not going to hurt you."

Jesse lowered his voice to a strong whisper. "Good thing he can't see you. He's shaking all over."

"Yeah. I figured he might be calmer if he couldn't see to race around the fence line away from me." She kept moving toward the big black, her tone soothing and her hand outstretched. In a matter of minutes, she touched his neck, stroking him as he stood quivering, obviously unsure of what was to come. "It's all right. No one's going to hurt you. Shh. Come on, boy." Mercedes worked her way to his tail, stroking from his withers to his hip, then she paused.

She slid her fingers down his leg and with her other hand, pulled a curved piece of metal with a sharp point out of her back pocket. "This will only take a moment. Easy now." She lifted the black's hoof only inches off the ground, guessing he wouldn't allow more, then quick as anything, she dug the point of the hoof pick under the rock wedged in his heel and popped it out. She set the hoof gently on the ground then walked to the stallion's head and untied the bandana. The horse snorted and trotted to the far side of the corral where she'd placed hay earlier that day.

"Don't think I could have done better myself. Well, maybe I could." Jesse gave a rueful grin as she looked up.

Mercedes scowled, working hard to keep her irritation and anger at this man in the forefront of her mind. He shouldn't be here—it wasn't right or natural or, or—anything. "So why are you here? I don't see you for years then you show up on my ranch?"

Jesse straightened, and his face grew serious. "Twilight, my best mare, busted a rail on the corral fence, then backed into it and sliced her hip open. Warren cleaned it, but neither of us wants to tackle sewing it up." A scowl flashed across his handsome features. "He claims you know what you're doing."

She bit her lip to keep something rude from escaping. The horse was hurt, which was all that was important right now. "Why didn't you get Doc Hadley?"

He shrugged. "Believe me, I tried. He's busy and can't get there until this evening. I think it'll be too late to stitch it by then. The wound will have dried out."

Mercedes sighed. "Right. It will have. Needs to be stitched right away. How long has it been now?"

Jesse pulled out his watch. "About an hour or so, I think." He looked up. "You don't have to come. I know how our fathers felt about each other." He jumped off the fence then untied his horse's reins. "I'll see what I can do for Twilight. No need to bother you—a woman shouldn't be dealing with such bloody business, anyway."

Frustration boiled to the surface, and this time, Mercedes didn't try to hold it back. "Women deal with cuts, blood, and grime all the time, and you know it. We skin the rabbits the men shoot, clean the fish, doctor the family when there's an injury or sickness and the doctor can't come." She shook her head. "I have carbolic acid and chloroform in a bag in the house along with other supplies. I'll get it and come."

He took a step back, drawing his horse after him. "Maybe I made a mistake. I shouldn't have bothered you."

She held up her hand and stopped him. "I'm not coming because you asked. Twilight needs to be sewn up properly, and she needs that wound cleaned so no infection sets in. So don't argue, unless you think you can do a better job."

She could clearly see the war taking place mirrored in Jesse's eyes and expression, but apparently common sense won as the muscles of his face relaxed.

He gave a brief nod. "Fine. Warren says you're competent, so I'll have to trust his judgment."

She swung around and headed to the corral gate. Right now she wished she'd said no to this arrogant man. Why had he even bothered to come for help if he didn't trust her competence? When she'd heard he'd returned to Tucson, she had prayed she wouldn't have to see him, even though another part of her heart had prayed for something entirely different. It would appear she'd have to squash that section of her heart and her hopes, and the sooner the better.

CHAPTER THREE

JESSE COULDN'T BELIEVE HOW MUCH MERCEDES had changed since he'd seen her. She'd been blossoming into a young lady at the age of sixteen, but at twenty-one she had matured into a lovely woman—in spite of the trousers and untucked shirt that had probably belonged to her father—now thoroughly stained by dirt.

He cast her another look as he rode beside her back to the ranch. She hadn't taken time to change into the split skirt she always used to wear or comb her hair that had loosened from her braid. Black curls clustered around her collar and over her shoulders, her hair even longer and thicker than he remembered.

He worked to harden his heart against the memories of pulling those locks and putting frogs on her head, then ducking to avoid her swinging fist. How he'd loved those idyllic days of childhood. He clamped down on his thoughts—they weren't children any longer. If only there was a way to go back. Part of him longed to restore the relationship they'd once enjoyed, but it appeared that too much hurt had flowed between the families to change things now.

They reined to a stop in front of his barn sooner than he'd expected. Jesse shook himself—time to get down to the business of tending to his mare. "What do you need me to do?"

Mercedes dismounted from her horse, her booted feet landing softly in the dirt, then she reached up and untied her black leather bag from behind the saddle. "How tame is this mare? Think you can get her down in her stall? A small dose of chloroform will help keep her calm so I can stitch her. But she's got to be down first, or she could fall onto the side I need to work on."

"Shouldn't be a problem. I told Warren and Johnny to strip the stall and get clean straw in there before we returned."

"Good." She followed him through the open door of the barn and glanced around. "Not much has changed in here since we were kids." Her words were soft and almost sad.

Jesse strode forward, determined not to react. Yes, not much *had* changed, other than a cancelled contract from their biggest buyer that almost cost them the ranch. All because Mercedes hadn't told him that her horse was sick. And even if she hadn't realized it, her father should have—and his father never forgave either of them. It might not have hit Jesse so hard if the gelding he'd been riding—the first of their horses to contract the sickness—hadn't been an orphaned foal he'd hand-raised and loved. That had cut deep. And she'd never come to him and apologized—never acknowledged her part in the disaster.

"Warren? Johnny? Anyone in here?" The words bounced back in the cavernous barn. He swung open Twilight's stall and noted the fresh straw. But where was the mare? A nicker from two doors down answered his call, and Twilight poked her head over the half-door. "There you are, girl. Come on, let's get you moved." He glanced at Mercedes. "You ready?"

"You might want to get one of the other men out here first, in case you need help getting her down." She stepped into the stall. "I'll check over my things while you take care of that."

Jesse nodded and headed out. Ten minutes later, he and Warren had Twilight down. Warren stayed by her head, stroking her neck and crooning to her. Jesse cocked an eyebrow at Mercedes. "You sure you know what you're doing?"

She shot him a steady look. "I've done this before, Jesse." She sank to her knees beside the mare and tipped an open bottle against a clean rag, then held it close to the injured horse's nostrils. The mare jerked back, but Warren held her firm. Mercedes passed her hand down the length of the mare's nose and stroked the moist rag around her distended nostrils. "I won't give her much. Warren, once she starts to relax, would you hold this rag close but not over her nose?"

The ranch foreman nodded and took the rag.

Relief hit Jesse hard. At least she was taking precautions not to kill *this* horse. He watched carefully as she poured carbolic over the open wound, then leaned over the mare's hip and carefully inserted the needle. Nothing but compassion filled her face. What had he expected? Delight that his horse had been hurt? What a stupid thought. She had offered to come and hadn't even hesitated when he'd been the one to ask. Somehow he needed to shed the years of hurt, but he didn't have the foggiest idea how to begin.

Mercedes took the wet cloth Jesse offered, making sure her fingers didn't touch his. She wiped off the blood then nodded to Warren. "You can remove the rag now, but stay with her until she's able to get up on her own and stand without any trouble. And I'd suggest you keep an eye on her for an hour or so afterward, as well."

Johnny poked his head over the half-door. "I'm done with my chores, Miss Taylor. I'd be happy to stay with her if you'd like." His freckled face broke into a smile.

"That's very kind of you." She glanced at Jesse, and all she could see was the frown marring his handsome features. Come to think of it, other than that one grin over at her place, she hadn't seen the man smile the entire time she'd been with him. "That is, if Jesse doesn't mind." She sighed. "Jesse?"

He seemed to jolt out of his thoughts and nodded. "Yeah. That'll allow Warren and me time to get our work done. Thanks, Johnny."

"Anything to help Miss Taylor—and you, boss." Red rushed into the cowhand's ears.

Mercedes turned away, not wanting to encourage the young man, although he had to be her age or even a year or two older, from what she remembered. She looked at Jesse and saw his frown deepen. This was ridiculous. She turned to Johnny once again and smiled. "Thank you, Johnny. The mare needs someone with a quiet voice and kind heart to stay with her, so I'm guessing you'll do nicely."

"Yes, ma'am. I'll do my best." He edged inside the door and sidled along the side wall until he reached the mare's head. "I can take over, boss, if you want me to."

Warren nodded. "Right."

Twilight snorted and lifted her head. Johnny settled beside her and stroked her face. "Easy girl. You don't want to rip out those stitches, after Miss Taylor worked so hard to fix you up all nice and pretty."

Jesse grunted and pushed to his feet. He beckoned her toward the door then stepped aside so she could go first. "What do I owe you, Mercedes?" He pulled the door shut behind Warren as the man stepped out then walked on past them.

She bit her lip. She didn't often charge people. Normally, they gave what they could—when they thought about doing so. There was no way she was going to ask Jesse Townsend for anything, even if she *was* close to being broke. "Don't worry about it. That's what neighbors do."

"Nonsense." He dug into his pocket and withdrew a roll of cash. "Even if you aren't a vet, you probably don't do this just to be kind. How much?"

Something about his tone grated on her, and she took a step back. "I said you don't owe me anything. I need to head home now. I have my own chores to tend to." She tipped her head. "Take care of that mare, and if you see any sign of redness or swelling beyond what there is now, come get me, or send for Doc Hadley if you'd prefer. And by the way, I often care for animals out of kindness, as I hate to see them suffer." Her voice dropped and took on a slight bitter edge. "It's rare people think to pay me. Good-day." She pivoted and headed outside where her horse waited at the hitching rail, head drooping.

The sound of Jesse's footfalls followed her. She halted at the sound of wheels and a horse clip-clopping into the barnyard.

Mercedes pivoted and stared at the buggy, then glanced at Jesse.

His eyebrows rose, and the first smile Mercedes had seen in the last hour tipped up his lips. He stepped toward the carriage. "Miss Ellington? What brings you out our way?"

A young woman with long blond hair pulled behind her ears and cascading down her back reined her horse to a stop. She waved a gloved hand and smiled, displaying perfect teeth. In fact, to Mercedes's eyes, everything about this woman spelled perfection. The hat perched on her perfectly formed head was exquisite—not too large or ostentatious, and decorated tastefully. Her emerald-colored gown clung in all the right places, and the lace-edged collar drew attention to her long, graceful neck.

Suddenly Mercedes became aware of her trousers and old shirt in a way she never had before. She could wear fine clothing and stand up against any woman when the time required, but that wasn't often the case. If only she'd taken the time to remove these grubby trousers and wear her split skirt. She glanced down and grimaced. A blood stain. She placed her hand over the spot on her thigh, hoping to cover it.

Jesse was staring at her. "Do you know Miss Ellington?"

Mercedes shook her head. "I'm afraid I haven't made her acquaintance."

Jesse nodded. "Miss Cassandra Ellington, I'd like to introduce you to my neighbor, Miss Mercedes Taylor." He turned to Mercedes. "Miss Ellington moved here with her parents shortly after I arrived. Her father is our new banker. I'm surprised you two haven't met."

Mercedes shrugged. "My work on the ranch keeps me busy, and since Martin does a lot of my shopping when Clara isn't able to, I have no reason to go to town."

Miss Ellington's brows rose. "Oh, is Martin your intended, Miss Taylor?"

She choked back a laugh. "No. He's one of my two hired hands. Clara takes care of my house and does the cooking, which leaves me free to work with the horses and tend to injured or sick animals."

The young woman's eyes widened. "So that's why you're dressed in men's clothing. You're a real live cowboy—or should I say cowgirl?"

Jesse grinned. "Miss Ellington is from Boston. I was the first real-live cowboy she met when I came into her father's bank to introduce myself."

Miss Ellington nodded, her curls bobbing. "And quite the dashing one he was, too. All dusty from working, and wearing a big hat and spurs." She gave a little shiver. "Delightful."

Mercedes had all she could do not to roll her eyes. "If you don't need anything more, Jesse, I need to get home and make sure Martin is getting his work done. Clara will probably have dinner on soon. Good to meet you, Miss Ellington."

"Oh, would you please call me Cassandra? I haven't met many ladies in town yet, and I'd be pleased if we could be friends. I'd love it if you'd drop by for a cup of tea one day."

Mercedes blinked, not sure she had heard correctly. She couldn't imagine herself fitting into this woman's lifestyle. Besides, it appeared she had an interest in Jesse, and for some reason, that stung. "Thank you, but I'm not sure I'll have time."

"Please?" Cassandra clasped her gloved hands together. "You may even wear your trousers if you prefer. Our home is behind the bank. It's large and drafty and a bit lonely at times. Won't you come?"

Jesse shook his head. "Like she said, Mercedes is a very busy person. I've rarely seen her sit and drink a cup of tea in all the years I've known her."

Mercedes bristled. "Since you haven't seen me in years, you can't possibly know what I like or don't have time for." She pushed aside how silly that must sound, since she was the one who'd said she didn't have time. Something perverse nudged her forward against her good judgment. "Tell me when you'd like me, and I'll be happy to come, Miss Ellington."

"Oh goody!" The young woman clapped her hands. "But remember, it's Cassandra." She picked up her reins then hesitated and moved them to one hand. "I completely forgot. This is for you, Mr. Townsend." Reaching into a bag on the seat beside her, she extended an envelope.

Jesse stepped forward and took the missive, his fingers brushing Cassandra's.

Mercedes couldn't help but see the flush that crept up the young woman's neck as she pulled back her hand.

Cassandra clutched the reins again. "Please come at three o'clock tomorrow for tea, if that's convenient, Mercedes. I may call you Mercedes, mightn't I?" She waved a hand without waiting for a reply and clucked to the horse.

Mercedes swung her gaze to Jesse who stood staring at the envelope, a bemused expression on his face. He must be anxious to see what his lady-love had written. She stalked to the hitching rail and untied her horse, then mounted. "Let me know if Twilight gets worse; otherwise, I don't expect we'll be talking again anytime soon." Reining her mare away from him, she kicked it in the ribs harder than necessary and cantered out of the yard.

CHAPTER FOUR

JESSE RODE HIS GELDING INTO TOWN the next day, wondering yet again what was pushing him to go when he had no errands in town and unfinished work on the ranch. But when was his work ever finished? Mr. Ellington's note hadn't expressed a sense of urgency and had suggested he come at his leisure. Could it have anything to do with the fact Mercedes was due to arrive and have tea with Cassandra Ellington in only a few minutes? Would she wear the same rough work garb she'd worn most of her life, or dress up a bit for her tea party with the banker's daughter?

He clucked to his horse to quicken its pace as he crossed the last expanse of flatland before reaching the edge of the bustling town. As much as he loved his home and the challenging work, he occasionally longed for the simple days of pushing cattle down the trail to market, knowing his only responsibility was getting them there without any loss or injury.

He drew his horse to a stop in front of the bank then dismounted. There was no rush. Maybe he'd cross to the store and see if Matthews had the new kerosene lanterns he'd mentioned last time he was there. He stepped onto the boardwalk and looked up the street. Wagons rolled through town kicking up dust, two cowboys lolled in the doorway of a saloon across the street, and people moved with a sense of purpose down the boardwalk.

"Mr. Townsend?" A man wearing a suit stepped out of the store and strode across the street toward him.

Jesse had to think for a moment, then he extended his hand. "Mr. Ellington." He should have recognized the man who'd sent him the missive yesterday, but he hadn't expected to see him exiting the store. "Are you in a hurry to see me, or could I stop in after I place an order?"

The somewhat burly man nodded his graying head and smiled. "Certainly, certainly. I didn't realize you'd stop by this soon, as I know your property must keep you busy. But I'll clear my calendar and make time whenever you're able to get free. No rush at all." He lifted a hand and moved away toward the bank, pushing open the door, then pausing and looking back over his shoulder. Jesse's gaze followed the man as he wondered yet again why he'd been summoned to town. That might be a bit strong for how the request was worded, but it certainly had come with an expectancy that he would accept the banker's invitation. Whatever it was could wait a few more minutes.

He pivoted when a horse trotted past, raising another puff of dust. He glanced up and froze. Mercedes Taylor, wearing a split skirt in a light shade of blue, topped by a cream-colored blouse touched with lace at the sleeves and neck, sat astride a mare that was almost as lovely as the woman who rode her.

As he watched, she turned her head and a long curl dislodged from her upswept hair. A rush of color stained her cheeks, and she started to raise one hand then lowered it. "Jesse." She tipped her head as she trotted past, but her gaze strayed to the bank and the form of Mr. Ellington entering the door.

Jesse lost all interest in the general store and what enticing things it might hold. He moved slowly toward the bank, his gaze staying on the woman who appeared so different from the one who'd visited his ranch in old clothes, her hair astray. A slight pang of disappointment hit him when she didn't look back, but he brushed it away. They were no longer friends and hadn't been since he was sixteen. He certainly wasn't going to moon over a woman who apparently had even less interest in him than he had in her.

Mercedes tapped on the leaded glass pane of the ornate front door of the house she assumed to belong to the Ellingtons, but her mind stayed fixed on Jesse standing in front of the bank. Was it a coincidence that he'd arrived in town at the same time as she? Not that it was any of her business if he was paying a visit to the banker, but she couldn't help but remember the note Cassandra had brought the day before. Could her father want to discuss a possible courtship before he allowed his daughter to spend too much time with the rancher? She tossed her head and stilled her thoughts as footsteps echoed on the far side of the door. It wasn't her business, and it was best to forget it.

Expecting to see Cassandra, she pasted on what she hoped would pass as a pleasant smile as the door swung open. She hoped this visit would be short. She'd like to get a few other errands taken care of and head back to the ranch. If it hadn't been for her stubborn pride rearing its head at Jesse's smug assumption that she wouldn't want to take tea with a new friend, she never would have left all the work waiting at home.

A young Spanish woman stood inside the foyer, wearing a clean white apron over her long dark skirt, her hair pulled back in what appeared to be a painfully tight knot at the base of her neck. "You are Miss Taylor?" Before Mercedes could reply, the woman stepped aside and gave a brief curtsy. "Please. Come in. Miss Ellington waits for you in the parlor."

Mercedes stepped inside the parlor. Cassandra Ellington rose from the deep green damask sofa, smoothing the linen fabric of her perfectly draped skirt as she did so. She held out a pale hand that must rarely see the sun and took a step forward, her face dimpling with a smile. "How delightful to see you again. I was hoping you wouldn't change your mind about coming. Please, sit." She beckoned toward a chair pulled near the sofa. "Sonja will bring tea in a moment."

Mercedes eyed the elegant upswept hairstyle that must have taken hours to achieve. She had been so certain she would find condescension in Cassandra's eyes, but she saw nothing but welcome and a sparkle of joy. Relaxing, she allowed herself to smile in return, suddenly happy she'd come. Maybe making a new female friend wasn't such a terrible idea after all. Other than her housekeeper and cook, she spent very little time with other women, slipping in and out of church on Sunday mornings, then rushing back to the ranch. Ever since Papa had died, she'd found it harder to get out, especially as the funds grew tighter and the bills more demanding. Mercedes sank into the comfortable chair. "Thank you. Tea sounds delightful."

Sonja entered the room balancing a heavily-laden tray. She stopped in front of Mercedes, poured the tea, placed a plate of lemon cakes on the table between them, then exited the parlor, pulling the door shut behind her.

After chatting for several minutes about inconsequential things, Cassandra leaned forward and touched Mercedes arm. "I'm so glad you decided to come. Now please tell me, will you move to town after you sell your ranch? What are your plans? If you don't have anything solid figured out yet, I'd be happy to help you decide. In fact, we have plenty of room here until you find another house."

Mercedes lips parted, but no sound came out for several long seconds as she tried to take in what the young woman had said. Finally, she uttered a croak. "What?" She shook her head and set the sprigged china cup of tea onto its saucer with a clink. "I have no idea what you're talking about."

"Oh dear." Cassandra placed her fingers over her lips. "I assumed my father would have spoken to you before he talked to Jesse . . . er . . . Mr. Townsend . . . about purchasing your ranch. I'm so sorry. Apparently I've spoken out of turn."

Mercedes pushed to her feet. "Please explain. What does Mr. Townsend, or your father for that matter, have to do with my ranch or where I choose to live?"

Cassandra rose as well. "I've already said too much. Won't you forgive me and forget it for now? I'm sure it's nothing important, or I misunderstood. Let's finish our tea and visit, and you can pop by the bank and chat with my father before you head home if you feel it's important. More than likely I've exaggerated, as well as speaking out of turn."

Mercedes shook her head and plucked her shawl from the arm of the chair where she'd placed it. "Thank you, but no. I don't think I could concentrate on anything else with this hanging over my head. I'll bid you good day, and thank you for inviting me."

She knotted the shawl and walked toward the door, then paused, not wanting to hurt the young woman who'd been nothing but kind, if a bit clumsy in what she'd revealed.

Pivoting, she smiled. "I'd like to return the favor and have you visit the ranch sometime. I'm so sorry to rush off, but I do feel I need to discover what your father is thinking. Thank you again."

She slipped out the door before Cassandra could reply and headed for her horse, determination straightening her spine. Was Jesse at the bottom of this, and had he gone to the bank after setting up some kind of plan with Mr. Ellington behind her back? Jesse's father had always coveted the water on their land, and maybe this was Jesse's way of honoring his dead father. She would know soon enough.

CHAPTER FIVE

JESSE SHOT OUT OF THE PLUSH leather seat on the other side of the banker's ornate desk, shoving his chair back hard. "What? Why are you asking me if I want to buy Miss Taylor's ranch? She'd never sell it, and I'm shocked you'd talk about such a private affair to anyone other than Miss Taylor. Is she aware you're talking to me?"

Mr. Ellington rose and waved his pale fingers that didn't appear as though they'd ever done an hour of work in the sun. "Sit down, Mr. Townsend. Please. I didn't mean to startle or offend you, and I didn't care to speak to Miss Taylor until I knew if I had someone interested who might be a solution to her problem. I may need to call in her loan soon. I assumed if I had someone she knew and trusted who might want to purchase her ranch, it would be easier for her."

Jesse shook his head, appalled at the other man's reasoning. "That's not the way we do things out here in the West. We don't go behind a ranch owner's back and try to sell their property. We work with the man or woman and see how we can help them." He snatched his hat off the edge of the desk and plunked it onto his head. "Good day, sir." He stalked to the office door, grasped the handle, and gave it a yank.

He bolted through the open doorway, intent on getting out of this building. Mercedes stood right across the threshold. He plowed into her before he could stop his forward momentum.

"Ouch!" She glared at him and staggered backward, then caught herself and straightened. "It's you. I should have known you'd rush here to talk to Mr. Ellington. I know our families parted with unkind words, but I'm disappointed that you wouldn't come to me before scheming with the banker."

She lifted her chin and stepped aside to allow him access to the bank foyer, then kept moving toward the banker's office.

"Mercedes, wait!" Jesse extended his hand and took a step after her, but it was too late. A few people close to the door were already whispering amongst themselves over the collision and the words Mercedes hadn't tried to soften.

How could she possibly think he was a part of this? He'd been shocked to his core when Mr. Ellington had told him about the debt against the ranch and given him first chance to purchase it. And what was this about the debt Mercedes's father owed the bank that she couldn't pay off? Wasn't she making a living selling horses and cattle? She didn't have a big herd when it came to cattle, and she operated with only a few ranch hands, but surely it hadn't come to this.

He stepped outside and rammed his hat on his head, determination fueling his steps. He'd get to the bottom of this and see what he could do to help, whether Mercedes liked it or not. He wouldn't see a neighbor run off the place that had been her family home, even if they were no longer friends. A pang smote him at the thought. No longer friends. At one time he'd hoped for more than that, but then all the ugliness started between their families, and nothing was ever the same again. He headed for his horse. Maybe there was a way to rectify that as well.

Mercedes tapped on the door of Mr. Ellington's office. She wished he were in a room on the other side of the bank, rather than so close to the tellers' cages, but she'd probably already set the gossips' tongues wagging by her tart comment to Jesse. Her cheeks burned at the memory, and she hesitated. At the sound of the banker's invitation, she pushed open the door.

Mr. Ellington slid his chair back from his desk and stood. "Miss Taylor. I wasn't expecting you. I understood you were having tea with my daughter, but please, come in." His voice was low and well-modulated—certainly not the ogre she'd expected.

She stood for a moment, suddenly unsure. Was there more going on here than what she'd believed? There was only one way to find out. "Thank you, sir. I was hoping you'd have a few minutes to spare. I'm sorry if I interrupted anything between you and Mr. Townsend."

He stepped around the desk and gestured to a padded leather chair. "Not at all. We'd finished our business before you arrived. Please, have a seat." He waited until she had perched on the edge of her chair, then resumed his place behind his desk. "Now. How may I help you today?" His face creased in a slight smile, and his eyes held a genuinely caring expression.

Confusion clouded Mercedes's mind for a moment. Could she have misjudged the situation, or had Cassandra been misinformed by her father? This man certainly didn't appear to be ready to snatch her ranch out from under her without so much as a by-your-leave. She clasped her hands in her lap and managed a smile. "Thank you. I hope you won't mind if I get right to the point."

He tipped his head in acknowledgement. "Not at all."

"Your daughter and I were visiting when she mentioned something that startled me." She bit her lip as a frown furrowed Mr. Ellington's brow, hoping she hadn't caused trouble for Cassandra. "I'm sure she was only trying to help, but she said she assumed I already knew or she wouldn't have spoken out of turn."

He leaned forward and laced his slender hands on his desktop. "Yes? Go ahead, Miss Taylor. What did my daughter tell you?"

Mercedes thought back to the conversation, wanting to be accurate. "She asked where I planned to live after I sold my ranch. Since I have no plans to sell my property, I was a bit taken aback. She went on to explain that you had spoken to Mr. Townsend about purchasing my property."

He steepled his fingers. "I'm sorry you had to find out that way, Miss Taylor. And in all fairness, I first spoke to Mr. Townsend about your property today. I erred in saying anything to my daughter. I assure you, it won't happen again."

Mercedes sucked in a shallow breath. "Please explain what's going on. I know my father owed the bank a bit of money, but I've made payments whenever I've been able. Surely you aren't considering calling the note?"

"I'm afraid so." He held out a hand to forestall her outburst as her lips parted. "Let me explain. I haven't been the head of this institution long, but since I took over I've been reviewing the books. I must say I'm appalled at what I found. The previous president loaned a rather large sum of money to your father in bits and pieces over the years prior to his passing—with a more substantial amount not long before he died. The understanding on that sum was that if anything ever happened to him, the funds were to be used to pay accounts in advance at the general store and feed-and-grain, as well as the blacksmith. Some of the money was to go into purchasing more blooded stock which you'd train and sell to the Army and other buyers, but we've not seen as much in the way of repayment as is required. Certainly not enough to keep up with the interest, much less pay down the principal. I'm afraid I have no choice but to call in the note, unless you have funds available to resolve the issue very soon."

Mercedes's hands shook in her lap, and she gripped them more tightly. "How soon? And how much? If I am I able to bring the interest payments up to date current and start making more consistent payments, would that take care of the problem?"

Mr. Ellington shook his head. "I'm afraid not . . ." He pulled a paper out of the stack to his right and adjusted his glasses. "Let me see." Running his finger down the page he nodded. "This is the most up-to-date document." He leaned forward, the paper extended.

Mercedes took it and closed her eyes for a brief moment. Surely there would be some way she could repay this note. Papa wouldn't have been so foolish as to put them deep into debt with no hope of recovering. Her gaze followed the column of figures until she reached the bottom, and she let out a gasp. "Oh my!" The document fluttered to her lap and she sank against the upholstered chair.

CHAPTER SIX

JESSE PACED THE HARD-PACKED DIRT IN front of the Taylor barn. What was taking Mercedes so long? Surely she wasn't still in town. It had been close to two hours since he'd run into her at the bank, and it only took thirty minutes or so to ride from town to her ranch. Could she have met with an accident? Concern coursed through him as all sorts of images assaulted his mind. He strode to the hitching rail and untied his horse. He reached for the saddle horn and paused, then turned his head toward the lane leading to the barn. Hoofbeats. And not coming in any hurry if his ears were working correctly. He pivoted and shaded his eyes against the glare of the late afternoon sun.

Mercedes sat astride her horse, not using the customary sidesaddle preferred by genteel women, her split skirt covering her legs. She reined her horse to a sharp halt a few yards away as her gaze met his. "What are you doing here? I didn't think you'd have the nerve to come here after scheming with the Ellingtons to get my property."

He winced. "I'd like to talk to you, if you'll allow me." He wrapped the reins of his horse's bridle over the rail and waited.

She nudged her mare forward then stopped at the hitching rail, her gaze never leaving his face. "All right. Talk. You have five minutes."

He stepped over to offer her a hand to dismount. Mercedes laughed. "I ride as well as you do, Jesse. I'm not a city girl like Miss Ellington." She swung down and grasped her horse's reins.

Jesse moved to a nearby fence and leaned against the top rail, working hard to present a calm exterior. *Might as well get to the heart of the problem.* He drew in a deep breath. "I had no idea Ellington was going to ask me to buy your ranch."

She raised a brow but didn't reply. Turning her back, she led her horse into the barn. "I saw Miss Ellington hand you a note. Surely you must have known something was going on. Time's running out, Jesse. Talk in here if you have anything more to say."

"You're not being fair, Mercedes. Hear me out. Have I ever lied to you in the past?" Frustration made his voice brittle.

She pivoted to face him, and her features softened. "No, you haven't. Not once. Which is what makes this even harder for me. Mr. Ellington did tell me it was his idea, but how do I know you didn't plant that idea by discussing it with *Miss* Ellington during one of your chats? She's obviously smitten with you, and she seems quite open about sharing what she knows with others. All it would take for her to go running to her father is you mentioning how much you admire my ranch and wish it was yours."

He leaned against the wall of the stall while she unsaddled her horse, his gut churning with emotion. "Well, I didn't. I like Miss Ellington well enough, but I don't discuss other people's business with her—or even my own, for that matter. As much as I appreciate your ranch, I have enough on my plate. Mr. Ellington sent me a note asking me to stop by the bank when I had time, but he gave me no hint of what he wanted until I arrived. I'm guessing he came to me because our land adjoins. Nothing more." He straightened. "So what's this about needing to sell? He said your father's line of credit ran out, but shouldn't that have been cancelled after his passing?" He almost ducked, wondering if she would take a swing at him for butting into her personal business, but he couldn't help if he didn't understand.

Mercedes nodded, but her heart sank at his response about *liking* Cassandra Ellington. Not that it was any of her business who he decided to court. None at all. Best to let it go. "That's what I assumed. But Mr. Ellington said Mr. Walton, the old president, and Papa were friends, so he kept on extending credit to me at stores. I assumed Papa had paid accounts in advance so I wouldn't have to worry. I knew he'd borrowed some at the bank, and I've been making payments. But to be honest, I'm not great at paperwork and accounts."

She swiped a brush over her mare's ribs then turned to face him. "I should have dug deeper. Mr. Walton sent me bills each month, but apparently they barely covered the interest. I have no idea why he didn't come speak to me about it before he left town." She spread her hands wide. "Now I'm apparently in debt, and I have no idea how I'll dig myself out."

"Maybe I can help. You sell horses for a living along with a few cattle. Let me buy three or four horses. I have the cash right now, and I can always use a few more head." He gave her a hopeful smile. "I'll pay fair market price. It's not like it's charity or anything."

Mercedes pressed her lips together to keep her mouth from gaping in surprise. Why would Jesse do that for her after all that had passed between their families, and even between the two of them? It was too much. And no matter what he claimed, it *was* charity. She'd been on his ranch. He had plenty of horses and couldn't possibly need more. She shook her head. "Thanks, Jesse, but I don't think so. I apologize for not trusting you earlier and for accusing you unjustly, but I won't take your money."

His smile faded, and he bristled. "Why not? Isn't my money good enough for a Taylor?" Bitterness tinged his tone. "Always the stubborn one, aren't you, Mercedes? Too much pride, just like your father. You won't accept help even if it means you'll lose your ranch."

She scrunched her brow and stared. "What is that supposed to mean? Papa wasn't a prideful man—he accepted help if he needed it. But he didn't accept charity. It's one thing to have neighbors help rebuild a barn when it's been damaged, because you know you'll do the same for the next person. But that's different than taking money from selling something you know isn't needed." She crossed her arms over her chest. "I'm not willing to do that. I don't care to be beholden to you in that way."

"What I meant was your father had his chance to get help from my father more than once, but he turned it down. Sure, he hoped we could get water rights to the creek running through your property, because your father didn't understand how to use that water to its fullest. Pa offered to help him channel and capture it. All he asked for was part of the water in return. Your father thought we were trying to take something that belonged to him, and couldn't see past his own pride to realize Pa was trying to do something that would have benefited them both. I guess the apple didn't fall far from the tree."

He pivoted and stalked toward the door. "Sorry you won't allow me to help. I hate to see you lose the ranch your family worked so hard to keep." Yanking open the partially open door the rest of the way, he stepped outside and disappeared.

Mercedes leaned her head against her horse's withers and sighed. She had done it again—made Jesse mad. How many times had she allowed her good sense or temper to get in the way when they were kids and sent him home in a huff? But there was no possible way she could accept his money. There had to be another option. Papa wouldn't have tolerated the thought of a Townsend bailing her out, even if it meant losing the ranch.

She frowned as a thought struck. Had Jesse been right about Papa having too much pride and her following in his footsteps? She shoved the idea aside. Papa might have been stubborn a time or two, but she was being sensible, not proud. It wasn't right to take Jesse's money when he didn't need the horses and felt sorry for her. She didn't want his pity. Heat crept into her cheeks. There'd been a time when she'd wanted much more than pity—or friendship for that matter—but she had long since given up on that hope.

But what to do about the ranch? Her ranch hands wouldn't be any help. They didn't have any stronger business sense than she did. Not that she considered herself inept, but it bothered her that she hadn't realized she owed so much money or that Papa hadn't paid her accounts at the stores in town. How foolish to have gone along as though all were well without checking for herself. Jesse was right to think less of her, but she wouldn't admit to being proud. She was simply trying to protect herself and do the right thing, exactly like Papa always had. She bit her lip. At least, that's what she remembered.

What had Jesse meant about his father offering to help her father with the water and he'd refused? She didn't know anything about that. Could he be making it up to look better? Her mind returned to his question—"Have I ever lied to you in the past?" No, he hadn't. At least not that she knew of, and she couldn't fathom a reason he would now.

She gave one final swipe to the mare then exited the stall. How foolish. Jesse didn't have a finagling bone in his body. But didn't men change when they were in love? He'd said he liked Cassandra Ellington. Was it possible he would accept Mr. Ellington's proposal to purchase her ranch, and the offer to buy horses was done so she wouldn't figure it out?

Enough. This was stupid. All the guessing in the world wouldn't change anything. But she knew what she'd seen in Cassandra's face when the woman mentioned Jesse's name. All she could do was pray Jesse hadn't changed that much and wasn't in love with Cassandra. Because there wasn't a thing she could do about it if he was.

CHAPTER SEVEN

JESSE GATHERED HIS REINS AND SWUNG onto his horse, then lifted a hand at his neighbor who stood in the doorway of his barn. "Thanks for your time, Mr. Matthews."

"Sorry I can't help, Townsend. But I don't need any more horses at the moment. I could stand to sell one or two of my own. Too bad about Mercedes's ranch bein' in trouble, though. My wife and I have known her and her family since she was this tall." He held his hand down to his knees. "Sure hate to see anyone lose land their family has worked so hard to keep."

Jesse's jaw tightened. "I didn't say anything about Miss Taylor losing her property. Where did you hear that?"

Matthews waved a dismissive hand in the air. "My wife was in the bank when Mercedes came stormin' out of Mr. Ellington's office, mad as a wet hen and spoutin' off about losin' her place and you tryin' to take it. Not that either of us believed that, mind you. We know you better than that, even if you have been gone a few years. Figured Mercedes Taylor has a bit of a temper, like her pa used to have, and whatever was wrong would blow over soon enough. But now that you come askin' about buyin' a couple of her horses, it makes me wonder if it weren't more serious than we reckoned. How long does she have?"

Jesse didn't want to lie, but it wasn't his business to tell tales, either. "Sorry, I can't answer that, Mr. Matthews. It's not up to me to discuss Miss Taylor's affairs. I simply came to pass the word that she's got several head of fine stock ready to sell, in case you or anyone else might be interested. You'll let people know if you run across someone in need of a good horse, right?"

The older man nodded, then wiped his sleeve across his forehead. "Sure will. Mighty warm today. Feels like a thunderstorm might be buildin'. Been so dry, I hope we don't get no lightnin'."

Jesse glanced at the sky. "There's not a cloud in sight."

"Nope. Not right now there isn't, but that don't mean nothin'. You been gone so long you forget how fast storms can build in these parts? Shucks, boy. It's a good thing you came back home before you lost track of who you are and where you belong."

Jesse grinned and raised a hand in farewell. "Sure thing, Mr. Matthews, I remember. And I agree. It's good to be home, although the house is a lot quieter without Pa there."

"Good man, your pa. Always said so. Although I think he was unfair blamin' Mercedes for a couple of your horses dyin' when hers came down sick. Weren't her fault. No way she could'a known her horse was carryin' somethin' that would pass along to your stock. She was only a young girl and didn't have all the know-how about animals she has now." He shook his head. "Not that it's any of my business, but it hit that girl hard when your families broke ties. Mercedes told my wife it were her fault, and she'd never forgive herself for the death of your horses. But I think it went a lot deeper than that. She blamed herself for losin' your friendship, as well."

Jesse's chin jerked up. "It wasn't her fault. I mean, I guess I thought it was at the time." Heat crept all the way to his ears. "Thinking back on it, I know better now. We simply drifted apart. It's not like we had an understanding or anything."

The older man gave a dry laugh. "Pretty nigh everybody in the county figured the two of you would marry one day. You were as close as a boy and his pet hound dog—inseparable since the time you first went to school—my wife told me that, plain and clear. She also said it don't seem right, your family puttin' all the blame on that little girl. Ain't no wonder she started doctorin' animals after that. Tryin' to make amends, that's what she's been doin' all these years. Figures if she can save other animals from pain, sufferin', or death, maybe it'll make up for a little of what she thinks is her doin'."

Jesse nearly choked. "Are you sure? I mean, I was upset at first that my horse died, and wished she'd told us that her horse was sick, but that's only one of the reasons our families parted ways. Her pa wouldn't let my pa have water rights from the creek running through his land, even though it was close to the property line that adjoins our ranches. That's what started things. Her pa was too stubborn to do things any way but his own."

Matthews wagged his head. "Nope. You don't know the straight of it. Before your ma died, she told my Gwen that she always felt bad about what your pa said to Mercedes, but she couldn't go against her own husband and try to make it right."

A chill raced over Jesse's body. "What did my pa say to Mercedes?"

"He told her it were all her fault—that she killed his stock and your horse, and that you'd never forgive her for it, no matter how long you lived. I knowed he were mad, but it weren't right to take it out on that girl."

Jesse gripped the reins so tight his fingers hurt. "Thanks, Mr. Matthews. I didn't know that. Guess I have some explaining to do to Mercedes—if she'll give me the chance. And until then, I'd really appreciate it if you'd keep what your wife heard in the bank to yourself."

"Sure thing, neighbor. Like I said, it's good to have you back. I hope things will be put to rights all the way around. You ought'a keep in mind how you felt about that little girl a few years ago, before things were spoken between your families that never should'a been said." He lifted a hand, pivoted, and disappeared into the barn.

Jesse spurred his horse and cantered down the lane leading to the road back to town, feeling as though angry hounds were nipping at his heels. Shame washed over him in waves at what his father had done and at the thoughts he'd harbored against Mercedes for years. Now it was too late to make it up to her—and right when he was starting to realize how much he'd like to do that.

The day after Jesse left, Mercedes patted the neck of the mare that she brought out of the barn, hating to part with Majesty, but knowing it must be done. "You sure you won't consider one of the other mares I showed you, Mr. Finnegan?"

"Nope." The brawny Irishman took off his hat and ran his hand over his red hair, then plunked the hat back on. "'Tis the one I've had me eye on. She's a nice sized mare, and won't birth tiny, wee babes, like some o' the other stock in the county. She's young, strong, and comely. Will ye budge on your price a bit, lassie? What yer askin' seems a bit steep to me."

She shook her head. "That's because I don't want to sell Majesty. I'll come down by twenty dollars if you agree to take one of the other mares."

"No, 'tis her I want. If yer willin' to sell her, I'll pay yer price, even if it does nearly empty me purse." He withdrew a leather pouch and loosened the drawstring. "Gold coins all right with ye? I don't have any paper money on me at the moment."

"That's fine." She almost blurted out that the bank wouldn't care what it was, as long as it was legal tender and would go toward her debt. Even though she would rather sell one of her other mares, she had to admit the higher price on this one would help a lot. "I sold two geldings this morning that I'll be delivering later to the Lester ranch. I can't understand why there's been a sudden rush for people to buy horses. What made you think about coming over here today, Mr. Finnegan?"

The Irishman counted the gold coins into her hand then stuffed the bag back into his pocket. "That young neighbor of yers, Jesse Townsend. He's got quite the persuasive tongue in his head, he does. I'd almost think he'd been born in the land of the Blarney stone, if I didn't know better. He showed up at me place yesterday, tellin' me you have some of the best stock in the county—and he mentioned this one in particular." He jerked his thumb at the mare. "I'd told him not long ago I was lookin' fer another broodmare, but I'd been thinkin' of buyin' one from him." He hunched a shoulder. "Not sure why he decided not to sell me one and send me to you instead, but I must say I'm glad he did."

He reached out and stroked the mare's neck, then picked up her lead rope. "This girl is right fine, she is, and no mistake. I won't even be moanin' to me wife about the price I had to pay. The mare will be worth it, or I'll eat my hat."

Mercedes stammered an answer, but the Irishman didn't appear to listen. He swung aboard his horse and trotted down the road, leading the mare behind him.

Mercedes stared at his retreating form, her mind reeling. Jesse sent him to look at her mares, especially this one, telling Mr. Finnegan he'd decided not to sell? So did that mean that Mr. Lester had gotten the same message? The Townsend ranch was renowned for their horseflesh as well as their cattle. That was one of the things that had raised her father's ire so much—he could barely compete with his neighbor when it came to sales, and it had turned him green with jealousy at times.

Should she go to Mr. Lester and give him his money back and tell him to buy his saddle stock from Jesse instead? But what would the man think of her if she did? He'd already paid her and expected delivery this evening. Would it be right to go back on her word, even if Jesse brought this about and sent his own business to her? Sure, he wasn't buying horses he didn't need, but he was sending business he could certainly use. His father had died several months ago, and it had to have set them back a bit until Jesse arrived and took over.

Not that she minded the Townsend ranch's success. She'd always been quietly disappointed in her father's attitude toward their old friends. She loved seeing other people prosper and believed there was more than enough business for both of them. Besides, knowing the Townsend family's business was expanding had helped ease some of her own guilt over the horrible loss of their stock when her mare had been sick and spread the disease to their herd.

That was one reason she wouldn't—no—couldn't—accept Jesse's help. She should be the one figuring out ways to make amends, and instead, she had been prickly and proud—exactly like Papa. Maybe the apple hadn't fallen far from the tree, as Jesse had said.

What should she do? Tell Jesse he should take two of his geldings to the Lester ranch and give him the money she'd received? Or was that still pride talking, proving she was too proud to accept help. Somehow she knew that was the case, and somehow the pride had to be broken.

She shook her head, hating the despair that she felt settling in and not knowing how to stop it. If Jesse wasn't so smitten with Cassandra Ellington, maybe she could talk to him about all of this, and at least try to be friends again—but that would be awkward if he did end up marrying Cassandra, knowing how she had once felt about Jesse herself. Mercedes wanted to heartily dislike the young woman, but she couldn't.

Cassandra had extended the hand of friendship and been sweetness itself. Just because Jesse appeared to desire her was no reason to blame Cassandra.

Why did life have to get so complicated? If only Jesse had returned a few years ago and they'd gone back to their old friendship. But was friendship what she really wanted from Jesse—and had she only cared for him in the past? Or had her desire gone much deeper now that she was a grown woman and no longer the schoolgirl he'd left behind? Jealousy wasn't a trait she cared to encourage in herself, but when it came to the thought of Jesse and Cassandra together, the green-eyed monster was hard to shake.

CHAPTER EIGHT

MERCEDES COULDN'T STAND IT ANY LONGER. She had to see Jesse and make things right. Even if he was in love with Cassandra and ended up marrying her, they could still be friends. Couldn't they? After all, Jesse had tried to save her ranch. Was she so shallow and proud that she would let their past or his feelings for Cassandra stand in the way of being a good neighbor? The sales she'd made the past couple of days had helped a lot. With that money she could pay the loan down by half, and maybe Mr. Ellington would give her a little more time to come up with the rest.

She swung up onto her stallion, Duke, her father's favorite and the one horse she would never part with and gathered the reins. Time to go eat crow and thank Jesse for his help. Trotting out of the ranch yard, she glanced at the sky. Sultry with heavy clouds. They could sure use the rain, but somehow it didn't have that feel. It had been dry for too long, and crops were starting to wither.

She shot up a quick prayer for the water they desperately needed and tacked on a short request for the strength to say the right things to Jesse, then hightail it for home before she tipped her hand in regards to her own feelings for the man. No sense in letting him see she still cared—more than even she wanted to admit—only to get her heart broken when he made his courtship of Cassandra public. She'd had more than her share of heartbreak over the years, and she steeled herself against even a smidgen more.

Ten minutes later, she reined to a stop in Jesse's ranch yard. Awfully quiet for the middle of the day. Not a horse being worked or a cow bawling, and no men in sight. Maybe they'd gone to a far pasture to fix fence or check on stock. Her shoulders drooped. She wasn't sure how long she could hold onto her courage and resolution to talk honestly to Jesse. Her horse swung toward the lane leading to her ranch then Mercedes hesitated and reined to a stop. She should at least go to the house. Jesse's housekeeper, Molly, would probably be inside working and might know where to find him.

Sliding off her horse, she wrapped the reins around the hitching rail in front of the house. Why was everything so quiet? It wasn't normal—at least the dog should have rushed out barking to greet her.

Mercedes strode to the door and gave a light rap on the frame. She waited a full minute, then stepped off the porch and walked to the back of the house. The kitchen opened onto a porch, and a window was positioned over the dry sink. Molly could be working and didn't hear her knock. She smiled as the memory of the woman's deep-throated voice singing old hymns flooded her mind. So many good things had taken place in this house during her growing up years. If only the bad hadn't come and wiped all of that wonderful history away. Where would she and Jesse be now in their friendship?

Blood rushed to her cheeks and warmed them as her old dreams of marrying Jesse returned. Of course that wasn't possible now, but at one time she'd believed it would happen. She tapped on the door next to the window and waited. Still nothing. Stepping over to the window, she peered inside, but nothing moved. How strange.

Shoving open the door, she called in a soft voice. "Molly? Anyone here?" The kitchen was orderly as always, with nothing out of place and no sign of a problem. Maybe she'd simply gone to town to shop, but where was everyone else? There was no way Jesse would leave the ranch unattended.

Mercedes pulled the door closed behind her. Time to check the barn. She should have done that to begin with, but as quiet as it was, she had assumed no one was there, either. A minute later she stood inside the massive building, allowing her eyes to adjust to the dim light. "Jesse? Warren? Anyone out here?" A chill ran up her arms. She rubbed them in spite of the warm weather. Something was wrong, and she intended to get to the bottom of it.

She rolled her eyes and blew out a breath. Jesse loved working with leather. More than likely, he was repairing a saddle or bridle. The harness room was on the far side of the barn. If the door was closed, he wouldn't have heard her call.

A couple dozen strides later, she stood in front of the wide open door, staring at the disorder inside. A bridle lay on the floor where it appeared to have been dropped or flung, a saddle stand was tipped over with Jesse's best saddle sprawled on the wood floor.

She sucked in a sharp breath as her gaze landed on the area next to the fallen saddle. Blood. And not just a few drops. She knelt beside it and reached out a hand. Still wet. She drew back.

Fear clutched her throat, making it difficult to breathe. Had Jesse been seriously injured? Had Molly hitched up the buggy and driven him to town? Surely he hadn't been shot—they hadn't had cattle or horse thieves close by in some time, although it was possible. The sight of the blood didn't bother her, but the thought of Jesse being injured had her hands shaking so hard she could barely control them.

She didn't want to lose him, and she finally admitted it. It wasn't only his friendship she wanted, it was his love—and she would fight for it if she had to. One way or the other, she had to let him know she cared—if he was still alive.

She sprinted across the barn to the buggy shed then slid to a halt, her chest heaving. The buggy was gone. The men must be out on the range, and Molly had taken Jesse to town. If she rode hard, she might catch them and be able to help. A moment later she was on her horse, galloping from the ranch yard, praying with every stride that Jesse was all right. She desperately wanted a chance to talk to him before it was too late.

Jesse guided Molly up the steps to the doctor's office across the street from the bank and opened the door. "Doc? You here?"

The man's voice came from the exam room. "Have a seat, I'll only be a minute."

"You might want to hurry, Doc, we've got a head wound

here that's been bleeding something fierce."

Molly plopped into the doctor's chair with a groan and stared up at Jesse. "I hate putting you to so much bother. You had to leave your work to bring me to town, and that's not right."

"Hush now. You're more important than any amount of work." Hurried footsteps sounded behind him, and Jesse swiveled to see Doc.

The middle-aged man came through the door, followed by a mother towing a young boy by the hand. "Bring Tommy in again if that cough doesn't improve in the next couple of days.

He hurried to Molly's side. "What have we here? That you, Molly?" He knelt next to the woman he'd known for years and gently touched the cloth Jesse had wound around her head.

"One of the cowboys get mad at what you served him?" His tone was jovial but he turned serious eyes to Jesse. "Looks like you got a good compress on it, but there's blood seeping through. Let's get her in the exam room and take a look."

Jesse helped Molly to her feet and walked her to the doctor's private room, containing a potbellied stove, a long, clean work counter on one wall, another wall of shelves and drawers, and a cot in the center with a stand next to it. "Sit up on the edge of this bed so I can take a look. Jesse, how about you tell me what happened."

"All I know is what Molly told me, but I'll do my best. I'd been working in the harness room, but had to step outside for a few minutes. Molly came looking for me, and apparently she was in a bit of a hurry. The light isn't good in the barn, and I didn't have a lantern lit. As she came through the door, she tripped and fell into the corner of a wooden saddle rack. I heard a crash and ran inside. By the time I got there, she was lying on the floor unconscious, with a gash in her head."

He reached out and patted Molly's shoulder. "Like to scared me to death. Other than a bullet wound, I don't think I've seen a person bleed that much."

The doctor grunted and dipped a rag in a pan of warm water on the stove. "Not surprising. Head wounds can bleed pretty bad. Makes it appear the person is dying when they're not. How long was she out, do you think?"

Jesse removed his hat and ran a hand over his hair. "Not much longer than the time it took me to get from the back of the barn to the front. She was coming to when I knelt down beside her. I was afraid to move her at first, so I ran to the house and got a pile of towels to try to stop the bleeding."

Doc nodded. "That was the best thing you could do. Then you got her straight here? Did she faint again on the way?"

Molly sat up straighter as the doctor probed her scalp wound. "No sir, I did not. I wouldn't have the first time if I hadn't hit so hard. Good thing I have a tough noggin'. Never done that in my life before."

"Nothing foolish about it, Molly." The doctor glanced at Jesse. "I'm going to keep her overnight, if you don't mind losing your housekeeper for the better part of the day. I need to watch her. I'm going to need to put a few stiches in this cut as well. You can go along home if you'd like."

Molly's face contorted like she was going to cry. "No sir. You're not keeping me overnight, no how. I've got work to do, and I been away from it too long already." She shook her head then winced and grabbed the edge of the cot. "Oh, I'm dizzy."

Jesse grasped her hands and held them. "You're dizzy because you got hurt. You'll stay right here until Doc says you can go home. I'll get something to eat in the café, and I'll let the men come to town later to do the same. We'll live. I'll come pick you up in the morning, if Doc thinks that's all right."

"That should be about perfect, as long as I don't see any complications arise. She should be ready to go home by then."

Molly waved him off and closed her eyes. "Then you get on out of here right now. Shoo! You don't need to watch him sew me up like some old torn quilt, and I don't need to worry about you going hungry. Get yourself over to that café and find something to eat, if they've got anything worth having, that is."

Jesse laughed, happy her sense of humor was intact. "Yes, ma'am. Now you mind the doctor, you hear?"

She puffed out a hard breath. "Guess so. Go along now."

Jesse stuffed his hat back on his head and stepped out onto the boardwalk, allowing his eyes to adjust to the light. Heavy clouds had built in the west toward the ranch, but there was still a smidgen of sun peeking through over the town. He headed toward the café then slowed his pace as he noticed Cassandra pulling the door of the bank shut behind her. She turned toward him.

He raised his hat in salute and would have kept walking, but she signaled for him to join her. All he could think of at the moment was Cassandra telling Mercedes about her father's desire that he purchase Mercedes's ranch. The memory rankled. It wasn't as if the lovely young woman facing him didn't have good qualities, but his interest in her had been brief at best. Knowing she had talked out of turn had only strengthened his desire to keep her at arm's length.

He crossed the street, his boots slogging through weeks of dust. If only those clouds would provide the much-needed rain the country was praying for. Stepping onto the boardwalk a couple of strides from Cassandra, he nodded. "Miss Ellington. I hope you're having a good day."

Her lips quivered, but she pressed them together in a firm line. "Mr. Townsend. I saw you stop at the doctor's office. Is everything all right?"

"I believe it will be. Molly, my longtime housekeeper and cook, hit her head and requires stitches, but the doctor believes she'll recover. She's staying the night so he can keep an eye on her. Thank you for asking." He started to move around her but she held out her hand.

"Please. I was hoping to talk to you. In fact, had you not come to town today, I was planning to visit your ranch tomorrow."

Jesse winced then felt badly when he noted soft color blooming in her cheeks. He hadn't meant to embarrass her, but he had no desire to have her visit again. The last time, Mercedes had been there, and if he wasn't mistaken, she had the idea he was interested in Cassandra—something he must set right, and the sooner the better. "How may I help you?" He kept his voice formal, not the once jovial tone he'd used when he'd met the young woman. It was probably his fault if she was interested in him, and somehow he needed to alert her to the fact that his feelings didn't go beyond friendship—if that.

"I want to apologize." She lifted her chin and worked to muster a tiny smile. "For my poor behavior with Miss Taylor. I understand she was none too happy when she arrived at the bank to talk to my father and saw you leaving his office. That was entirely my fault. I should never have said what I did or assumed she knew what was going on. I will be expressing my regret to her as soon as I have the opportunity."

The rapid sound of hoofbeats coming up the street halted the words Jesse planned to say. Cassandra's apology was the last thing he'd expected. She had more depth than he'd thought, he'd give her that. He gave a quick bow. "No need to apologize. But thank you."

A horse reined to a hard stop in front of the bank, and Jesse pivoted.

Mercedes sat astride her father's stallion as the horse pawed the ground, the dust billowing around his hooves. Her stormy eyes stared straight into his. "So you're not dead or injured after all. I was worried, but I guess I had a hard, fast ride for nothing." She shot Jesse a long look that spoke volumes, then tugged on her horse's reins, backing him into the street and away from the boardwalk.

CHAPTER NINE

MERCEDES'S HANDS SHOOK AS SHE GRIPPED the reins. She had wasted her time and energy on Jesse Townsend, believing his life to be in danger, only to find him talking to Cassandra Ellington. She should have known. What had he been doing, butchering a chicken in his tack room? It didn't matter, she'd changed her mind about apologizing for her past behavior. He could court Cassandra if he wanted to. She would stay on her own ranch and out of his life from now on. Mercedes spun her horse and pointed him toward home.

"Mercedes. Miss Taylor! Please wait." A clear but firm woman's voice came from behind her, but Mercedes kept moving forward. She had no desire to talk to anyone right now, least of all the woman Jesse was so obviously smitten with. Although in all fairness, he hadn't been looking at the young woman with cow eyes or holding her hand, but that was probably reserved for private.

"Miss Taylor. I shall start shouting if you don't stop." Cassandra's bell-like voice wasn't far behind.

She slowed and glanced over her shoulder. Cassandra trudged through the dust, her hem held up above her ankles for all the world like she didn't give a fig who might be watching. Mercedes had to smile. She had tried so hard to dislike the woman, but her engaging, forthright personality somehow managed to worm its way past her defenses yet again. "All right. Fine. I'll stop, but I'm not waiting long."

She glanced past Cassandra to see Jesse staring at them where he appeared frozen on the boardwalk a few yards away. She raised her voice. "I'll talk to you, but I have no desire to speak to anyone else." At this point, she didn't care that it sounded petty. Her heart hurt after seeing the man she'd thought severely wounded casually talking to another woman. What an idiot she had been to overreact. Embarrassment hit her with renewed force, and she almost turned her horse again to head for home.

Cassandra must have read her mind, as she reached up and grasped the reins. "I won't keep you long. I've been wanting to see you and planned to ride out to your ranch. Won't you come to the café or to my home for a cup of tea so we can chat in comfort and have a bit more privacy?"

"I'm afraid not. I've wasted too much of the day as it is. I need to get home." Mercedes tried to keep her tone from turning harsh, but it was hard with that kind face looking up into hers. No doubt she was covered in trail dust and looked a mess. Jesse couldn't help but see her in a poor light. "Can you tell me what you needed?"

Cassandra nodded but didn't release her grip on the reins. "Yes. I'm so very sorry for speaking out of turn and upsetting you when you visited my home. My father was furious with me, but even if he hadn't been, I'd be angry with myself. I'd so hoped you and I might be friends, and I ruined any chance of that by talking about my father's business before he had a chance to do so. It was unthinkable of me, and I do apologize." Her warm eyes suddenly twinkled. "But I've heard you've sold a number of horses recently, and it sounds as though Father isn't going to call your note, so that's very good news."

Mercedes gave a soft gasp. "He's not? Are you sure? He hasn't said anything to me yet."

Cassandra clapped her fingers over her mouth and groaned. "Not again. Oh dear. But he said . . ." She sighed. "I guess I've done it again, haven't I? But at least it's happy news this time. Why don't you stop in and see him while you're here so he can explain? I believe he was going to send a letter out to you, but I assumed that would have been done by now, since he mentioned it yesterday at breakfast." She waved a hand in the air, releasing the reins. "Nevertheless, it wasn't my place to speak, and I'd be so grateful if you wouldn't tell Father I did so. Please?"

Mercedes gazed down and smiled in spite of herself. "I promise. And thank you for telling me and for your apology. I think I'll wait for that letter he plans to send, so he won't wonder why I stopped in. I did stop by with a deposit a couple of days ago and asked that most of it be put against my loan. Maybe that's what helped to change his mind."

Cassandra smiled. "Thank you. And one more thing before you go, if you don't mind?"

"All right." Mercedes patted her restless horse.

"I am not interested in Jesse Townsend, nor he in me. In fact, if I had to guess, I'd say he's downright aggravated with me for what I said. I've already apologized to him, but I want you to know that I have no designs on him." She gave a sweet smile. "I understand the two of you were very close at one time. Maybe it's not too late."

Mercedes could only stare as she tried to get her bearings. "Well now. I'm not entirely sure what to say."

Cassandra stepped away from the restless horse. "You don't need to say anything to me. But he certainly appears as if he'd like to say something to you." She nodded toward Jesse. "Oh, I forgot. You might not know that Jesse brought Molly to the doctor's office. Apparently she was injured and required stitches."

Her heart plummeted and a wave of red rushed to her cheeks. Molly was hurt. Here she'd been blaming Jesse for not being injured and coming to town to flirt with Cassandra. Shame washed over her. She hung her head for a moment, then looked up. "I'll go see her now. Thank you—for everything, Cassandra. You've been a true friend. I'd love to take you up on the offer to come see you again, or have you come visit, if you'd still care to?"

Cassandra gave a sly smile. "That would be lovely. I believe Molly will be staying here overnight. Jesse might need company on the way home."

Mercedes swung her horse toward the doctor's office and all but bolted to the ground to rush inside. The last thing she could do right now was face Jesse. She'd been such a silly goose, thinking the worst of him yet again. She didn't know how she could ever possibly make it all right, or even how to begin. And she didn't totally believe Cassandra. She might not be in love with Jesse, but that didn't mean he didn't feel that way about her.

CHAPTER TEN

JESSE STILL COULDN'T BELIEVE THE CHANGE in Mercedes. He'd decided to skip going to the café, in the hope he might be able to speak to her when she exited the doctor's office. Her eyes had been blazing when she had faced him on the boardwalk, then her expression softened. Mercedes had jumped from her horse and raced into the office after talking to Cassandra. She must have learned of Molly's injury, but he'd give anything to know what else the two women had talked about.

What could Cassandra have said that would change Mercedes's attitude so quickly? More than likely the same apology she'd offered to him, but that wouldn't have altered her anger at him. And why in the world was Mercedes angry, anyway? He scratched his head. Women were beyond his comprehension.

The door to the office opened, and Mercedes stepped out. As she raised her eyes to meet his, her face instantly colored. Had he done something to cause that? He pushed out a smile. "Howdy, Mercedes. It was kind of you to visit Molly. Is the doctor done stitching her head?"

"Yes." She stayed where she was then glanced back, almost as though she wanted to run inside again. "She told me what happened. I'm so glad you found her and were able to bring her to town. I thought . . ." She bit her lip, turning her face away.

He took a step closer, standing at the base of the steps leading to the porch. "You thought what?" He scrunched his brow. "Did you know Molly was hurt when you came to town?"

"No." She sucked in a deep breath. "I stopped by your place to talk to you. I saw all the blood in the tack room. I couldn't find you and I thought . . ." She shook her head. "Never mind. It doesn't matter. Molly is going to be all right. That's all that matters."

Jesse knew he was missing something important, and suddenly it hit him. "You saw the blood and thought I was hurt? You were worried . . . about me?" Hope bloomed in his heart for the first time since he'd returned.

She turned her face away, soft color suffusing her cheeks again. "Possibly." The word was so soft he wasn't sure he'd heard it. "Then I raced to town. I saw you and Cassandra talking and knew you were fine. I need to get home now. I've been gone too long." She met his eyes briefly then walked down the steps, passing him, and gathered her reins.

"Wait. Please?" He moved closer. "My buggy is here, and I need to get home as well. You mentioned you came to my ranch to talk. Would you ride with me in the buggy and tie your horse behind? I'd like to know what you wanted to talk about, if you still care to do so."

She worried her lip then nodded. "I suppose that will work. If you don't push me to talk. I need to do some thinking first, if you don't mind."

He didn't understand what she needed to think about, but as long as she rode home with him, he could stand not knowing.

A few minutes later, her horse was tied to the rear of the buggy and they were leaving town. Silence enveloped them, leaving Jesse more than a little uncomfortable. He cleared his throat. "So Molly told you what happened?"

Mercedes nodded.

"You said you came by the ranch to find me and saw the blood."

She nodded again.

He blew out a breath in frustration. "Blame it all, Mercedes. You never used to have trouble talking. You used to chatter without ceasing when you were a kid in pigtails. Why are you so quiet now?"

A smile barely touched her lips. "Yeah, you were the silent one. Always teasing me about talking too much. That used to make me want to wallop you."

He arched his eyebrows. "It did? Guess I didn't have a lot to say at times."

She laughed, and the sound filled him with joy. Then she

sobered and turned her face away. "Kind of like me right now."

"Ah come on, Mercedes. You said you came to the ranch to find me and talk. Don't tell me you already forgot what you came to talk about?" The wagon rolled into a rut and out, bouncing the buggy and throwing Mercedes against his shoulder. Jesse barely restrained himself from putting his arm around her and pulling her closer, but he'd probably get slapped for his efforts. He well remembered the time when he was fourteen and had tried to kiss this black-haired girl. His face still stung thinking about it. "So you gonna tell me or what?"

She shifted her weight away from him. "I suppose I'll have to. I mean, I need to, and I prayed, and I know it's what the Lord wants me to do, but it's hard."

"I'm not an ogre, you know. You can tell me anything you want to. We used to be friends once upon a time. In fact, there's something I'd like to say to you as well. When I was over at Mr. Matthews's house a few days ago, he said something that made me think and has caused me some worry."

She turned to face him. "I can't imagine what that might be."

He'd been hoping she would offer to speak her mind first, but he'd be the gentleman and do the right thing. "Well, it's about something my pa said to you that I never knew about until recently." He gripped the reins harder and slapped the horse's rump. "Get along there." Jesse pulled in a slow breath and gathered his courage. There was every possibility she'd never forgiven his father and had believed what he'd said. And in a way, he guessed she had that right, as his actions hadn't shown her any different.

Mercedes kept her gaze straight forward, and her body ramrod straight, as though steeling herself for some kind of blow. "And what was it he said?"

"That it was your fault my gelding and his other horses died, and that I blamed you and would never forgive you for it."

"And you never did." Her words came out in a whisper so low he barely heard them.

The words punched him in the gut so hard he felt sick. Why had he allowed so many years to pass with this not resolved? He'd been an idiot. It was time to set things right.

Mercedes wasn't certain she believed what she'd heard. Jesse hadn't known what his father had said to her so many years ago? She had always assumed he did—in fact, that Jesse had said as much to his father, who only passed it along to her. But she had to know for sure. This was too important to brush over. "Why?"

He gave her a quizzical look. "Why what? I don't understand."

"Why did you act like you hated me after your horse died and cut off our friendship?"

He ducked his head for a moment, then raised his gaze to meet hers. "I was young and stupid. I guess I believed my father that you should have known your horse was sick and not ridden with me that day. It never occurred to me that you were as devastated as I was and hadn't known there was a problem. My father was angry—but I realize now it wasn't only about the horses—he resented your father for not allowing him to channel a portion of the stream onto our land. I think that colored everything that happened after, including what he said to you. I wish I'd known, Mercedes."

"Would it have made a difference? Would you have gone against your father at the time and remained friends with me?"

"I'd like to think so, but I'll admit I still had a lot of growing up to do. I'm so sorry."

Mercedes struggled with her feelings for a brief moment. It would be so easy to stay angry, but she'd turned all of that over to the Lord recently and asked His forgiveness. Now Jesse had done the same to her. How could she accept God's forgiveness and deny Jesse's request? "I forgive you, Jesse. I realize now your father wasn't expressing what you felt, even if you were upset about your horse at the time."

She shifted on her seat and gathered her courage. "And I need to apologize as well. I never told you how terribly sorry I was when Jasper died. I know how much you loved him, and due to my own pain, I withheld my sympathy and carried a grudge all these years. I was so convinced you hated me and would never want to be friends again, that I never once thought about what you were going through. My mare lived, even though she was the one who carried the sickness, and your gelding died. It should have been the other way around."

She bowed her head. "Not long ago, the Lord convicted me for my pride and stubbornness. I asked Him to forgive me, but I hope you will too. I'm sorry for not trying to reach out to you and for being hurt ever since."

Jesse touched her fingers, then withdrew his hand and looked straight forward.

Mercedes's heart sank. He must be thinking of Cassandra to not even want to touch her. "It's all right, Jesse. I know you have feelings for Cassandra. I like her a lot myself, even though I didn't want to at first. I hope you and I can at least be friends and good neighbors again. I want the war between our families to be over."

Jesse's lips parted as though to speak, but the words were cut off in a mighty explosion that rocked the buggy. Jesse had all he could do to control the horse as it bolted forward. "What in the world?"

Mercedes peered around the top of the buggy and gasped. "Lightning. It struck not far ahead of us, and the dry grass is on fire. Jesse, the wind will drive it straight to my ranch. Stop the buggy!"

He pulled the horse to a halt, speaking low words of reassurance to the spooked animal.

Mercedes jumped from the buggy and raced to her horse tied behind. "It's only a small flame right now. I'm going to ride ahead and see if I can put it out." She flung herself into the saddle and spurred her stallion forward toward the growing fire a hundred yards ahead.

CHAPTER ELEVEN

"MERCEDES, WAIT!" JESSE YELLED, BUT SHE was already astride and galloping toward the fire. He prayed he'd be able to control his nervous horse and not overturn the buggy, but he couldn't allow Mercedes to try to fight that fire on her own. She didn't so much as have a bucket or water. His gut clenched with fear as the smoldering fire grew. What did the woman think she could do? Whatever it was, she could easily put herself in danger.

He kept a tight grip on the reins, but urged the horse into a lope with the buggy bouncing along the road behind it. The fire was a few yards to the side of the road in a rocky patch of ground, so maybe it wouldn't spread fast. Another rumble of thunder sounded right before a jagged bolt ripped through the sky. Thankfully this one didn't appear to make contact with the earth.

Mercedes slipped off her horse and stripped the saddle, then separated the blanket from beneath it and raced toward the nearest flames. She swung the blanket over her head then thumped it down on the smoldering grass. Sparks flew into the air, spreading to another patch of grass and igniting those.

The horse and buggy reached the edge of the road closest to the blaze. Jesse drew to a stop, set the brake, and jumped down. "Mercedes! You're making it worse. The sparks are spreading the fire. Stop!" He dashed forward but she didn't appear to hear him.

Mercedes raced around the edge of the fire to the front, apparently intending to head it off if possible. Suddenly, her foot caught against a rock. She tumbled to the ground, the blanket flying from her hands and landing near her head in the flames. It quickly ignited, and sparks flew into the air. Several landed on her skirt, beginning to smolder.

Jesse ran for all he was worth, horror gripping him as he saw flames burst to life near the hem of her skirt and begin to travel toward her knees. "Mercedes. Your dress! Roll out of the way. Get into the dirt."

She wasn't moving. As he drew close he saw why. A welt was rising on her forehead, and her eyes were closed. He fell to his knees and grabbed her shoulders, then pushed, sending her rolling into a patch of dirt devoid of rocks. The fire on her skirt sputtered but didn't go out. Jesse grabbed handfuls of dirt then tossed them on the still smoking material. Once he was assured there was no more danger of fire on her clothing, he scooped her into his arms and headed for the buggy. She had forgotten to ground tie her stallion, and he could see the animal on the road headed toward the ranch.

Gently he placed Mercedes on a patch of dry grass near the buggy, then stroked her hair away from her face, checking the lump. Water. He had a canteen under the seat. He tore his kerchief from around his neck and poured water over it, then knelt beside her. "Come on, honey. You have to wake up. You can't be hurt too bad." He dabbed her cheeks and forehead with the damp cloth, being careful not to touch the welt. "Please, Mercedes. Wake up."

He slipped his arms around her shoulders and cradled her in his arms. "You like to've scared me to death with that stunt. Nothing is worth your life, not even your ranch. I can't lose you, honey." Placing a careful kiss on her forehead, he continued to whisper, not even sure what he was saying anymore. He'd known since childhood that he cared for Mercedes, but this all-consuming love born of the fear of losing her almost flattened him. How could he have not realized how much he loved her?

"What did you say, Jesse?" Her eyes fluttered open as she stirred in his arms. "Why are you holding me?" She struggled to sit up but fell back again and moaned. "What's wrong with my head?"

"You hit it pretty hard on a rock when you tripped, then your skirt caught on fire. It's out now. I think you'll be all right, but you need to lie still. We'll get you in the buggy and back to my ranch."

"The ranch! The fire. I remember now." She pushed to a

sitting position and looked wildly around. "It's spreading. Why didn't you help me get it out? Why did you let it burn? I'm going to lose everything if it reaches my house and barn." A choked sob came out between her parted lips.

"Because saving you was more important than saving material things." He released her and cradled her face with both hands. "It appears you heard some of what I said as you were coming to. I love *you*, Mercedes, not Cassandra. There's no way I was taking the chance of losing you to this fire. I know you're stubborn and have a hard head. You proved that with this fall, but I'm not taking any chances with your life. It's too precious to me."

She stared at him in wide-eyed wonder. "You don't love Cassandra? But I thought . . ."

"I had no idea you thought that until today, but no, I don't."

Another rumble smote his ears. He looked up. "Mercedes. Hold out your hand."

She puckered her brow but did as he said, then gasped. "It's sprinkling."

He grinned. "Let's get you into the buggy. It appears there's more rain coming." By the time he'd carefully helped her onto the seat, the heavens had opened and the rain came down in earnest. He clucked to his horse. "Do you mind getting wetter? I'm afraid the wind is going to blow it in here before I can get you back to town. I want the doctor to take a look at your head before we head home."

She laughed, her voice bubbling with joy. "Mind? I'm thrilled. Almost as thrilled as I am that you don't love Cassandra." She stuck her hand out of the buggy. "We've needed this for so long. Do you think there's a chance it will put out the fire before it reaches my ranch?"

Jesse pulled the horse to a stop, and it stood with its head lowered. "Yes, I think there's a good chance. It's coming down hard now, and I can barely see. But why do you care so much that I don't love Cassandra? Is there a chance you might have affection for me in a way I hope you do?"

She gave a shy smile. "I was conscious for a minute or two before I opened my eyes."

He snorted a laugh. "You little minx! How much did you hear?"

"Enough to wonder if you're going to propose, or at least kiss me." Her dark eyes gleamed as she stared up into his.

"Yes, ma'am, on both counts. But I'd sure love to get that kiss and be assured of how you feel about me, before I take the chance of proposing." He bent over her and pressed his lips to hers in a gentle, tentative kiss.

Mercedes moved closer and slipped her arms around his neck. After a few moments, she pulled back and smiled. "That was a good start, but it didn't seem to me that you really love me. That was more like a friendly kiss."

He gave a small groan of frustration mixed with anticipation. "Let's see if I can fix that." This time he didn't let her go until she had melted against him, returning every bit of the passion he felt. He lifted his head. "Better?"

"It'll do for now until you get a bit more practice." She grinned. "Did you know Mr. Ellington is extending my note?"

He gave a start of surprise. "To answer your unspoken question, no, Cassandra did not tell me that. All she did when I saw her in town was apologize for causing us both trouble. But why tell me that now?"

"Because I know the next thing on your list was to propose. I want to make sure it's not out of pity or to help me save my ranch." She cocked her head to the side. "It isn't, is it?"

He released a deep laugh of pure joy. "Not in the least. How about I show you what it's all about, and maybe you'll believe me this time."

She lifted her head and closed her eyes. "It would be my pleasure, Mr. Townsend. I assure you, a little more practice would do both of us good."

As Mercedes lifted her chin for his kiss, gratitude overwhelmed her. God had blessed her mightily by saving her ranch and giving her the love of this good man. To think she could have missed all of this if she'd held on to her pride and refused to forgive. She gave a contented sigh.

Jesse stroked his finger down her cheek, sending tingles of anticipation through her. "Everything all right? Is your head hurting? I can get you to town right away if you'd rather."

She opened her eyes. "It hurts a little, but I'm fine. In fact, at the moment I'm thanking God for reuniting us." She leaned her head against his chest, listening to the steady beat of his heart. "I'd only hoped for a renewed friendship, but instead I've been given a love beyond compare."

The End

If you'd like to learn more about Miralee Ferrell or sign up for her newsletter, visit her website: www.miraleeferrell.com

HAVE DRESS, WILL MARRY

BY YVONNE LEHMAN

CHAPTER ONE

Wildcat Mountain, Kentucky
1892

DESPERATE TIMES CALLED FOR DESPERATE MEASURES. If ever there was a desperate time it was now. Julie Hayes had no other option.

Besides, why should such a question be limited to men?

All her life when Julie had asked such questions, the answer had been, "Because you're a girl." This was one time only a girl could do it. And she would. What could be worse than the predicament she was in already?

Her thoughts went to articles about women fighting for their rights that she read in the newspapers and magazines James Greely brought to her each time he returned from Lexington after his transactions there with the jeweler.

Now, James apparently wasn't returning, and Russell Cutler, her step-- she didn't like to put "father" on that, said a warrant would be put out for his arrest.

Her expression must have shown her shock. "Don't worry, hon. Just like you've taken over the teaching in James's place at the school, you can replace him in taking the gems down to Lexington."

Hope sprang inside her. This could be her chance to get away. He seemed to read her mind. "And if you don't return with the money, you can join your sweetheart in prison." He grinned, self-satisfied.

"Russ," she choked. "I won't do it. You can't make me."

"Little girl, I'm your daddy, and I can do whatever I like."

"You're not my daddy, and I'm a grown woman."

He had acknowledged that after her mother died, and Julie took over the cleaning and cooking, besides working at his General Store.

"Well, it's like this. The store hasn't brought in much money lately. James hasn't come back with my money." He shrugged. "You could help out with the debt."

A wave of understanding wafted over Julie. She should have known what he was after. Her mother's gems. He'd mentioned them often enough. But her mom had made her promise to use the gems for her own well-being. Her mother had found them in the abandoned mine and Russ, himself, had evaluated them, like he did for others who found gems in the mine. Russ had a business of buying the gems from those who wanted immediate cash, then Russ sold them to a jeweler for what he called a "modest profit."

She turned and he grabbed her arm. "You don't turn from me."

She faced him and squirmed out of his grip. He had never hurt her, but she didn't doubt he would at the slightest provocation. He'd become a different man since her mother died and he'd begun to frequent the saloon.

He grinned. "I'll give you a couple days. It's either replace James or give me the gems. We're family, and you have an obligation to help out. Think it over." Russ stomped out of the fine house that her mother's money had helped buy.

Julie didn't need to think it over. If he got the jewels, she'd be stuck in Wildcat Mountain at his mercy.

So, it was now or never. Fall had come to the mountain, and snow would soon follow. And it wasn't escape she needed, but someone she could trust who would offer protection. That led to only one conclusion. Who else but that good-looking circuit-riding cowboy preacher?

Her heartbeat sped up. That was, of course, only because he was the answer to her predicament. The former preacher, elder Doc Sullivan, had tried to scare everybody into heaven, but judging from the three times Brother Timothy had preached, he had a less lengthy, gentler way.

And he was pleasant on the eyes. She stopped those thoughts and asked forgiveness. When she and Amy, and some of the other women talked about his dark curly hair, and the twinkle in his dark brown eyes, and how the smile that dimpled his cheeks could trigger a fast heartbeat, Granny

Simms made a tsk-tsk sound with her tongue and said 'a-body needed to look upon a preacher with eyes of faith.

Julie wasn't sure what that meant, but when he stood in front of the church and talked, she often closed her eyes to keep from sinning.

Today, she had to be courageous and bold. That's why she was wearing her best blue linen dress beneath a full skirt and blousy top. She would take her gems, and only one bag containing her mother's wedding dress, a picture of her parents, a square of quilt, and a few personal items. Elation swept over her, as if a whole new wonderful life was opening up to her.

That's probably how a prospective bride would feel.

And that's how she felt when the first indication of his arrival was the beige color of his wide brimmed cowboy hat and the brightly colored yellow and red bandana around his neck. She stood in the churchyard like the town's people did on every third Sunday when the saddleback preacher was due, weather permitting. They couldn't be sure if he'd be delayed by needy persons awaiting him along the way, or nature gone awry with rock slides, flooded trails, or even a coal-mine mishap somewhere.

Others saw him too and began making their way inside the building that consisted of one large room filled with benches separated by an aisle down the middle, which served as a school five mornings a week. On Preacher-Sunday, it became a church where women sat on one side and men on the other, eager to hear the word of the Lord.

"You coming?" said Amy who had stopped in mid-conversation to watch the preacher.

"Save me a seat." Julie heard Amy's disparaging sigh which meant she'd much rather find out why Julie dismissed her. But Amy headed toward the church.

As soon as Brother Timothy dismounted and tied the horse to a post, he turned.

Julie stood right in front of him.

"Good morning, Miss Hayes." He removed his Stetson and exposed dimpled cheeks.

She had a speech planned. But she saw Russ leave a couple of men he'd been standing with and head toward her. She had to do this quickly. She forgot the preliminaries, and thinking the preacher's eyes looked like warm dark chocolate, she asked her question with urgency. "Brother Timothy. Will you marry me?"

CHAPTER TWO

TIMOTHY SULLIVAN STARTED TO TELL HIMSELF he didn't know why he had to catch his breath when she asked if he would marry her, but of course he knew. This was the third time he'd come to the mining area, but that first time flashed in his mind.

He knew he wasn't cut out for being a preacher. All the way up the mountain he'd planned how to tell the people he was a temporary fill-in. He'd have to preface that with the story of his saddleback-preaching grandfather having been killed in the train accident a few weeks prior.

He couldn't very well say the Rolling Hills Church pastor and elders made him feel like he'd be sinning against God and his grandfather if he didn't do this. He prayed God would give him the words.

He'd heard Doc Sullivan, as his grandfather was called although he wasn't a doctor, talk about the needs of the people in Wildcat since the gem mine stopped yielding several years ago, and the poverty of nearby coalminers. Timothy hadn't known what to expect--maybe that they'd be covered with coal dust or something.

They hadn't been. Most were not as well-dressed or as educated as city folks but were every bit as clean, smart in their ways, and maybe even more well-mannered. The congregation had dwindled since the gem mine closed, and they'd not been able to get a preacher who wanted to live in the dying town.

A stout woman with a voice to match, handed out copies of "When We All Get to Heaven," making him wonder if they'd already heard about the accident. She played the piano that could use some tuning. Everyone stood and sang about, "what a day of rejoicing that would be."

Timothy got up and looked out at about fifty staring, questioning eyes. Then he had seen her. She'd entered, looking like a ray of sunshine, and holding onto the arm of an older woman he later learned was Granny Simms. She wore a perky little hat like the kind his sister wore when she went to town. But all his family members had dark hair and dark eyes. This one had hair the color of golden wheat rolled beneath that hat.

He tried not to stare as she led the older woman to a seat where a red-headed young woman motioned to them. The way he was thinking more about her and her dress being yellow as if it mattered, he felt even more convicted about having taken on something that might be an abomination to the Lord.

Before attempting a sermon, Tim had to tell the congregation what had put an ache in his heart. He kept his head down while talking about the wreck, until sobs reached his ears. He'd looked up to see women sniffling and wiping tears from their faces. Some men wept openly and put a hand or a sleeve up to their eyes. Many blinked, looked down and tightened their lips. He'd never be the kind of man his grandfather was.

He'd taken so long talking about the accident and answering questions they flung at him, which never would have happened in a city church, he decided to let his sermon be on John 3:16. His grandfather would already have preached on the passage, but they nodded and rocked and women smiled like they were hearing that for the first time and liked it. He reckoned a person never tired of hearing about Jesus loving them.

After church he'd been introduced to everybody and figured putting all the names with the faces would take longer than he expected to continue being a circuit rider. The image of the pretty girl in a dress the color of sunshine stayed in his mind because she was so different from his lifestyle of cows, horses, dark-haired, dark-eyed family, and the even darker sense of gloom since his grandfather's death.

He'd learned she was Miss Hayes, who helped out at the school, and thought that might be why she and James Greely, the schoolteacher, had seemed to enjoy a special relationship. He'd noticed that they migrated to each other in the church yard after services while Timothy stood at the doorway shaking hands.

And now, this third time he'd come to the mining town, she stood before him, looking at him like children did after a service when he opened up a bag of hard candy he promised if they'd be good in church. His grandfather would have scared them into being good, but Tim preferred bribing them.

And now, when Miss Hayes said in a rather desperate tone, "Will you marry me?" it was like his life flashed before his eyes, and he struggled for the right words and inadvertently they came out as, "Yes, of course."

But he wasn't sure the elders in the church having laid hands on his head and saying he was ordained gave him the right to perform a marriage ceremony. Right as he opened his mouth to say he'd need a few details, they both turned their attention to someone striding toward them.

Timothy expected James Greely, the only man around he thought might be a good match for Miss Hayes, but instead it was Russell Cutler, an elder and one of the better-dressed men in the church. Was he the groom? He was old enough to be Miss Hayes's father.

Then she said the strangest thing. "Maybe you can bring the book the next time you come."

Timothy's gaze returned to her, and the look in her eyes reminded him of someone who suddenly happened onto a rattlesnake. Her expression quickly changed from fear to a smile and she said, "That's a wonderful idea."

She turned toward Mr. Cutler who extended a hand. He had a smile on his face but a question in his eyes.

"We were talking about how helpful it could be for the school children," Miss Hayes said, "if we used *The Christmas Story Book for Children*."

Timothy didn't remember such a conversation but hoped he'd said that instead of something about a lovely woman with corn-silk hair, pretty dresses, and soft blue eyes who looked at him like he was a delectable piece of candy. Must have been his grandfather who promised the book.

She lifted a hand, said, "Amy's saving me a seat," and hurried away.

"A Christmas book?" Cutler cast a curious glance. "That's a few months away yet."

Timothy laughed lightly as he headed for the church, and Cutler fell in step beside him. The last stragglers were going inside. He too wondered why she'd mention a Christmas book while the leaves on the trees were beginning to be a great reminder that an artist's painting was a poor imitation of God's creation.

He knew snows came early on the mountain. Trails could be treacherous even in good weather. "Don't know how many times I'll get up here before Christmas," Timothy said, wondering if he might make a special trip with that book. "Grandfather said sometimes he simply couldn't make it."

Cutler nodded and mentioned someone who wanted a visit from Timothy. They walked on into the church and Timothy saw Miss Hayes sitting next to the red-headed girl he'd learned was Amy, who sat beside Granny Simms. Miss Hayes appeared more solemn than usual. Maybe because her fiancé wasn't in church today.

Timothy recalled his grandfather saying he counseled young couples before they married. He didn't feel qualified to do so, being a twenty-five-year-old single man himself. He'd have to wait until he could speak with James and Miss Hayes. He would advise them to find an established preacher, such as the one in Rolling Hills or Lexington, instead of one who was circuitous and temporary.

No, he didn't feel qualified to counsel a pretty woman like her on how to be a good wife to some man. He could use a little counseling himself. On second thought, he'd gotten counseling all his life, mainly from his grandfather who said the way to treat a wife is to say, "Yes, ma'am" a lot and love her with all your heart.

They both had laughed. But something had worked for his grandparents. Grandfather could stare down a gun-totin' scoundrel or a snorting bull, but when he looked at Grandma his dark eyes softened to warm brown. His eyes showed what he felt in his heart.

Reminding himself he needed to be thinking about the love of John 3:16, Timothy removed his hat and joined in singing, "Shall We Gather at the River?"

CHAPTER THREE

AFTER CHURCH, TIMOTHY BREATHED A SIGH of relief when Miss Hayes didn't approach him again but hurried away with the other young woman. Maybe she realized it wouldn't be proper for them to talk about her upcoming marriage, without her fiancé present.

As the congregation dispersed, an elder gave him a list of requests and invitations from persons wanting him to visit, many because of sickness, others about life and faith questions.

It was late afternoon before he finished his duties, and the last one was a couple back in the cove who couldn't get to church for a while and wanted to know if they'd still get to heaven.

He decided it was harder work trying to preach and think and counsel and comfort than it was to tame a wild horse. He patted his big brown best friend, Buddy, as he rode back down the mountain. After a few miles along the winding trail, they both needed to stop in the grassy spot by a creek and rest a while.

Buddy was drinking from the creek, and Timothy sat and leaned against the trunk of a shade tree. He munched on the tasty little corn pone Granny Simms had fried up for him and brought to church because she liked his sermons, short and to the point without any "galley-waggery," she said.

He was chewing on that when he heard a strange sound. His mind revealed a flash of possibilities as he jumped up and looked around.

No, wasn't a barn owl. Theirs was a short high-pitched shriek.

Mountain lion? They'd probably pounce and growl later.

He'd heard that a bull elk sounded like a freight train. The bull on the Sullivan Ranch didn't come close to resembling an elk.

The sound was like pee-GAAA.

Then he knew.

Peacock.

Yes!

Now where did he get that information? Oh yes, his sister Becky. Every time she came home from the university she shared interesting, if not helpful, bits of trivia. A peacock could sound like a female's high-pitched shrieking.

Uh oh!

But a peacock's shrieking wouldn't be accompanied by horse hooves pounding the ground. Then he saw something streaking though the trees of the winding trail above him. At least it seemed to be on the trail. But if the rider was in control, why the shrieking?

He jumped up but stayed near the tree in case he had to duck behind it. Then he saw the female rider was pulling back as if to stop the huge animal instead of leaning forward to gain control.

"Jump!" he yelled, before they were on him. "Jump off!"

The next thing he knew the pounding hooves grew fainter and stopped. He glanced up. There was none other than Miss Hayes, whimpering and hanging onto a tree limb above him with her skirt billowing and her blue undergarment swaying, exposing her ankles.

All he could think to say was, "Jump."

"Noooo," she moaned. "My dress. My dress."

He didn't know what a dress had to do with anything. She should be concerned about her bones. "I'll catch you," he said, hoping he wasn't lying. He would try.

"My-my hands won't let go."

He assessed the limb. It was a small one hanging down from a bigger one, and *it* might let go. "Just a minute."

Was that a wildcat, or did she growl?

He brought Buddy over, swung up into the saddle, and maneuvered the horse beneath her. "Okay, you're only about two feet from the horse's back. Now drop."

"What if he runs away?"

"He won't." Timothy didn't bother to mention he might buck

and they'd both break their necks. He planned to count to three but suddenly she sounded like a peacock again and twisted as she dropped. His hands shot out and with a little shifting, she was right there in front of him, sidesaddle, and brushing at her skirt.

She should not be so concerned with the possibility of her legs showing. He'd been more concerned about having to set them if she hit the ground and broke them.

Buddy grunted and shook his head like he wasn't exactly pleased, then decided the patch of clover was too tempting to resist and began munching. Timothy knew a little about temptation and figured he'd best get his arms away from around Miss Hayes lest his breathing mimic hers. They'd both sound like runaway horses.

Timothy dismounted and lifted his arms for her, but she shook her head. "We're not safe out here." He wondered if she was spooked by the sudden chill of late afternoon and the breeze moving the tree limbs turning the mountainsides into a labyrinth of waving shadows.

"Please," she urged. "Take me home with you. I'm in danger."

"Someone is following you?"

"He will." Her fear was obvious. "And we have to find the horse. Please, please. My bag is fastened to the saddle horn."

Timothy untied Buddy and hoisted himself up behind her. She began talking in a more relaxed tone of voice. "I didn't have time to explain this morning at church. I needed to say more about the marriage."

Tim figured there were more pressing things to think about at the moment. Like having his arms around a frightened woman, and one who indicated she was being pursued. And there was the matter of a runaway horse who might be lying on the trail or suffering somewhere alongside it. And what in the world was he going to do with her?

He'd begun to think he was hearing impaired that morning when she said, "Will you marry me?" and quickly changed to the subject of a book. But now, if he was hearing right, she was saying something even stranger.

"Our marriage," she said timidly, "will be in name only."

CHAPTER FOUR

Near Sullivan's Ranch near Rolling Hills KY

SITTING SIDESADDLE, JULIE TURNED HER HEAD enough to see Brother Timothy's baffled expression. He gazed along one side of the trail, then the other, avoiding eye contact.

He cleared his throat. "Before we get into that, let's talk about who you're running from. If he reaches us, I'll know whether to shake hands or shoot first." He laughed uncomfortably.

"Shoot first, if it's Russell Cutler."

"Is he trying to marry you against your will?" Her head and shoulders turned sharply toward him. "No! Russell is my stepfather."

"He's trying to make you marry somebody?"

Julie sighed. Brother Timothy had no idea what she was getting at, and she didn't quite know how to come right out and say it. They rode in silence except for the gentle clip-clop of the horse along the path and the steady rolling of the nearby creek. Small animals scurried away, and there were sounds of squirrels or the breeze in the trees.

Julie didn't know how to explain her problems. She was more fortunate than many on Wildcat Mountain. "I think," she said finally, "Russell is doing something illegal concerning the gems that come from the abandoned mine. James hinted at that. James left, and Russ wants me to take his place."

"He can't force you to do that," Timothy said.

"I live in Russell's house. I work in his General Store without pay because I'm family, so I have no money." Julie heard the desperation in her voice as she tried to get him to understand. Her mother's jewels were all she had in order to make a life for herself, and it wouldn't be wise to mention them. "Now that James hasn't returned, I'm helpless. Escaping is the only answer, or I'll be stuck there with Russell Cutler for the rest of my life."

She took a deep breath. "I need someone to protect me until I can be free of him."

"So," he said, "you plan to marry James so he will protect you, and that's why you said in name only?"

She dared not face him but knew he would be watching her profile. "Not . . . James."

"Then who," he said, obviously bewildered, "Who is the groom?"

Her shoulders rose with her deep breath. "I've thought the answer to my problems might be marrying James." She shook her head. "But . . . he didn't come back."

"Then . . .?"

She could almost hear him thinking and figured he would dump her as being somewhat out of her mind. He pulled the horse to a stop. "Miss Hayes, you're over eighteen, aren't you?"

She was embarrassed about that too. "Yes, I am. I'm twenty-three. That makes me a spinster. And there's no one in Wildcat Mountain I would consider marrying except James. Now that's not a possibility."

"Then . . . why . . . who?"

She turned her head so he couldn't see any part of her face which she knew was ashen. She felt as though the blood had drained from her entire body. Was he beginning to understand? Maybe her words were coming alive in his mind that she had to get away--she needed protection--James was gone--she asked Brother Timothy to marry her . . .

And here she was on his horse with his arms around her.

He got off the horse. Surely, since he was a preacher, he wouldn't leave her on the mountain, all alone. Already, darkening shadows crept closer. But she'd rather face a wild animal than the likes of Russell Cutler. As time passed, she noticed how much lighter the landscape became. They were out of the mountains and before them, looking like a giant washboard, were deep green rolling hills bathed by the soft gray of dusk.

"Shh," he whispered and walked off the path. Bullet was

limping along through the trees. Brother Timothy soothed, "Easy, boy. You'll be all right."

She asked Brother Timothy to hand her the bag tied behind the saddle, and he did. Awareness washed over her. Clutched in that bag against her body were the only possessions she had in the world. But that was more than she had up on the mountain. Up there, everything belonged to Russell Cutler.

The horse allowed Timothy to check his hoof, then feel along the leg. He led the horse over to where she was sitting. He looked up at her. "I think the horse must have pulled a tendon. I'll see if we can lead him home."

She wondered if he meant her home or Wildcat Mountain, but he mounted behind her. He led the horse alongside them and soon they reached more level ground. The sun had set and the sky deepened from blue to gray.

"Oh, look at the cows," Julie said.

Timothy chuckled. "Believe me, I know what they look like."

Feeling foolish, she tried to explain herself. "Of course I know what a cow looks like, but I've not seen so many grazing and others walking together like that."

"Supper time," Timothy said. "They're heading for the barn."

Her gaze stretched further, to the long white structure that looked more like a fine mansion than a place for cows.

"They seem like contented cows," she mused. "And why not? They can roam as they please, then have someone else prepare their supper."

He chuckled again, as he stopped the horse and dismounted. He might have thought her clever, saying that. After opening a gate, he made a sweeping motion with his hand. "Welcome to Sullivan Ranch."

Julie marveled that what her eyes took in, which seemed to have no stopping place, was Sullivan Ranch. Up on Wildcat, vision was restricted by groves of trees, and forested mountainsides.

Brother Timothy mounted Buddy again. While leading Bullet, they trotted up to a farmhouse, larger than any on the mountain. The white two-storied clapboard with its wrap-around porch surrounded by a banister looked inviting. But she had no idea what she'd find in that house.

Anxiety welled up inside her. Her thoughts had been what

she was running away from. Now she wondered what she had run to.

They rode around to the back, and a rider approached on a big black horse and tipped his hat to Julie. Brother Timothy dismounted and told the man he greeted as "Henry" about the lame horse. Henry said he'd see to it and led Bullet toward a stable.

Timothy held out a hand. Julie handed him her bag which he set on the ground, then lifted his arms to her. She felt so right in them as he helped her down and set her on her feet.

She reveled in feeling the strength of his arms, the nearness of his body, the closeness of his face, and wanted to express her gratitude for his giving her this sense of safety. Lifting her chin, she looked into his eyes. His warm breath grazed her cheek. Before she could find words, he released her, shifted his gaze to the ground and picked up her bag.

Falling in step beside him, she looked up and became aware this was a really big house. It reminded her of newer homes that were pictured in magazines James brought from Lexington.

Timothy opened a screen door and stood back for her to enter. She took a few steps onto a porch and stopped. The lower part of the wall was wooden. The upper part screened-in. A long table with matching wooden chairs sat near the outer wall. A round table was off to one side while a swing hung on chains at the opposite end.

Looking over her shoulder, Julie tried to visualize the wide-open spaces that anyone out here would see. This was so different from her world.

Her gaze focused on Brother Timothy, a new realization dawning. Who lived in this big house?

"Don't look so worried," he said as gently as he had talked to the horse. "They won't bite you."

They? Did he have a wife and children? Had she assumed he was not married? Taking a deep breath, she tried to prepare herself for whoever *they* were.

Brother Timothy must think her a terribly foolish woman. The good Lord must think her worse than foolish, having humanly thoughts about this preacher-cowboy. How could she have been so impulsive?

As soon as he opened the back door and she stepped into that hallway, the aroma almost made her swoon. She'd had very little lunch and no supper. The scent of something delicious made her suspect beef stew.

She hardly heard Timothy's words about setting her bag on the narrow table against the wall, beneath a row of hooks on which hung several cowboy hats.

He led her into the kitchen, a spacious room where four people sat around a long table. Two males who resembled Brother Timothy, one older and one younger, jumped to their feet and stared at her. A pretty dark haired woman about Julie's age questioned with mischief in her eyes. The gray-haired woman smiled, then rose and began walking toward them.

"This is . . ." Brother Timothy cleared his throat, then looked at her. "I don't believe I know your first name."

"Julie," she said softly, barely glancing at the curious-eyed group.

"Miss Julie Hayes," he said. "This is my grandmother, Olivia Sullivan. My sister, Becky. My brothers, Grant and Ryan."

The grandmother looked on while Becky said, "Hello, Julie," and the brothers said, "Howdy, ma'am."

"Miss Hayes has met with a little trouble," Brother Timothy said. "She needs a place to stay for a while."

Julie's quick glance revealed the older brother looking skeptical but the younger brother and sister seemed pleased. Her heart stopped when she observed Grandmother Sullivan inspecting her thoroughly, reminding her of the way Russ looked at a jewel through a magnifying glass. Finally, the older woman's brows lifted, her eyes widened, and her head moved from side to side. She sighed. "There is no way we can have a girl like this come in and take up residence in this house—"

CHAPTER FIVE

"GRANDMOTHER?" TIM INTERRUPTED, UNABLE TO BELIEVE this inhospitality.

Becky ground out, "Gran!" at the same time Tim spoke, and he heard the sudden intake of breath from his brothers.

He stared at his grandmother, and he was first to break the stare. She was head of the family now, not that she hadn't always been even though Grandfather had claimed that position. He had always seemed ready to reconsider if she didn't agree with him. She would smile. and Grandfather would get that twinkle in his eye.

Tim's glance around revealed his siblings were as shocked as he.

Grandmother's gaze sought Grant who mumbled, "We *are* dealing with a lot right now."

That was an understatement. For Grant, more than the rest of them.

When Grandmother's eyes met Becky's, his sister pleaded, "She can stay with me in my room."

Tim was about ready to ask for a private conversation with his grandmother, but she clicked her tongue. "What's that look on your faces? Don't you know me at all? You don't even let me finish my sentences."

Tim knew she was a generous, kind woman. But she was also as good at breaking a horse, birthing a calf, and toting a gun as any man, and could be more likely to get her way by speaking, because she used real words instead of cussing.

So which one was showing up?

"Come over here, honey." Gran held out her hand to take Julie's arm and led her to stand beside Becky. "Ryan, I saw how you looked at her when she came in here. This pretty little missy doesn't need any more of that eye-gazing like she's some mouthwatering morsel for you to eat."

A laugh escaped Ryan's throat until Gran's glance turned it into a cough, and he tried to display a stolid expression. Tim saw a moment of pain cross Grant's face as he glanced at Julie, and thought the cause wasn't this woman, but the one who had broken his heart.

Tim decided to study the hem of his grandmother's long skirt instead of look into her eyes. She seemed to be waiting for something so his gaze finally met hers. He felt the need to take a deep breath through his nose, and his nostrils drew together when he did.

"What I'm saying," Gran continued, "Is that she can't live here with you three buckaroos roaming the house. So right after supper, you need to pack up and move to the farmhouse. You can eat here, but you'll not be sleeping here."

"Oh, no," Miss Hayes moaned, but Ryan drew their attention. "Gran, I'm just a boy."

After Tim and Grant finished guffawing and Becky stopped laughing, Gran gave him her warning look.

"I know you're only a seventeen-year-old boy. But you've claimed to be a man ever since you were twelve-years-old and a piece of fuzz showed up on your chin." She looked up at the high ceiling and back. "Now you'll do like your brothers, get your stuff, and hightail it to the farmhouse."

Tim glanced at Julie with a nod, indicating everything would be fine. She was safe now. The warmth in her eyes reached him, causing a combination of pleasure and discomfort. Maybe it was the way her lips formed the silent words of, "Thank you."

Gran took charge. "Becky, show Julie where to freshen up before she eats."

Becky led Julie from the kitchen. Grant and Ryan returned to their place at the table. "Tim," Gran said, "Your grandfather would be proud of you."

With a twitch of his head, Tim headed from the room with a question rolling around in his mind. What would his grandfather do in a situation like this?

The answer hit him like a bolt of lightning. Doc Sullivan would help Julie Hayes reunite with James, the man she'd expected to marry, before she became so desperate she would marry someone else . . . in name only.

He could not fathom how a man could agree to such a plan, considering the appeal of the lovely Miss Hayes.

Did she think . . . a preacher would?

CHAPTER SIX

When Becky led her out of the kitchen and into the hallway, Julie's focus seemed to fail her. She felt weak and placed her hand on the wall.

Becky caught hold of her arm. "You don't look like you can make it to my room. Let's go over here." She apologized as she opened a door, and they entered a small room with a toilet in the corner, a box tub, and a couple of sinks. "This is where we can clean up after working outside."

"It's fine." Julie took a deep breath. "I . . . need to wash up and sit down."

Becky pulled a stool over to the sink and turned on the water.

Julie sat and as soon as she put her hands beneath the flow, she cried out and jerked them away. Turning them, she saw they were red and scraped.

"Oh," Becky exclaimed as if she were hurt. "Can you wash them?"

Julie nodded. "That surprised me. I didn't realize they were scraped like that. I've felt . . . numb." She returned her hands to the water, and after the initial sting, they began to throb, but the cool water helped.

Becky took a cloth from a shelf and wet it. "Here, wipe your face with this. Do you need to lie down?"

"I need food first, if—if that's all right."

"Of course it is. Let me tuck your hair in place." Their eyes met in the mirror's reflection. Julie felt as faded as she looked seeing the contrast. Becky was as dark as Julie was light. She felt Becky had the same kind of personality Brother Timothy had, gentle but strong.

Becky took a small box from beneath the cabinet, lifted the lid, and took out a jar of salve. She applied it to Julie's hands and wrapped them with gauze. "You can take the gauze off later. You need the salve, and you probably don't want to eat with greasy hands."

Julie really wanted to eat even if she had to munch it like a cow or lap like a dog.

They returned to the kitchen, and a wave of nausea hit her. Surely the aroma of food wasn't doing that. She began to tremble. Her surroundings blurred, and she swayed.

"Miss Hayes?" That was Brother Timothy's voice from somewhere behind her. She felt strong hands on her shoulders and leaned against what must be his solid chest, reminding her of the ride on the horse with his arms around her, making her feel safe.

Ryan jerked a chair from the table, causing it to scrape across the floor. He set it beneath her about the time her knees buckled.

"S-sorry," she mumbled as the two men guided her down onto the chair.

Becky held out a glass of water, and they both held onto it as Julie took a sip. "She needs to eat," Becky said.

"Oh my," Grandmother said, "your hands are hurt."

"I—I . . ."

The older brother set a bowl of food on the table.

"Let's scoot her over to the table," Ryan said.

"I can walk."

"No," Brother Timothy said. He and Ryan picked up the sides of the chair, as if she were a child on a pat-saddle made by two people holding onto each other's wrists. Despite her fatigue, hunger, and embarrassment, she felt the urge to giggle. Or maybe cry at all this caring attention. They hauled her over and set her in front of the bowl of stew that smelled wonderful and had lumps of meat, potatoes and carrots in it.

Her hands shook as she reached for the spoon Gran took from a drawer and handed to her.

"I can feed her," Becky said, making Julie feel like a wounded animal.

"I'm feeling better already," Julie said. "For a minute I felt like I was still on the runaway horse."

"Oh my, no wonder you're shaking," Gran soothed, pulled up a chair, and sat on the side of it facing Julie. She touched

Julie's arm and closed her eyes. "Lord, let us be to this girl what she needs. Bless the food. Amen."

Gran lifted the spoon, but Julie took it. "I think I can. I'll lean over." She did, taking broth only. The hungry grumbles in her stomach screamed for more of the tantalizing food as good as its aroma promised.

She thought some of her weakness was the realization of what happened that day and her trembling now was probably because everyone was staring at her. Brother Timothy and Ryan walked around to the other side of the table as if to see her better. She took a bite of potato, chewed, and swallowed.

"I think I was numb," she said, "and barely starting to feel . . . things. It's all so . . . unbelievable." They were silent, as if waiting for an explanation. At least they deserved one. "I was hanging from a tree, and Brother Timothy saved my life."

"What?" The stolid older brother who stood apart from the others came to life. He stepped toward her. "Who did such a thing?" he demanded about the same time Becky stifled an audible squeal of protest and Gran moaned, "Ohhhhh myyyy . . ." Gran's caress of her shoulder felt like a mother's touch.

"We've never had a woman hanged around here," Ryan said roughly. "Was it men or women who hanged you?"

"Ryan," Brother Timothy said forcefully. "We've never had anybody hanged around here in about fifty years."

Ryan's head jerked toward his brother. "Yes, we have. Remember that horse thief over in—"

"Never mind." Brother Timothy raised his hand. "Miss Hayes wasn't hanged by the neck. She grabbed a tree limb to get off the runaway horse. She was hanging by her hands."

Julie wasn't sure if the sounds being made were sympathy or what, but Ryan laughed heartily. Others returned to their places at the table.

"Brother Timothy saved my life," she said again, around the carrot in her mouth.

Ryan slapped his hands together. "Does that mean she's going to be our sister?"

Julie realized Brother Timothy was *brother* to three others in this kitchen. "Oh, maybe I should call him Preacher Timothy."

Becky gave a short laugh. "Around here, he's plain ol' Tim." She shrugged. "Or just Timmy."

Timmy? Julie could never be so informal with him. He was

a preacher and her hero. Maybe her future husband.

"Tim will be fine," he said, and Julie wondered if he'd stop calling her Miss Hayes. His glance moved to her bowl, fast losing its contents. "I could use some of that stew."

Grant thrust his thumb to the side along with a glance, saying, "It's in the pot," at the same time Ryan said, "On the stove."

Julie wasn't sure if that was good-natured ribbing. The two brothers looked smug while Timothy shook his head and grinned. The dimples softened his ruggedly handsome face.

"Sit down, Timmy," Becky said. "I'll get your stew. You deserve it after saving someone's life. It's great having another female in the house."

"Is this a visit, or you here for good?" Ryan asked.

"I don't know," Julie said after swallowing hard. "I can't go back. I've been afraid for a long time. I need to be . . . protected."

"Well, we can do that," Ryan proclaimed, his young face animated and his dark eyes flashing with confidence. "All of us can shoot a rattlesnake between the eyes and split him right up the middle, rope a calf, ride a bull, tame a wild horse—"

"Yeah," Grant said, "but can you mend the back fence like you've been told every day for the past two weeks?"

Ryan looked across at Julie and shook his head. "Don't mind him. Grant gets the big head because he's a Rolling Hills deputy and locks fellows in a cell and throws away the key."

"And don't you forget it," Grant warned.

Julie couldn't help but smile at Ryan. Her quick glance at Timothy revealed he was as eager for that stew as she. The contents of both their bowls were vanishing. She knew Ryan would like to be someone's hero, perhaps hers. But Timothy already was. He'd saved her life and brought her home. As if feeling her eyes on him, Timothy glanced at her and looked quickly down.

"Um," Ryan mumbled, gaining her attention. "What are we protecting you from? Or . . . who?"

"Hold it," Timothy said. "The reasons for Miss Hayes being here is a private matter for now." He and Grant exchanged glances, indicating this might be a legal matter since Julie needed protection. Julie didn't want a confrontation with Russell Cutler. She wanted to be away from him.

When Becky took her bowl to be refilled, Julie leaned away

from the table and against the chair back. The movement took her thoughts to the caress of the soft cotton dress beneath her outer clothing.

The caring ways of this family were like soft cotton.

Soothing as the salve on her hands.

She was reminded of the stray kitten that had appeared one morning at the school. They all let go of their personal problems and ministered to that scraggly, starving little thing. They felt needed.

Maybe this family was looking upon her as a diversion from their recent loss of Doc Sullivan. She welcomed their ministrations. She wished she could do something for them.

Feeling safe, and welcomed, she thought of those around her. How wonderful to be part of such a family. Gran accepted her on sight. Grant seemed skeptical, but kind. Ryan was delighted. Becky was pleased.

And Brother Timothy. He's the one who brought her here. Was he glad? Or maybe he thought he had no other choice.

Her gaze returned to him. He looked down at his stew. She couldn't read his expression.

Maybe he was just hungry.

CHAPTER SEVEN

THE LAST WORDS GRANT SPOKE TO Tim, after Gran shooed him and Ryan out of the kitchen was, "We'll talk later."

Yes, where there was a hint of anything illegal, Grant would be intent upon hearing it.

"I'll be right back," Tim said to his grandmother who began taking care of the leftover food. "I want to get a few books from the parlor."

She smiled. "You go ahead. We're not going anywhere." He knew she meant her and the dishes.

Tim walked down the hall and met Ryan who came down the stairs with a box of his belongings. "Your schoolbooks still in the parlor?"

Ryan gave him a look. "I can't get things from my room and from the parlor all at the same time. I'd like to put this in the wagon, if that's all right with you."

"Only asking." It seemed nobody could open his mouth to Ryan without his thinking it some kind of reprimand.

Tim walked past Becky's room on the left and on into the parlor on the right. It was a cozy room for family to gather or to be with friends or to sit near the fire and read a good book. Each of his siblings and he had sat at that desk in the corner, literally burning the midnight oil and studying for their classes.

In here, he felt closest to his grandfather, and also missed him the most. They'd spent many hours reading and talking about the Bible. He'd felt like he was Grandfather's favorite, but in truth he and his grandfather were able to spend more time together on the ranch. Grant had been living his own life in Louisville for a while, Ryan was young and in school, and Becky at college. Nevertheless, Grandfather had made him feel special.

He selected a couple theology books and a leaflet on prayer. He considered something by Victor Hugo but decided he'd best keep his mind on religious matters for a while.

The sound of feminine voices and light laughter wafted across the way, and his thoughts turned to Julie and Becky. Miss Hayes fit right into his family. But that's how his family was. Never turn away a person in need. Even go and find them, like his grandfather had started doing early in his life as a circuit-riding preacher.

He went to a shelf and searched the children's book section. Sure enough, there it was, *The Christmas Story Book for Children*. Satisfied, he put it atop the other books, left the room, and walked on past the sound of muted female voices.

After setting the books on the table beside Julie's bag, he walked into the kitchen and began clearing the table while Grandmother prepared the bin of soapy water for washing dishes. He wondered how Julie washed dishes up on the mountain. He remembered when there was no running water and certainly not heated water in the house. These modern conveniences were a blessing, especially to women.

Well, the Sullivan men too. While growing up, the boys had their turns at household chores, just like Becky had hers out on the farm, not only with planting and harvesting, but with the cows and horses.

"You boys will make some woman a good husband one of these days," his dad and grandfather had said many times.

. . . *Not in name only*.

At that unseemly thought, he had to juggle the stack of bowls, and they clattered slightly when he set them on the countertop next to the bin of water.

Grandmother looked at him, then at the bowls. "I'll need a little more of that hot water." She glanced at the pot on the gas stove.

He wondered if that gleam in her eyes meant she thought he might be in hot water.

No, he decided as he brought over the water. She lifted her hands so he could pour it in. She was simply eager to get his report. Since the train wreck, this had become a ritual each time he returned from the circuit, like Grandfather used to do. Gran wanted to hear all about the people and changes that had taken place like births and deaths and marriages. She especially wanted to hear about the clan back in Bear Cove that she claimed as relatives, although they hadn't seen each other in many years.

Before long they'd finished and the kitchen was swept. Cornbread and a few pieces of pie, made from their own Sullivan's apples, were securely covered on the sideboard. Grandmother always left something out for what she called, "her bottomless-pit boys." It'd be gone before bedtime. Tim was putting the big stew ladle in the drawer when he heard Ryan exclaim, "What in-?"

Tim rushed out into the hallway and sure enough, Ryan had Julie's bag open. A piece of quilt lay on the table and Ryan tried to stuff something white back into the bag.

"What are you doing?" Tim barked. "That's Miss Hayes' bag."

Ryan spread his hands. "I didn't know that."

"Well, you knew it wasn't yours," Tim accused.

"Yeah," he said. Then, "No. Sometimes you bring things home with you. Preacher-payment, you say, like Grandfather did."

Ryan was right about that. Maybe he wasn't snooping. But the way he'd shoved that white material didn't look too good. "Are you trying to tear that up?"

His tall, lanky, younger brother had a beet-red face, indicating he really hadn't known that belonged to Julie, or else was sorry he got caught. "Maybe we should fold that instead of shove it," Tim suggested.

Ryan pulled it out. Gran gasped. "Oh, my. Turn your heads."

Tim and Ryan turned after exchanging a questioning glance.

"My, my, this is pretty," Gran was saying. "Looks like a wedding dress. That's why I said don't look. It's bad luck for a man to see the bride's dress before the wedding."

"Grandmother. She's not—we're not—"

"Oh, I'm not saying you are. But she's a Miss and you're not married. We don't want to chance any bad luck."

"What kind of bad luck?"

After a moment, Gran said, "Why, I don't know. I've never heard of anybody finding out. Okay, it's folded and put away. You can look now."

Tim turned, looked at her and at the bag, then at Ryan

propped against the wall, giving him a smug look.

Tim started to get his stack of books but was stopped short by Ryan's quiet declaration, "She's in the family way."

After an eternity of stunned silence Tim heard a ringing in his ears and a voice that sounded like Gran saying, "You want your mouth washed out with soap?"

"I heard her say it," Ryan replied calmly. "She said she has to get married. And soon."

Tim's immediate reaction was to punch his brother, make him take it back, say it wasn't true. But it sounded very much like what she'd said when on the horse with him.

Ryan raised his eyebrows, picked up his books, and walked out the back door.

Tim hoped he could swallow the sour taste that had risen from his throat.

Grandmother said softly, "Well, when a girl runs away from home, it's a serious matter." She patted his hand that grasped the side of the table. "You've brought home a lovely girl."

"Yes," he agreed absently, staring at the wall. "But what am I going to do with her?"

He wasn't sure he'd said that aloud, until Gran replied, "That's for us to consider together." She paused. "Isn't it?" And when he didn't reply immediately she spoke softly. "Why Timmy, I believe you're smitten."

Smitten? "No, I—I—" He could only shake his head and knew the warmth he felt would show in his face. But he couldn't fall for someone who . . . "She came to me because she needs . . . a preacher."

"I have faith in you," she said.

That's what his grandfather had said. That's what the church leaders had said when they voted on him to ride the circuit. He had to try and think like a preacher. But how could he, a temporary substitute circuit-riding-preacher, ask . . . who is the father? James? If so, did he have his way, then abandon her? Or . . . did Russell Cutler force his attentions on her?

Tim knew why he'd rather be out with the horses and cows. This situation was way beyond his abilities, whether as a man or a preacher. He picked up the stack of books and turned to go out the door.

He'd never felt so confused or incompetent, even in his grandfather's pulpit or at a brush arbor, since the moment Miss Hayes literally dropped into his arms.

CHAPTER EIGHT

JULIE FOUGHT NOT TO FALL ASLEEP in the porcelain claw-foot tub. This was the first time she had ever bathed in anything other than a wash tub, where the hot water hadn't come from the faucet but from a pot on a stove. She tarried as long as she dared, lest her eyes closed.

She left the bathroom in one of Becky's nightgowns. Holding her folded clothing, she faced Becky who had changed into a gown and was propped against pillows at the bed's headboard.

When she and Becky had come into the room, Julie had reacted with surprise. "Twin beds?"

"I know, I know." Becky had grinned. "Preachers are condemning them. Discussions fly fast and furious. But I'm not married, and I want my visiting friends to stay in the room with me, but have their own bed."

Julie had nodded. "I've seen these advertised in magazines."

Now she was eager to climb into that other bed and prop up on pillows like Becky. She glanced at her clothes. "Should I wash these in the bath water?"

"Put them on the chair by the door," Becky said. "Lillian comes once a week to wash our clothes."

Julie grimaced. "These are all I have with me." She put them on the chair seat. "I left in such a hurry--"

"Don't fret." Becky gave a dismissive wave. "You and I are about the same size."

Julie placed her hand on the side of the chair back. "Oh, Becky. You're all so good. And you don't even know me."

"But I want to." Becky's dark eyes flashed with interest. "I want to hear all about this adventurous story of yours. Why you were hanging onto a tree limb and . . . um . . . fell into Timmy's arms."

Julie tried to ignore that sly look in Becky's eyes, as if she wouldn't mind if she were really in Tim . . . um . . . the preacher's arms. But she mustn't think of that right now, although the thought made her feel as comfortable as the soft gown caressing her body.

"Oh, Becky." Julie spread her hands helplessly. "I never even talked to him before today. And then . . . I asked him to marry me. I want to marry for love," she said as if that had anything to do with her having Brother Tim's arms around her. "But I don't know what to do but get married. It's the only solution to my predicament. I have to get married. And soon!"

"Ummff," Becky gasped and quickly covered her mouth with her hand. Her big brown eyes were huge. Just as quickly she uttered, "Sorry."

Julie lifted her hands, palms out. "Oh, you don't understand."

"Yes, yes, I do." Becky wiggled a finger toward the other bed, indicating Julie should go there.

Shaking her head at her ineptitude with this conversation, Julie turned down the quilt and sheet, propped the pillows, climbed in, and leaned back.

Before she could decide how to tell her story, Becky turned with her shoulder against her pillows and faced Julie, looking like a juicy secret was about to come her way.

"Oh, Julie," Becky said. "I'm not going to judge you. I have a friend in college who had to get married. That was a shotgun wedding if you ever saw one. Her dad, grandpa, uncles, brothers—"

Julie couldn't help but laugh, thinking maybe her situation wasn't as dire as it could be. "I'm not in the family way," she said. "No chance of that. I'm not saying this right, but—"

"You're not . . . ?" Becky glanced toward Julie's stomach.

Julie shook her head. Becky began to laugh. Then they both did.

Finally, Julie told her the main problem was Russell Cutler wanting to involve her in what might be illegal. The only thing Julie didn't tell her about was her mother's gems.

Becky in turn, revealed her own adventurous spirit. "You see," she said, her eyes wide, "Although my brothers didn't compete with me, I competed with them. I learned to rope, and brand, and shoot, and plant, and harvest, and train horses . . ."

On and on she went. Julie loved it. She'd never had anyone talk with her so personally. "And then," Becky continued, "after the university in Lexington opened its doors to women, and Grant was already going there, and then Timmy, I made that a goal. I would not let those brothers of mine be smarter than me."

They both laughed. "Oh, I doubt they are."

Becky looked down and picked at the quilt. "I've had my . . . stupid moments."

Julie lifted her eyebrows and waited.

"I'm kind of running away too," Becky admitted. "I left school. I used the excuse of the train wreck that took grandfather's life." She paused to blink away moisture and took a deep breath. "That was true, but also I needed to get away from a professor at the university. We began seeing each other." She paused. "And then he admitted he isn't . . . free."

"M-married?" came out of Julie's mouth, and she abruptly clamped her hand over it. "Sorry. That surprised me."

"Ha!" Becky said with a toss of her dark hair behind her shoulder. "What do you suppose it did to me?"

"Men can fool us," Julie admitted. "They can be different in private than in public. I learned that from my stepfather."

"Was he terrible to you?"

"Not physically," Julie admitted. "But if I stayed there I'd never get away. When I found out James wasn't coming back, I knew I had to leave."

"James will come back for you, won't he?"

"He would be afraid to go back to Wildcat. We were good friends. I think maybe we would have married if Russ hadn't started sending him down to Lexington with the gems he buys from people who find them in the abandoned mine."

"You love this James?"

Julie sighed. "I haven't had the luxury of thinking much about love."

"Well," Becky said jovially, "in case you do, I have three brothers I'd like to marry off. One's a little young. One is still broken hearted. But the other—"

"Oh!" Rather than allow herself to reveal the quickening pace of her heartbeat at that thought, Julie reached behind her head, snatched a pillow, and tossed it past the night table at Becky's face.

Laughing, Becky grabbed one of hers and threw it at Julie.

Their laughter stopped at the tap on the door. "Come in," Becky called as they both pulled the quilts up to their chins.

Gran entered with Julie's bag. "You might need this." She set it on the chair and came over to the bed. "Now let me look at those hands." After her examination, she smiled. "You might end up with a blister or two, but they're going to be much better by morning."

Julie had never felt so welcome anywhere since her early childhood when she lived with her mom and dad.

"Good night, girls." Gran smiled and left the room.

Becky rearranged her pillows and extinguished the soft glow of the gas lamp.

"You know," Becky mused as she scrunched down under the quilt, so Julie did too. "It's much more fun having a pillow fight with a sister than with rough-housing brothers."

"Nice thought," Julie said. Someday Becky would have those sisters. And one of them would be the kind of woman a preacher would want for a wife.

CHAPTER NINE

TIM HAD MIXED FEELINGS AS THE wagon rolled along the path to the farmhouse where he'd spent the happiest days of his life, visiting his grandparents. It also reminded him of the loss of his parents when he wasn't much older than Ryan was now. Accepting the losses hadn't been easy, emotionally or spiritually.

Maybe he should be more understanding of Ryan's attitudes. Somehow, though, strangers back in the mountains received his comments more easily than his siblings. He reckoned the same applied to him too.

And he had to admit, his frustration wasn't so much with Ryan, but with what Ryan heard Julie say. It threw him, like a bucking horse could do.

They'd never been a quarreling family. After Grandfather's death, Grandmother said, "It's fine to grieve. We likely always will. But don't dwell on what you've lost. Dwell on what you have and work toward creating a good life and serving the Lord."

Remembering that, he decided to be more tolerant with Ryan, but he didn't want to discuss Julie's personal life with him or Grant, only the legal aspect. While he was making coffee a knock sounded on the back door. That must be Homer, the foreman.

"Come on in," he called.

"Saw lights on and thought I'd check if you need anything. Lillian hasn't stocked any food, but she can bring something."

"Thank Lillian. But we brought pie up from the big house. There's plenty. Here, I'll dish out a couple pieces."

"Well, I can't refuse your grandmother's pie," Homer said

with a grin that plumped his cheeks and widened his eyes beneath his bushy gray eyebrows.

As he left, Tim called, "Oh, tell Lillian we'll eat breakfast with Gran in the morning."

"Will do. But she'll come up and see what needs to be done here."

Soon, Grant and Ryan came in from having taken care of the horse and wagon. When Tim approached Grant and asked to speak to him, Ryan asked, "Can I be in on this too?"

Tim shook his head. "Sorry. Not this time. It's private."

"Fine, fine. Why don't I go sleep with the hands in the bunkhouse if I'm not part of this family?"

"It's not that, Ryan," Tim said. "This is a private matter and maybe criminal."

"Sure, I'll go to my room." He scoffed. "Like a good little boy."

Tim didn't know if that was hurt or anger in Ryan's eyes before he stalked down the hall to his room. But this was not something he could share with his young brother. He could only share with Grant about Julie's suspicions and fear of Cutler.

"Now let me see if I have this straight," Grant said. "Miss Hayes suspects Russell Cutler of criminal activity because of something James Greely told her."

Tim nodded.

"And she's running away because she's afraid of Cutler?"

Tim was reluctant to say what he must. "Ryan overheard her say she's . . . in the family way."

Grant's forkful of pie returned to the plate, and he studied it for a long moment. He finally scratched a place beside his lips then looked at Tim. "So," he said, "Ryan overheard something that implies Cutler has personally violated her."

Tim got choked on that. He shook his head. "I hadn't thought that. I was thinking she and James . . ."

Grant's brows formed a straight line. "That's what I got from this, since she's running away and is afraid of Cutler."

"But she has a wedding dress in her bag, so she planned—"

Grant took a sip of his coffee and stared at Tim over the rim. He swallowed and set the mug down. "Tim, legally this is hearsay. James told Julie. Julie told Tim. Ryan eavesdropped. We don't know if she's in the family way by consent or force."

He lifted his hands. "Julie or James will have to make an accusation before any action can be taken." His lips tightened. "Julie is not a child."

"If she's in trouble and doesn't accuse, then what do we do with her?"

Grant pointed a finger. "She's your project. You brought her here."

"I had no option. This was dropped in my lap so to speak. Literally." He grimaced. "She came to me as a preacher who could help."

"Well?" Grant questioned.

"Well, what?"

Grant's eyebrows lifted over amused eyes. "You're the one who told me about that duck statement. What was it?"

Tim grumbled, hoping he wouldn't act up like Ryan had a way of doing. "Yes. Yes. The good ol' writer James Whitcomb Riley wrote that when he sees a bird that walks like a duck, swims like a duck, then he calls that bird a duck."

Grant chuckled.

Tim tried, but this was far from funny. Miss Hayes had every reason to consider him a preacher. He stood in front of those church goers up on Wildcat Mountain. However inept, he gave a sermon. One sermon really, three times. He visited the sick. He comforted the hurt and grieving. He listened to sinners confessing. So, Miss Hayes had every right to seek a preacher's help. And he was the one she picked. But that's because she had no other choice. He'd felt kind of pleased about that, until it started becoming so complicated.

Grant took pity on him. "You can do what this family has always done with any stray creature. We take care of it, no matter its condition."

Miss Hayes, a creature? Well, yes. A creation of God and a mighty fetching one too. But she happened to have—conditions.

Tim got up to get the coffee pot from the stove and pour another cup.

Ryan strode in. "Can I have some of that coffee?" He looked at them with belligerence. "Or do I have to drink milk?" Ryan had come in the back way. He'd obviously gone out his bedroom window or the front door and listened from the porch.

"Dagnabbit, Ryan," Grant growled. "If you want to be treated like a man, then act like one."

"Were you out there listening?" Tim asked.

Ryan shrugged. "Thought I ought to know if I'm going to be an uncle."

Warning himself to stay calm, Tim simply stated, "I never did more than nod briefly at her up on the mountain."

Ryan gave him a sly look. "You brought her here kind of disheveled."

Grant warned, "That's enough."

Ryan sneered. "Yeah, why don't we all just pray about it?" He stalked off, leaving Tim and Grant to exchange helpless glances. Without their grandfather, how were they going to contend with Ryan's belligerent attitude?

Tim rinsed the cup out and set it on the counter. "I'll talk to Julie in the morning," he said. He took a mug from the cabinet and poured coffee into it, then added cream the way Ryan liked it. He remembered that not too many years ago Ryan's mug would be mainly milk, with a little coffee. He didn't bother to knock on the door, but opened it, walked on in, and set the mug on Ryan's desk.

Ryan stretched his neck to peer at the cup and grumbled, "'bout time you did something right."

Tim's heart softened at the good-natured ribbing. "You can say that again."

"Don't count on it." Ryan took a gulp of coffee and mumbled, "Mmm."

Rather than count on too much, Tim nodded, said "Good night," and left the room. On the way down the hall he knew what Ryan had said sarcastically was what Tim needed to do seriously.

In his room, without lighting the lamp, he sat on the side of his bed and bowed his head. He opted for a mental conversation with the Lord. *What in the world is going on here? Am I being punished for taking on a preacher's responsibility when you didn't call me to do that? Is that why you put that pretty girl in my life, the first girl who ever made me even consider more than the farm and the ranch?*

Tim waited. The Lord didn't appear inclined to respond. His only options remained—either find James and turn Miss Hayes over to him, or turn the situation over to Grant who would turn it over to the proper authorities.

If Cutler forced himself on Julie, would James want to marry her?

If he loved her, he would, trotted across Tim's mind.

If he loved her?

If James loved her, would he see things as Tim did?

As a man who had allowed his wandering emotions to capture in his mind the picture of that beautiful woman, he visualized a little boy or girl who would have golden hair and sky blue eyes.

Tim recalled being almost four when he learned his mother was carrying a baby. He already knew about animals that produced offspring. After Becky was born, he held her as she grew and found her the most fascinating thing he'd ever seen. Didn't matter if she smiled or cried, he held her, thinking she was as cute as any newborn calf or filly.

But Tim had to face reality.

His grandfather had taught him early in life, that when tempted to judge another for sins or mistakes, to remember the words of preacher John Bradford who, when seeing a man being led to the gallows, said, "There but for the grace of God, go I."

Tim knew how easy it was for humans, young ones in particular, to become engrossed in their own emotions and not heed the consequences.

With a bit of chagrin, he thought about the time Grandfather caught him and Alice Ann in the hayloft, gave them both the sermon of their life. That led to Tim's recommitment to the Lord and his determination to live a moral and respectful life.

Lying in bed, looking out the window at a moon-drenched landscape made it easy to think of love and attraction. That happened rather naturally.

When he turned his face from the window and gazed at the dark ceiling his thoughts dipped deeper. The Bible taught that love was not only natural feelings, but love is action. One mustn't judge others, but they are to see the fruit in their lives. Character mattered.

And if Tim were James . . . there would be more to consider than natural feelings. Like a horse with a broken leg. It might be your favorite. But you have to shoot it anyway.

Well, they wouldn't shoot Julie, but if Cutler abused her, he might entertain the thought of shooting him.

Love was not the only issue here.

And suppose Cutler hadn't dishonored Julie. Suppose

James didn't want to marry her, regardless.

Tim rolled to his side away from the window and closed his eyes. He hoped and prayed that by morning his thinking would clear.

CHAPTER TEN

IF NOT HIS THOUGHTS, THE EARLY morning sky was clear as Tim and Grant rode down to the ranch house. The sun began to spread the promise of a glorious fall day of hills and valleys in many shades of green with a background of mountainsides in riotous color. They'd been taught to be thankful, lift their eyes to the hills, and remember the one who created their spread, their cattle and crops.

Tim gazed out over the land. Hands would have been at work before the sun rose to nourish the crops. He thanked God for blessings as he and Grant followed the aroma of bacon cooking in Grandmother's kitchen.

Tim didn't know how he might react to Miss Hayes. Grandfather had taught them that one can live a lifetime of doing good, then one wrong action can tear it down forever in the eyes of others.

But he didn't think badly of her. Maybe . . . even more protective.

When they walked into the kitchen, Grandmother was alone. She took a pan of biscuits from the oven and put them in a bread basket.

On their way to the table Grant said a quick, "Thank you Lord for this food and these biscuits. Amen." He grabbed one and bit into it by the time the basket reached the table.

Grandmother's sharp eyes turned toward them. "Ryan ate and is off to school."

Grant made a noise, but Tim figured it was more about the biscuit he was buttering instead of what Ryan might have said while eating his breakfast. "I guess he told you all about our conversation last night?"

"Of course."

"It wasn't his place."

"He's family," she chided. "Weren't you ever young?"

Tim grimaced as Grant said, "Not me," and chomped down on his biscuit.

Young? *Let's see*, Tim pondered. *I've aged considerably in the past couple days*. He went to the cabinet and grabbed plates for the eggs Grandmother was cracking into the skillet.

Julie and Becky didn't appear. After finishing breakfast, he said, "If you would, Grandmother, give Julie the book I put on the hall table. I'll try to get back about mid-morning to . . . um, show her the farm."

While Grant rode off to check on the crops, Tim headed for the stables, looking forward to continue his training of the thoroughbred.

When he returned at mid-morning, Julie opened the screen door as he dismounted. He avoided her eyes, but garnered the image of a trim woman wearing a dark brown split skirt and tan shirt. "Nice outfit," he said.

"It's Becky's."

He supposed he'd taken it for granted when Becky wore it. Not that it mattered, but he should have known. Julie brought only one bag and the main item in it had been a wedding dress. Feeling awkward, he mumbled, "We can walk down to the stables." It wouldn't be proper to ride together on his horse since she already had her wedding dress and planned to marry . . . someone.

Tim said in his best preacher-like tone, "I was wondering, Miss Julie. You mentioned...marriage in name only."

"Oh," she breathed and shook her pretty head of golden hair, shining in the mid-morning sunlight. "I couldn't wait any longer." She turned her face toward him, and he saw the helplessness in her expression. "I don't like abandoning the school children. Or my friends. But I was desperate."

Tim looked at the grass in front of them as if needing to step carefully. Yes, she would have thought of the time factor as well as her reputation.

"And I thought marriage was the answer. Maybe I just need to be . . . protected."

Now Tim was pretty sure Julie's proposal was meant for him, not James. On the horse, she made it clear the marriage would be in name only, meaning she held no particular affection for him, but would marry out of fear and desperation.

It would be too painful to allow himself to fall in love or marry a woman who didn't return that love. Marriage vows were said for better or worse, sickness or health, rich or poor. A man should be willing to commit to the negatives, but he also wants the positives.

"Thank you for the book," she was saying, sounding animated. "To tell the truth," she said and he hardly heard her words over his own thoughts. Could he ask about her intimate, personal life so they would know how to help her?

". . . I mentioned it so Russ wouldn't know what I was really talking about to you."

Marriage. She'd asked him to marry her. Perform a ceremony? Be a husband?

"But if I teach again, I can use that book."

If? Did that mean if the situation is resolved with Cutler and she returns to teach with James?

They reached the stables where cowboys nodded, tipped their hats, and a few gave him a grin and sly glance. Tim returned a warning gaze. "How's her horse?"

Henry hunched a shoulder. "Not quite ready for riding the range."

"Bullet's a little too headstrong for me anyway," she asserted, but he'd already reckoned that she wasn't adept with a horse. "I rode my mama's old mare on the mountain. But most of the time I walked."

"All right, how about Buddy? He's already familiar with you."

"He might want to get away from me too."

Tim wondered if she was thinking about those who left her by death or James who abandoned her, but she patted the horse's neck and laughed lightly. No, she wasn't thinking negatively. He was the one doing that.

"He will be fine. See, he likes you."

Her face turned to him. Their eyes met and their gazes held. He should look away but was captured by the question in her eyes.

Was she asking if he liked her? Was she asking if anyone liked her enough to marry her? Or was she simply questioning about the horse?

He busied himself with readying a horse for himself, and they led the horses from the stable.

They rode over the range, and Tim delighted in her awe and exclamations about the cows and thoroughbred horses grazing on the Kentucky bluegrass.

"It looks green to me," she said.

"But it's blue in June. Then the tiny blossoms cover the land for miles and miles." June popped into his mind. Eight months from now.

Her laugh was light. "I feel like I'm seeing for miles."

"Fifteen or twenty, at least."

"On the mountain," she said in wonder, "the views are beautiful, but distance is limited. Here, it's like my vision goes on and on."

Tim agreed. "My eyes adjust in the opposite way," he said. "Here, I'm accustomed to watching the running of herds of cattle and horses. I know where the ponds and creeks are. I can see corn fields in the distance. In the mountains I wonder what wild animal is around the next bend or behind the next tree."

"I like both."

Tim agreed again. "So do I. But here, I feel more—free."

"So do I. And . . . protected."

Tim longed to do that. He tried telling himself it was because she looked at him with those blue eyes so full of gratitude, and he liked having a woman beside him as he rode the range, and he liked the idea of being her protector. But he must face reality.

If anything, Tim was only a substitute, like being a substitute circuit rider. The real one she wanted was no longer there and someone was needed.

He did not know how to approach the subject of her condition. Perhaps he didn't need to. He would try to make her feel comfortable enough to confide if she wished. He would befriend her, keep his distance, not think like a man at all, but try to think like his grandfather-preacher. After all, her heart and emotions weren't free. They were tied up with James or Cutler or a life growing inside her. Or all three.

"You seem like such a happy person, Miss Julie. How do you manage that in the midst of your . . . um, present situation?"

Her face and eyes lifted to the sky, as blue as her eyes. The sun glistened on her golden hair. She was bright as a new penny.

"I think you're testing me, Brother Timothy."

Okay, she was seeing him in the preacher mode. That was good.

"When we have the Lord's presence in us we have hope and peace even in the times of trouble. The loss of my dad was devastating. Losing my mother was worse. I had no one really close. I hurt and grieved terribly, and still do sometimes, but I am glad Mother and Dad are in heaven with Jesus." She added quickly, "You know that, having lost your grandfather."

Tim nodded. "Yes, our faith makes it bearable."

"And I'm happy to be here. You've all taken me in like family. Someday I will repay you."

"Our pleasure," he said, and looked into her face then. Pleasure, yes. He was looking at a person of beauty, gratefulness, goodness, strength, and courage. He could admire her willingness to have a better life. One needed to look at the complete person, not only one aspect.

And he did. But he would have to be careful not to think too highly of someone else's intended, if that was the situation.

On second thought, maybe he should tell her about his dream of supervising the farm since she was impressed with the idea of him being a preacher. Maybe she would no longer have that gleam in her eyes, or look at him with that smile on her pretty face, or talk about how wonderful they all are. She could begin to see him as a cowboy, not a protecting preacher who could marry in name only.

She was doing fine on Buddy, so he led them to the back forty.

"Things are changing quickly in the cities," he said. "And change will come to the small towns. The cars, electricity. Boys need a place to ride their horses, and have morning Bible studies. Hearing a circuit riding preacher every few weeks or so isn't enough." He spread his hand, indicating the vast landscape. "I'd love to turn this into a camp."

"Oh, I can see it," Julie said. "Up on Wildcat, there's very little schooling. Many parents don't see a need beyond their children learning the basics. They'll go into coal mining. Many spend their time in the abandoned mine area, looking for gems, hoping to find one that will make them rich."

Tim dismounted. "I can show you where I'd build my own house, over by the creek where I can take the boys fishing, then hear it rolling all night long. You want to see?"

"Oh, yes. I love that idea." She gave a delighted laugh as she slipped down into his waiting arms. He moved his hands away from her waist as soon as he felt she was firmly balanced on her feet, and he stepped back, almost losing his own balance.

She fell in step beside him as they walked down to the creek. He could imagine the young boys would be fascinated with her telling about riding a runaway horse down the mountain, and she could make all kinds of analogies about that.

She could tell about the dangers, but that she ended up safe in the arms of . . . he cleared his throat . . . Jesus, of course.

CHAPTER ELEVEN

"MEMORY QUILT?" GRANDMOTHER QUESTIONED ONE COOL evening while she, Julie, and Becky sat in the parlor in front of the lighted fireplace. Julie enjoyed such evenings when they would stitch a loose seam, sew on buttons, and knit or crochet. She hadn't had time for knitting or crocheting while on the mountain. Julie showed them the memory quilt her mother and Granny Simms had encouraged her to start.

She explained the small pieces representing life with her parents, including scraps from childhood clothes. There was lace, and one from a crocheted doily. She stroked a tan square printed with the outline of darker flowers. "This is from my doll that was left outside during a three-day gully washer, mud and all. The scrap is clean but no longer white with red flowers."

They smiled. Julie liked telling about her life before her mother married Russell Cutler. She sighed. "I have scraps about many good times at Wildcat. And I definitely want to make one about Sullivan Ranch and all of you." She spread her hands. "That will be a big one."

"I like this idea," Becky said. "I guess it's easy to remember what each piece represents."

Julie thought of her personal things still in the house at Wildcat. "I have notes about them. But not with me."

"Now there's something you can do while I'm away at college. Write the story behind each one. With my expertise in journalism, we'll make a book about memory quilts." She laughed.

"You may be joking, Becky," Grandmother said. "But that's a good idea. We quilters use scraps from worn clothing and some from sentimental pieces. But I've never heard one called a memory quilt."

Julie watched Grandmother staring at the quilt, then she lifted her gaze to Julie's face. "You know, this is about the size of a baby quilt."

"It is, isn't it?" She smiled. "I was thinking more of a table covering or a wall hanging. See the edging. I have one side finished and need to stitch the others."

Julie did not tell them that her jewels were tucked away in the finished side of the quilt and the corner folded to keep them secure.

She laid the quilt on the coffee table. "See, I turn the edge. Then I turn it under again and stitch it. That leaves an opening for a rod."

"Ingenious," Becky said.

"Yes," Gran said, with a glance at Becky. "Quite nifty."

Julie had thought she would be lonely after Becky returned to college to stay in the Lexington boarding house until the weekend. As eager as she was for Becky's return for those long talks and being teased about Tim, she also looked forward to the return of the wedding dress.

It had never been cleaned, was worn only once but had become wrinkled. Becky assured her the cleaners could do a better job of getting the wrinkles out than she could with a flat iron. Several times after her mother's death, Julie cried while hugging her mother's clothes. All were given away except the wedding dress. Julie had imagined the scent of her mother was on the dress. But having it cleaned seemed a way to let go of the past and be active in the present. She would keep it for sentimental reasons.

She briefly worried that Russ might find her. But mainly, she forgot everything when riding over the ranch with Tim. She loved the way he looked sitting in the saddle, as if he'd been born there. Much of the time his eyes were shielded by the cowboy hat. At other times he'd lift his head and looked at her with those dark brown eyes. So often they held a hint of gold, as if lighted by the sun.

She liked to sit on the screened-in porch and watch Tim out there, training, tending, or riding horses and sometimes racing them around the track. She could no longer deny it. She was hopelessly, irrevocably in love with that circuit-riding-cowboy-preacher.

During that week, Ryan came in after school to see his Grandmother and eat something she fixed especially for him. Sometimes he sat on the porch with Julie, and she explained the quilt to him. He wanted to know all about her life with her parents.

It was Friday when Tim went to pick up Becky from the train station. Gran was packing food for him to take early Saturday morning for his circuit riding to Bear Mountain, Coalville, and a brush arbor back in a cove. He would be gone for several days.

Julie missed him already, but knew the importance to people waiting for their turn to hear a preacher. "There's always a room, a lean-to, or a stable where I can spend the night," Tim said when she asked how he managed overnight.

Ryan was setting the table and talking about his school subjects that Julie asked about while she helped Gran with dinner. At the sound of a horse and wagon rolling up to the back, Ryan hurried out and soon returned with a long folded garment bag. Becky rushed in, opened her arms wide for welcoming hugs.

"Okay, boys," Becky commanded, "don't look. I gotta show them the wedding dress. It cleaned up beautifully."

"Who's the lucky—? Ow!" Ryan scowled at Tim who was tugging on his shirt and said, "Come on, let's take those bags to Becky's room."

"I'd like to know which one of us would have bad luck . . ." He looked around innocently and turned a sly grin toward Tim, who'd already turned, making a hasty departure from the room.

It seemed like Ryan was teasing her about . . . Tim.

The three women waited until footsteps returned down the hallway. When reaching the kitchen doorway, Ryan snuck a glance their way, but Tim looked straight ahead and the two of them walked out the back door.

Having known Ryan would look, the women chuckled and finally could take the wedding dress from the garment bag.

Each touched the soft material. "No wonder your mother

kept this," Becky said. "It's as beautiful as anything I've seen in the city stores."

"She made it," Julie said proudly.

"And kept it for you," Gran said, with a smile. She held it up to Julie. "Looks like a perfect fit."

Julie's eyes grew moist. She thought of the loving looks on her parents' faces in their picture.

"You have the dress," Becky quipped. "All you need now is the fiancé."

In her mind, she saw herself in that photo of her parents. She wore the dress. Who would be the husband with such a loving look on his face?

Feeling warmth in her cheeks, she moved to return the dress to the garment bag.

Yes, she had a dress. But...who, and when, would she marry?

Julie had sometimes wondered if Ryan paid her too much attention, and if he might misunderstand her being friendly. But since the day he teased her about Tim, and showed no jealousy, she knew they simply enjoyed each other's company. She began to recognize a routine. Many days, after he rode up to the farmhouse and stayed for a while, he'd come out and then disappear into the woods.

Curiosity got the better of her. One afternoon she told Gran she was going to take a walk. She went out the front and headed for the woods near the farmhouse. She found a path and followed it to a small clearing. She hid behind a big poplar several feet away.

Before long she heard the sound of boots tramping over twigs and fallen leaves. Then she knew what Ryan was doing. She closed her eyes, commanded her heartbeat to stay away from her throat. She dared not move nor make a sound. Long after the sounds became only birds chirping and animals scampering through the woods, she remained in that spot.

When deepening shadows threatened to obscure her way out, she followed the path. In spite of the rain that began to fall, she kept to the edge of the woods until far in front of the house before turning toward it.

Then guilt struck her. The Sullivans must never know what she'd done. She had betrayed the trust of those who took her in and treated her like family.

Fortunately, at supper the attention was on the food, all of it from right there on their land. Roast beef, mashed potatoes, snap beans, golden corn, and peach cobbler. As soon as the blessing was said and their plates filled, they would share their activities. Before any of them had a chance to share, Grant came in, obviously drenched, but walked on into the kitchen, holding his black hat with POLICE on the band. Something about his stance looked very official.

"A lot of talk about criminal activity is going on in towns and cities concerning Cutler." His tone sounded as formal as he looked. "Accusations are flying faster than a wild horse bounding over the fields and across the hollows."

"Oh," Julie exclaimed. "James accused Russell?"

"No, ma'am," Grant said, looking straight at Julie. "Accusations are being made by Russell Cutler. Not against James Greely, but against Miss Julie Hayes."

CHAPTER TWELVE

TIM WATCHED FEAR JUMP INTO JULIE'S eyes as she gasped. "Are you going to arrest me?"

"For what?" the inquisitor asked, gazing poker-faced.

"For-for . . ." she stumbled over her words. "What-whatever he accused me of."

"I haven't talked with him personally," Grant said. "The sheriff in Rolling Hills told me Cutler rode in claiming his prize horse is missing, along with some gems. He said a boy saw you leave with the horse."

"I'm not a thief. I borrowed the horse and rode it down the mountain because my mother's mare can't trot as fast as I can walk." Her hands lifted helplessly. "I didn't mean to bring this into your family. I'll . . . go away."

"Afraid you can't do that, ma'am. You admitted you have Cutler's horse."

"He can have it back. I can't ride that thing anyway." Quickly, she added, "Since he called me his daughter, my riding his horse wouldn't be a crime, would it?"

Tim couldn't sit and watch her squirm. "If Cutler cares so much about her, why hasn't he reported her missing?"

"The Chief asked him that. Cutler said he thought she was distraught about her boyfriend leaving. He expected she'd come back since there was a store to tend and a school with no teacher."

Her boyfriend? So her relationship with James was no secret from Cutler. "What else?" Julie sounded dejected.

"Cutler wants you to return to the mountain. But if you refuse, he said he will accept that and not press charges against you if you return his horse and his jewels.

Tim tried not to wonder why Cutler included gems. He took a deep breath. It was Grant's place to ask the hard questions. Not of Julie, but of Cutler. So much pointed to Cutler's being an uncaring scoundrel. "Was Cutler not concerned that she might be hurt?"

Grant shook his head. "He said if Bullet had thrown her, he would have returned to the mountain. Or . . . he might even wander into Sullivan Ranch since he bought the horse from Grandfather several years ago."

Julie moaned. "He knows I'm here."

"Likely. Otherwise he wouldn't have mentioned Sullivan Ranch. We employ workers from all over these valleys and mountains. Word would get around about a woman being here."

"What's going to happen to me?"

Grant's steady gaze matched the tone of his voice. "I'm an officer of the law, Julie. Now, we can keep you here as long as you want, as a friend. But not a minute longer as a fugitive, or a thief. My job as a deputy and Tim's reputation as a preacher are at stake."

"Oh." Her gaze met Tim's, and her blue eyes clouded with deep sorrow. "I never meant to hurt anyone." She looked down at her hands on her lap. "I don't have his gems. I never meant to steal the horse. I only needed to get away."

It seemed only she and he were in the room as Tim felt the distress she exhibited. While he was wondering how to ask what he wanted to ask, Ryan blurted out, "Are you afraid of him, Julie. Has he hurt you physically?"

She lifted a shoulder in a brief shrug, as if that were of no consequence. "No, he doesn't need to hit or fight anyone. He . . ." She searched for words. "He has to be in control. He's . . . I guess you'd say . . . selfish, self-centered."

She looked around. The questioning expressions encouraged her to continue. "He's not really mean. Only—well, for example he'd rather I work at the General Store 'til nightfall even after teaching half a day than work there himself."

Even Grant seemed relieved that Cutler apparently hadn't harmed her physically. "You didn't take any of his gems?" Grant asked pointedly.

"No," she said forcefully. The color that rose to her cheeks was likely chagrin that such a charge had been made.

"Anything more you want to tell us? About Cutler or

James?" Grant asked.

For a moment, Tim thought she was about to say something. But some things would be difficult to talk about, when it was personal. Finally, she said, "No. I don't."

Grant nodded. "The sheriff wants me to look into this. I'm in the business of checking out anything that hints of breaking the law."

Tim wished he could comfort her, but all he could think to say was, "And it's my business to . . . pray." With that he bowed his head and closed his eyes. "Dear Lord, help us get to the bottom of this and do what is right in your eyes."

As soon as he said, "Amen," Grant said, "All right, tell you what I can do. I will take Cutler's horse up to Wildcat Mountain and hope this is the end of it. You don't want to go back up there, right?"

"I feel bad about leaving everyone. And the children not having a teacher, but I can't go back and be under his control. And now," she looked around with a small smile on her lips. "After being here and your treating me like I'm family, I can't be content . . ." she sighed. "Otherwise."

Tim did not like the idea of her returning to Wildcat Mountain. An unmarried mother would be ostracized by most. They likely would not allow her to teach at the school. No doctor was up there, and how could she get off the mountain for one? She was better off here. She'd asked for *the preacher's* protection. He wondered what form that would take after Grant saw Cutler.

Two days later, Grant returned. He talked with them all at the kitchen table over coffee and pound cake that Grandmother said might sweeten the sour expression on Grant's face.

He gave a quick laugh and a dubious glance.

"Didn't things go well?" she asked.

"Yes and no," he replied. "He was glad to get the horse back. He gave the impression of being a respectable man who loves his stepdaughter and said he'd love to have her return."

"That sounds like the yes part," Ryan said. "What's the no?"

"Well," Grant said, looking around and then settling his gaze on Julie. "He says he forgives her for taking the horse. And if she returns his gems, all will be forgiven and forgotten."

"He's not telling the truth."

Tim broke in. "Julie, you said he told you James left with his gems and didn't return. Do you think he believes you're in on that?"

"I don't know what to think . . . anymore."

"What Cutler said to me, Julie," Grant informed them, "is that he will give you a week to think it over. Then you can return the gems or be arrested."

"Then it comes down to her word against his, right?" Tim said. "If she doesn't have his gems, then he can't prove anything."

"Cutler may think the threat will make her return to Wildcat. An accusation, true or not, can harm a reputation."

"What will happen to me if Russ follows through with that threat?"

"Then the sheriff will take it from there."

"Hey!" Ryan exclaimed. "And if they add the horse theft into it, maybe your hanging from a tree was a foreshadowing of what was to come." He leaned his chair back on two legs while laughing heartily.

"Ryan!" both his brothers shouted and Grandmother said, "Wash your mouth out with soap!" Her words sounded like a reprimand, not something he really should do.

He shrugged, stood, and walked over to the doorway. Julie thought he was probably trying to ease the tension. It might be the wrong time to joke, but it was clever. Becky talked about foreshadowing in writing, and Doc Sullivan had explained passages in the Bible being foreshadowing of events about Jesus.

It didn't really apply to her since the horse had already been returned—by a deputy. If she had to, she would give the gems to Russ, or the authorities, and she would have to endure whatever legalities ensued. If she had to, she could go back to Wildcat and live in Russ's house, or maybe live with Amy, or even in back of the General Store.

No way could she tell them about her jewels now. She would look guilty. In an effort to be protected she had come to the place where she would be arrested. "I'm sorry—"

"Don't look so worried," Grant said. "He's obviously

wanting money. We may try for some kind of settlement."

She could never allow that. They all seemed in agreement that they would even pay her way out of this. Then her gaze moved to the doorway where Ryan, who had been uncharacteristically silent for a while, was propped with one leg bent and his foot against the casing.

He gave her a long look, wore a slight grin, and then winked.

He knows. Julie opened her mouth. No air went in. She couldn't breathe or shut her open mouth.

"I-I–" she finally managed, but could say no more. "Ex-excuse me."

She got up and rushed to Becky's bedroom. She took the quilt from the drawer and ran her hand over the edges. No lumps.

Becky came in. Julie moaned. "They were my mother's jewels, not Russell's."

"Julie?" Becky's eyes held incredulity.

Becky stopped her when she began to try and explain. "Come tell the whole family."

She would look guilty. She was guilty of not telling them about the jewels right away. She hadn't been smart about this. No way could this family ever trust her again.

CHAPTER THIRTEEN

TIM TRIED TO READ HIS SISTER'S EXPRESSION when she and Julie returned to the room. Julie was holding her memory quilt. Becky seemed as confused as the rest of them.

Julie sat and glared at Ryan. "Did you take them?"

"Now look," came Grant's immediate response. "We may not always see eye to eye with our brother. But nobody goes around—"

"I do have them," Ryan said. "I put them on a high shelf in a can in the pantry. Right over there." While everyone stared, he walked to the pantry, then returned with the can.

"Why?" she gasped.

"For safe keeping, in case Cutler came here to search."

"Ryan!" Grant barked. "That's being an accomplice."

Tim didn't know what to think or feel. He understood her borrowing Cutler's horse. He didn't condemn or judge her for being with child. But—lying and stealing?

With difficulty, Grant asked, "Ryan, you went through her things?"

"I didn't go through her things," Ryan retorted.

"Then how did you know about . . . whatever's in that can?"

"The way she acted about that little quilt. Almost like it was a pet." He chuckled at his description. "And she kept saying she'd repay us someday like she really believed it. I figured she's too smart to run off that mountain, not having any way to make a living. The logical place to hide gems would be in the edge of that quilt." He shrugged. "It simply added up."

He looked from one shocked person to another. "I thought it would be interesting for Cutler, who'd probably come here, not to find any jewels and sneak back where he came from. No evidence, huh, Grant? I was doing what all of you said we would do, and that's protect her."

Grant chided. "But we don't shield a thief."

"I'm not—" Julie protested.

Grant raised his hand. "Your turn will come. Ryan, you knew she was being accused. Then you found jewels. You had to think she stole them."

He smiled at Julie. "No. I don't think she's a criminal. Not after the way she always said she didn't take Cutler's jewels. She never said she didn't take *any* jewels."

"What were you going to do with them?

"Return them after things are settled about Cutler. Then she could do what she wanted with them. Whether or not she stole them is her business, not my place to accuse or judge. My place was to protect her."

"That's unreasonably reasonable," Grant said, and shook his head like a dog after a bath. He turned to Julie. "You want to tell us about this?"

Ryan brought over the can and let the jewels fall onto the quilt.

"These are mine," Julie said. "My mother gave them to me." She picked up a ring. "This is my mother's engagement ring my dad gave her."

"It's beautiful," Grandmother said, looking closely at the gold band. "I've seen some like this. The prongs are like a little basket holding the cultured pearl. Lovely."

"Nobody's going to believe me," she said, and the tears flowed.

"Hold on," Becky said. "Don't talk 'til I get back."

Julie knew Becky had every right to grab the bag, return and throw it and Julie out of the house. She could hear her own breathing that had to be done through her mouth because her nose was stopped up from crying. Amazing it could do that when it seemed all the water inside her was rolling down her cheeks. Gran handed her a handkerchief.

Becky returned and handed Grant the picture frame holding the wedding picture of Julie's mom and dad. Becky tapped a place on the picture. "See, this is her mother in that wedding dress—"

"Oh, don't look," Grandmother said.

"I've already had my bad luck," Grant said. "Beautiful dress."

Despite the concern about Julie, and now Ryan, Tim felt a sense of relief. Grant never talked about his personal life since his heartbreak. His mentioning the dress was something positive. Maybe he was doing all right.

But . . . the dress? If the dress Julie has is her mother's wedding dress, what does that mean? He answered his own question. It meant the same as if she bought or made a dress. And she had this one cleaned, indicating she expected to marry . . . soon, whether for love or protection or her condition.

Grant nodded. "The ring on your mother's finger looks the same as that one. I'm talking like a deputy now to let you know what we're up against. This is your word against Cutler's."

She nodded. "I know you don't know if you can believe me. I didn't think of it as lying because I didn't steal anything from Russell. Except his horse."

"You borrowed that," Tim said.

"You may be able to prove the jewels, particularly the ring, belonged to your mother," Grant said, "But is there any way you can prove she gave them to you?"

"She's . . ." Julie whispered, "dead."

The quiet was palpable.

Julie looked down at the jewels on her lap. Maybe God was punishing her for seeking protection from the preacher, and having special personal thoughts about him. She must forget about winning his heart. He could never like or trust her again.

She had to think of some way to vindicate herself. "Only one other person knows about these jewels and that's Granny Simms. We worked on the quilt at her house, and she's the one who taught me to fold the ends."

Julie reached for the can and Ryan handed it to her. She put the gems in it and held it out to Grant. "If this will help, give them to Russell Cutler."

Grant handed the can to Ryan. "Put them on the shelf."

Julie no longer felt like part of their family, but like a fugitive. She was more trapped than when on the mountain.

Then Becky did the strangest thing. She reached over and took Julie's hand. "I believe you," she said.

Julie couldn't prevent the eye-flooding then and vaguely heard Grandmother say, "You fellows go about your business and let us girls have a good cry."

Julie didn't think she would ever stop.

Tim had to face the facts of what they must do to help Julie personally and legally. "I think it's time we questioned James Greely."

"Not we," Grant contradicted. "This is now official business. Your job is to see that things go on here as usual."

Grant's glance at Julie, then his gaze at Tim was like telling a witness or a suspect, "Don't leave town."

Tim was uncertain how to behave. However, he didn't want to accuse Julie or give her the impression he believed she was a thief. At the same time, he didn't know whom to trust. He couldn't even trust his own heart.

CHAPTER FOURTEEN

JULIE KNEW GRANT'S WORDS WERE A warning that she should not leave the ranch, which made her feel like she'd committed a crime. Maybe taking Russ's horse was a crime in a court of law. And if Russ did what he'd threatened and took out a warrant against her for stealing gems, he would be believed instead of her.

The Sullivans didn't question her. In the few spare moments Becky had when she came home for the weekend, she wanted to continue working on the memory quilt project. Their conversation generally included Grandmother, and they talked about Becky's classes and the professor's approval of her final paper about creating memory quilts as coverlets and wall hangings.

Tim kept busier on the ranch than when she'd first arrived. He took her riding a few times and continued to teach her the art of riding correctly and controlling a horse. Although he was always kind, like a preacher would be, he seemed distant.

After several days, Grant returned. But he wasn't alone. James was riding beside him. When James stepped onto the porch, she reached out her arms. James took her hands in his for a moment, then she clasped hers in front of her skirt. He started to speak, but Grant said, "We'll talk about all this when Tim gets here."

Grant looked over his shoulder. Not only was Tim approaching, but Ryan rode in from school. Ryan dismounted and upon discovering James Greely had arrived, he took on the stance one would expect of a deputy like Grant.

"What did you mean by leaving Julie up there to deal with Cutler? What kind of—?"

Grant stopped him. "Hold your horses, Ryan."

They went into the kitchen and introduced James to Grandmother who brought out cake and made coffee.

Ryan had thunder in his eyes as if he were having difficulty holding his horses. Rather than Grant, it seemed to be Tim who was closely scrutinizing them. Julie supposed that a deputy would look for any signs of criminality while a preacher would look for things unspiritual. But . . . wouldn't stealing horses and jewels be both criminal and unspiritual? Oh, what did they really think of her?

"I'm sorry, Julie," were James's first words. "For leaving you with all that responsibility." His brow wrinkled. "But what could I do? Russ is your step-father."

"I don't blame you. I . . . left too."

Julie listened carefully while James told his side of the story. Cutler did accuse him after the sheriff began to question him and the jeweler. In trying to vindicate himself, the jeweler revealed that James had brought Cutler's gems but had taken no money. The jeweler paid Cutler when he came to town looking for Julie.

Grant added to the story. "The record books of both Cutler and the jeweler have been confiscated. If there's to be a warrant for arrest it will be against them."

"But what if Russ still accuses me of taking his gems?"

"Then it's up to the sheriff to take it from there."

"Your word, Granny Simms's confirmation, and the ring your dad gave your mother indicates you'd be believed," Grant said, much to Julie's relief.

Her thoughts returned to James, obviously pleased to be returning to Wildcat. "My dad had dealings with the gem mines before they closed," he said. "Coming from a gem mining background, I'm not completely ignorant of things going on that might not be illegal, but definitely cheating."

He glanced uncertainly at Julie. "I didn't want to leave the school children. I feel that's my special calling." He took a deep breath. "Now I feel like a coward and a failure."

Tim spoke up. "You're not a coward for refusing to be involved in illegal or immoral activity." He stood, reminding Julie of his standing in front of the church at Wildcat. "The Lord is always ready to forgive us of sins and failings if we ask. Then we try to do what is right."

James nodded. "Julie, I'd love for you to return to Wildcat

with me."

"With you?" She put her hand to her forehead. "I can't make a move right now. So much to think about."

"Excuse me," Tim said, "I need to see about the horses."

"There's more cake," Grandmother said in the ensuing silence. James seemed to be studying his plate. Grant picked up his coffee cup and moved it to his lips. Ryan gazed at her with a look of amusement in his eyes. Becky poked her with her elbow.

What all that meant, Julie didn't know. But she wondered about that abrupt departure after Tim's brief sermon to James. Perhaps there really was trouble with a horse down at the corral. Or maybe he'd decided she should leave Sullivan Ranch and go back to Wildcat where she came from. After a short while, James left for Wildcat Mountain.

The following morning Grant departed for the city. Things went on as usual at the Sullivan Ranch, but Julie felt they were all waiting for Grant to come back with some kind of verdict. She felt even more strongly that Tim had some dire matter on his mind.

When Grant returned, this time Russell Cutler was with him. That frightened her. If Russ wasn't arrested, that must mean he accused her and Grant would then take her into town for questioning. Maybe he came to get her jewels and wouldn't officially accuse her.

After the family gathered in the kitchen, Grant laid out the facts while Russ sat with his head lowered. Grant said the cheating had been done on Wildcat Mountain. Russ would buy the valuable gems people found in the abandoned mine. He'd given them far less than the gems were worth. Russ discovered the jeweler tried doing the same thing to him which led to their becoming partners in their cheating.

"They pled guilty," Grant said. "They're on probation. In lieu of jail, the jeweler has agreed to sell his business and make restitution where he can. Russ will make restitution also. Whether they're sorry or if it's only to save their hide, I can't say."

Russ looked up then, and his eyes looked weary with circles underneath. "I am sorry, Julie." His gaze turned to Tim. "Preacher," he said respectfully, then glanced around. "After James left and didn't return, I was afraid Julie would leave me too. I wasn't thinking right, or caring much about anything after her mother died. That's why I urged her to use the money her dad left her to buy the house. It was for her. I guess I couldn't show my feelings well, but had to act kind of tough."

It seemed at the moment as if only the two of them sat at the table. "I used the wrong method in trying to keep you there," he said. "I did want somebody taking care of the house, working in the store, and I thought if I didn't pay you, then you couldn't get away. After living with your mom, I'm not good at being alone."

Julie could hardly believe what she was hearing. He hadn't mentioned the gems. He sounded sincere. But even if he wasn't, she didn't have to go back to Wildcat Mountain. And even if he wasn't being truthful, she could be. "I forgive you, Russ."

He shook his head. "I don't know how you could. I'm . . ." He shrugged. "She didn't steal any gems from me. Her mother gave me money for the house and the gems to Julie." He choked up. "Anyway, Julie, you can have the house. I'm no good up there anymore. They'll know what I've done."

"If you ask their forgiveness they'll give it," Tim said.

He nodded. "If they listened to Doc Sullivan, they will."

They all agreed, with soft chuckles.

"The Lord still loves you, Mr. Cutler," Tim told him kindly.

Russ nodded. "I used to know that. I guess I kind of blamed God for taking my wife. But I know better."

After a long moment, Julie said, "The house is yours, Russ. And, for what's it worth, I've been told that Amy's mother had her eyes on you before you married my mother."

His eyes grew wide, and he stared.

Julie grinned. "She's a good cook too."

She could hardly believe it. Russell Cutler actually blushed.

After Russ seemed convinced he could face his failures with courage, he left with the parting words, "I'm going to try and be the kind of man your mother thought I was when she married me, Julie. And not the kind of man I became after she was gone."

Feeling convicted about her own actions, she admitted, "I suppose I always resented you because you weren't my dad."

"That's all right," he said. "Maybe we can do better."

She nodded.

After he left they talked about how well things could work out for her. She and Russ could work toward being a family.

James wanted her to return to Wildcat. "But you're welcome here as long as you want to stay," Grandmother said.

Becky pulled on Julie's arm. "I want her here as my sister."

Even Grant gave an approving nod.

Tim's smile was thin, and his gaze didn't meet her eyes. She could not stay if he didn't want her here. That strange silence settled upon them again.

Grandmother said, "Maybe we all need to sleep on our decisions and talk about them another time."

"What?" Ryan blurted out. "How long are we going to postpone the most important question? Everybody acts like they can go about their lives like always. But somebody has a responsibility toward that unborn baby."

"Baby?" Becky rasped, and Julie wondered which of those three siblings was responsible for an unborn baby. Maybe the attention would be off her for a change.

CHAPTER FIFTEEN

JULIE SAW THE CONFUSION ON BECKY'S face while Grant and Tim looked at the floor. Grandmother regarded Julie with a kind, sympathetic expression.

Becky huffed. "What? Whose baby are you—?"

"Hers," Ryan said, pointing.

Julie looked at that pointing finger, and at Becky. It seemed to be pointing at Julie. She looked over one shoulder as if someone with a baby might be standing behind her.

Finally, Grandmother sighed. "We might as well be open about it. We all know about it, Julie, and will do what we can to help. But we need the truth."

"About . . . about the baby?" Julie didn't understand, but Grandmother nodded and smiled sweetly.

Becky slapped the table with the palm of her hand. "What are you talking about?"

"Come on, Bec!" Tim chided. "You were the first to know."

Now it was Becky's turn to say incredulously, "About . . . a baby?"

"Denials at this point will only lead to more trouble," Grant said.

Becky was the only one who didn't know? Julie didn't know how the others knew, but it wasn't really a secret. "I guess Russ told you. Mom was only seven months along. When I knew she was in trouble, I ran to get the midwife and then Russ. Both Mom and the baby . . ."

She stopped long enough to take a shaky breath, then swallowed hard. "Some said she was too old to have a baby. Russ blamed himself. That's when he changed so much. I . . ."

Becky put her arm around Julie's shoulders. Grandmother

came over with a handkerchief for wiping the tears.

Julie heard a few male sounds she thought were sympathy. Grandmother said quietly, "I'm so sorry, Julie. But . . ." she lifted Julie's chin and waited until they could look eye-to-eye. "We're talking about your baby."

Becky gasped as her arm moved away. "You have a baby?"

Julie stared at her, vigorously shaking her head. "No." She heard the uncertainty in her own voice but it was caused by the conversation, or accusation, taking place.

Julie squeaked, looking around. "Did Russ say I have a baby?"

"No," Grant said.

"I did," Ryan said. He told about the night he didn't mean to hear the conversation between her and Becky. "When you said you *had* to get married--"

Becky screeched and jumped up. "What is wrong with you? There is no baby."

"Re-really?" Tim said, looking pleased about that.

Ryan glanced around at eyes staring holes through him. "You mean she was talking about having to get married, so she could be free of Russell Cutler?"

"Oh, my," Grandmother said, shaking her head and sending Ryan a reprimanding glare.

Tim came over and knelt in front of Julie. Her breath caught in her throat. He took her hands in his. "Please, forgive me for jumping to conclusions."

"You thought I could . . . ?" She looked away.

"Julie." He waited until she faced him again. "Anybody can make mistakes. Can sin. Goodness knows I have. And I did in this. I should have come to you. I should have behaved as . . . your preacher."

She caught her trembling lower lip with her teeth.

He stared at her. "But none of us judged you. We thought someone took advantage, and it might have been Cutler."

"Not like that." She looked down at her hands in his, pressed against her skirt.

He moved his away and stood. "I can't expect you to forgive me right now. Maybe, with time."

Oh, she could. Is that why he wanted her to see James? Thinking she might be having James's baby? He had been so kind, even when he thought her a fallen woman. Her heart leapt at the thought he might care for her . . . personally. She mustn't act overjoyed, not at a time like this. She dared not look at Becky, lest they both burst into laughter.

Grandmother clicked her tongue. "I do declare. I've been planning to fix up a special room for the mother and new baby." She sounded disappointed.

"And I thought I needed to get you married to James," Tim said.

"I thought I might marry James to get away. But I don't think I could have. I like and respect him." She couldn't look away from him. "But, I don't . . . love James."

Becky scoffed. "You guys are the stupidest . . ."

The women began giggling while Tim and Grant exchanged glances. Ryan looked like he wished a hole would open up and swallow him. "I'm the one who started this. I jumped to conclusions about what I overheard and I guess . . . no, I *know* I added to the confusion. I'm sorry. It was wrong of me to eavesdrop."

"No, Ryan," Julie said. "You have every right to learn about the kind of person you've taken into your home. I wouldn't blame you if you eavesdropped deliberately. And, really, this makes me feel better. You're all so . . . perfect and I'm so . . ." she shrugged, "unsettled."

"Perfect?" Tim muttered, shaking his head.

"Per-fect?" Becky repeated, and added with a grin, "Maybe me. But not them."

They all laughed, easing the tension.

Except Ryan. He stood and grasped the back of his chair. Julie thought he might run out, like he often did. Instead, he continued to apologize. "I'm sorry, Julie, for all the trouble I've caused you, about the gems, about the baby. I'm to blame. They're all right about me. I act and speak before I think. Or worse yet, without thinking."

"Amen," Tim said at the same time Grant coughed and Becky made a-huh sound. Julie's glance revealed they were teasing him, not blaming. But she had to try and make him feel better.

"I have my faults too, Ryan. I've spied on you, and I know a secret about you."

They all looked at her as if she might hurt Ryan or embarrass him. They'd all come to his defense if she falsely accused or condemned. Exactly like they would do with any member of their family.

"Go ahead," Ryan said as if ready for a thrashing.

"The way you want to know everything, and notice things that others don't, all the questions you ask, and really care what others are thinking."

His face was flushed, and he looked down at his boots, like a child bearing up under a reprimand.

She said, "That's what Granny Simms said Doc Sullivan did. He could get people to tell him their deepest problems, and he'd listen. If he couldn't do anything else, just the listening made a difference."

Grandmother had a knowing look in her watery eyes.

The kind expression and slow blink of his eyes gave her the courage to go further while his dumbfounded siblings glanced at him and at her. "Another thing," she said, "I've even heard you yell like him out in the woods."

"That's called . . ." tears sprang into his eyes but he laughed, ". . . preaching."

Grandmother was nodding and didn't bother to wipe a tear that escaped her eyes. Becky placed her hand on Julie's and squeezed.

Tim mouthed, "Thank you." And most surprising was Grant, the tough stoic deputy who threw his arms around Ryan's shoulders and pulled him close. He mussed his hair and said, "Maybe it's time I answered some of your obnoxious questions."

At Ryan's startled look, Grant shook his head. "Let's have a bite to eat first."

"Sit down," Grandmother said. "I'll get the milk."

At the table, Tim said, "Ryan, you want to make the circuit with me next weekend?"

Ryan's mouth didn't close for a long time. Finally he said, "Grandfather wouldn't let me. Said I had to get my schooling first."

"Well, I'm not Grandfather."

"Why wouldn't he let me go with him?"

Grandmother spoke up. "He always said you each have to find your own way."

"And I've found mine," Tim said. "I'm not cut out to be a preacher. I'm a cowboy. My heart is with running the ranch."

"So," Ryan leaned the chair back on two legs like he had a habit of doing, but at everyone's widened eyes he returned to four. "You finally think I can do something?"

Grant scoffed, and Tim said, "Yeah, like going to the seminary in Louisville if you have any ideas of . . ." he cleared his throat, "yelling like Grandfather."

Ryan blanched. "You're tough."

"Tougher than you," Tim and Grant said at the same time. Then Grant added, "There's still a lot of milking and branding and herding and cleaning out horse stalls and mending fences ahead of you, boy."

Ryan grinned, as if he didn't mind at all.

Julie looked at Tim, who smiled at her, but there seemed to be a little sadness there, some kind of resignation. Would he blame her for saying those things about Ryan instead of letting Ryan reveal it himself . . . when the time would be right?

With trepidation, she watched him until he met her gaze. Then he winked, not like Ryan had done which indicated he knew a secret, but like . . . approval.

CHAPTER SIXTEEN

TIM COULD HARDLY BELIEVE HE NO longer needed to be concerned that Julie was in love with James, or was desperate to marry. Russell Cutler didn't pose any threat. He chided himself for not being happier that she no longer needed him or his family for protection or her livelihood.

Nevertheless, Grandmother said the next day again during dinner, "We consider you family." That was confirmed by each of them.

"What I'd like to do is go to the college. I want to teach. I can sell one or more of mother's jewels to pay for tuition."

"Yes." Becky clapped her hands. "That means a shopping trip and off to school together like sisters."

"I love that idea," Julie said. "I can get my belongings from the mountain, but they're not as stylish as yours. My one hat belonged to Mother."

Gran hmmed. "You think I could get my feet into those pointed toe shoes?"

Ryan spoke in a falsetto tone, "Should I get a feather or a flower for my cowboy hat?"

In a poor imitation of a girl, Grant whined, "Some cheek rouge would look great with your dimples, Timmy."

Grant hadn't joked or laughed in a long time, and Tim took advantage of that. "Grant, you want a gold or silver necklace to lay against that--?"

By that time, they were all laughing so hard they dared not put food in their mouths.

"Now," Becky said between spurts of laughter, "you see why I need a sister?"

Tim didn't laugh about that but glanced at Grant whose

knowing eyes and grin indicated he knew Tim did not think of Julie as a sister. Then Grant surprised him. "Tim, let's discuss that idea of yours for turning the back forty into a camp for boys."

Soon, they all contributed on how each could take part. Tim would be camp director, delegate authority, and teach Bible stories. Grant could take them on a jail tour so criminals could scare any meanness out of them. Ryan wanted to build a huge bonfire and tell ghost stories to scare whatever was left out of them after the jail tour.

"Are we feeling a little left out?" Becky asked.

"Well, we do still have a ranch and farm to run," Grandmother said, "and the boys will need that male influence."

"I can write about it from its inception to its becoming a reality." Becky looked at Julie with raised eyebrows.

Julie thought. "Maybe we should also have a two-week camp for girls, then we three can teach them that girls can ride and rope and brand and shoot—"

"And which part will you teach?" Tim jested.

"Um . . . memory quilt-making?"

Tim felt like smiling all over. His dream and his grandfather's vision of a boys' camp was materializing. What more could he ask?

He knew what he'd like to ask.

On a crisp, cool, moonlit evening in November he asked Julie to ride with him to the campsite.

"Oh," she said, after they tied the horses and walked over to a bench atop an incline beneath a tree. "This wasn't here before."

He motioned for her to sit and sat beside her. "This is where I envision my front porch will be. That is, if my wife approves."

"You have a wife?" she jested.

"No, but for the first time in my life I've thought more about that than about cows and horses."

"How flattering." She was trying hard not to be too

serious—expect too much.

"Indeed," he affirmed and grinned. "And the blame lies with you."

"Well, I've been blamed for a lot lately. Why not this?" She paused. "I . . . made you think of . . . marriage?"

"When you asked me to marry you up on the mountain, and then all that talk about marriage and babies and a wedding dress." He looked over at her, and dimples dented his cheeks.

"I have a dress, and I do expect to marry. If you look at the picture of my parents, you'll see Mother is wearing that dress. It's so beautiful. Simple but elegant. It's an ivory satin gown—"

"Hold it!" Tim said forcefully. "I'm beginning to picture it. Grandmother wouldn't like that."

Julie laughed. "Yes, bad luck."

"That's superstition, or just a bit of fun," Tim said, seriously. "Luck doesn't have anything to do with having a good marriage. I think it's putting God first, along with the blessing of—of—being in love."

Uncertain of how to proceed, Tim stood, reached for her hand. "Let's walk down by the creek." After she stood, he didn't let go of her hand. It felt warm, soft, and perfect in his larger, rougher one.

She didn't seem to mind as they walked along the side of the tumbling creek, high from recent rains. "I don't think of you as a sister," he said.

She didn't seem to mind that either. She looked up at him. "I don't think of you as a brother either."

"A preacher?"

She shook her head while still looking into his eyes. "A man."

He liked that. And then she said, "While we're talking about marriage . . ."

Were they?

"When I asked my mother how she could love Russell Cutler if she had loved my dad, she said there are different kinds, and the heart has room for many loves. When I wanted my life to change I thought James and I could have a good life together. We like and respect each other. But. . ."

"But?" Tim prompted.

"I don't want to start my married life as if I'm settling for someone or something. I want what my mother and dad had.

I want that spark of something like they had, that special love."

"Really?" He stopped walking and faced her. "How do you know about such things?"

She looked down. "Well, I watched them. And I- I've heard . . ."

He lifted her chin with a finger, and his voice softened. "Like the love I have for you?"

"What?" She couldn't have heard him right.

But he was silhouetted against a background of stars in a deep blue sky, and yet something in his eyes seemed even brighter.

"I love you, Julie. I tried not to, but I began to love you the moment I saw you."

"At first sight?" her heart sped up.

"I'm not sure it was love, but it was a fascination, an enchantment. As if . . . you were meant for me. At the same time I told myself you couldn't be."

"Well, I am," she said.

"Okay," he said. "If you insist."

"I do."

He held up his hand. "Not yet. A man wants to hear that after he proposes, when the time is right." He looked up at the limbs of a nearby tree. "Ryan talked about foreshadowing," Tim said. "I like to think that the day you fell from a tree limb into my arms was a foreshadowing of what was to come."

"Oh, now I have to climb trees?"

"No, you have to come into my arms." The cherished look in her eyes sent his heart stampeding like a runaway horse. "That's where you belong. For a lifetime."

"I like that," she said, finding the air hard to breathe, moving closer when his arms opened, and then closed around her. Looking up at him she said, "In fact, I love the idea. Even more, I love you."

She felt his warm breath on her lips and then the gentle brushing and then the taste of them. Yes, this is where she belonged. In the heart, and arms, of her beloved cowboy.

The End

If you'd like to connect with Yvonne Lehman
you may join her Facebook page
www.facebook.com/yvonne.lehman.3

THE HAND-ME-DOWN HUSBAND

BY VICKIE McDONOUGH

CHAPTER ONE

Silver Springs, Texas
June 1885

ELLEN STEWART'S PULSE SOARED AS SHE stepped off the train and onto the platform of the Silver Springs depot. A breeze only slightly cooler than the stuffiness of the railcar tugged at her skirts. She searched the crowd for her brother-in-law, Lance Garrett. Although she dreaded seeing him again, she was dying to meet her one-year-old niece Tessa for the first time. If only Isabelle were here too.

Ellen stiffened her spine as she moved out of the way of the other debarking passengers. Lance wouldn't be happy when he learned the reason she'd agreed to come to Silver Springs, but she was determined to do what was best for her sister's daughter—and that certainly didn't include being raised in the tiny Texas town. A squeal from a woman who'd been on the train snagged Ellen's attention. The woman hurried forward then hugged a man and woman on the platform. Four other people ambled toward the baggage car, while an elderly couple waited to board.

The wailing of a child drew her gaze to the stairs. Lance rushed up then with Tessa in one arm. He quickly scanned the depot. Tessa's face was red, and her sobs cut Ellen's heart to the quick. She forced a smile and lifted a hand, afraid Lance wouldn't remember what she looked like. The tall cowboy wearing boots, denim pants, a blue plaid shirt, and a black hat caught her gaze. He nodded and headed toward her, his lips pursed tight. He patted his daughter's back, then placed a soft kiss on her temple.

Ellen paused at the intimate action. From the letters Lance had sent her, she'd gotten the impression that Tessa was a nuisance to him. But that gentle kiss indicated otherwise.

"Sorry I'm late. Tessa picked a lousy time to fill her diaper."

Ellen's cheeks flamed at the crude comment. "Think nothing of it. I just arrived."

He glanced past her to the train. "I need to get your luggage. Would you mind holding Tessa for a few minutes?"

"I would love to—if she'll let me." She realized the little girl had stopped crying and was staring at her with watery eyes.

Lance looked at her for a long moment then cleared his throat and glanced away. The aroma of cows and leather wafted off him, and a frazzled sadness distorted his handsome face. "I suspect you look enough like her ma that she will."

Ellen glanced down at her niece, her cheeks warm from locking eyes with her brother-in-law. His comment about her looking like Issie had stunned her. "Afternoon, Tessa. I'm your aunt Ellen." She patted her gloves together then held out her hands. "Would you let me hold you?"

Lance rolled his eyes and shook his head. "This isn't a business meetin'." He passed the girl to her a bit roughly and headed across the platform toward the baggage car.

Ellen juggled Tessa to get a better grip on the little girl then walked over to the bench situated along the office wall and sat down. She wrestled her handbag out from under her niece. Tessa puckered up and looked in the direction her father had gone.

Scrambling for something to say, Ellen stammered, "Uh . . . I'm . . . your mother's sister, Aunt Ellen. I live in St. Louis, and your mama was my little sister. She was three years younger than me." She relaxed a bit as Tessa looked at her. Ellen smiled. "Your mama was an ornery little girl. She never wanted to do what she was told and much preferred causing trouble, but I loved her dearly."

Several minutes later, Tessa jumped when the train whistle blew and the engine started forward. Ellen gently patted her niece's back to reassure her as the noisy train departed the depot. She already missed home. She didn't intend to stay in Silver Springs long—only until she found a way to convince Lance that Tessa was better off in St. Louis with her, where she would be raised properly. Tessa would attend the best schools the town had to offer, as had Ellen and Issie. And life was safer in St. Louis. Isabelle would still be alive if she had stayed there.

Unlike Silver Springs, the big town was rarely hit by tornadoes. The last one had been in 1872, and it had been small. She cast a glance at the cloudless blue sky, thanking God for the pretty day. *Please, Heavenly Father, let me take care of my business and get back home before another bad storm hits this part of the country.*

Tessa pointed toward the train, now a black spot on the horizon, and jabbered a string of unintelligible words, making Ellen smile. The girl had her mother's blue eyes but her father's dark hair—a lovely combination. Something in the way Tessa frowned made Ellen remember her sister.

Issie had returned home from a visit to their aunt in Fort Worth full of stories about the handsome cowboy who'd won her heart. Several months later, Lance came to the house for dinner—slicked up, but still an awkward cowboy. He'd talked about his ranch in Silver Springs, his plan to raise cattle, and that he wanted to marry Issie. But when her father staunchly refused to give his blessing to their marriage, Lance stalked out of the house, while Issie had run upstairs crying.

The next morning, when Issie didn't come down for breakfast, Father sent Ellen to check on her. She would never forget seeing the disheveled room, with clothing on the bed, chair, and floor, and later, her father's wrath at the telegram they received telling them that Issie had eloped with her cowboy.

"Your mama was a stubborn lady."

She gazed across the empty depot, feeling abandoned. Where was Lance? Surely he wouldn't give her Tessa and then leave. She'd prepared herself for a fight—prayed God would give her the gumption needed. Lance had sounded despondent in the three letters he'd sent, which said he couldn't care for Tessa and the ranch. He needed her help. So she had come—for Tessa's sake.

Her niece started fidgeting. Ellen didn't know what to do. She had never taken care of a young child. She had been only four when Issie was Tessa's age. She bounced the little girl on her knee, hoping to distract her from whatever was upsetting her. "What's the matter, sweetie?"

The girl gazed up at her with an odd expression. Did she remind Tessa of her mother? Lance had said Ellen resembled her sister, but Issie had golden hair that gleamed in the sunlight like their mother's gold and diamond wedding ring, while her own hair was more brown than blond. Issie had a lively, bubbly personality, while hers was quieter. Ellen liked to think things through rather than jumping right into the fire and later being sorry that she'd gotten scorched.

She brushed a wisp of Tessa's silky hair out of her face. She leaned over and kissed her niece's head, feeling a motherly sensation she'd never before experienced. "Don't you worry, sweetheart. I'll find a way to get you out of this puny town. You'll love living in St. Louis."

A strangled sound drew Ellen's gaze to her left, and her heart jolted. Lance stood three feet away with a fierce scowl on his face. "Tessa isn't going anywhere except back to the ranch."

Lance tugged his daughter from Ellen's arms and stalked across the platform to the stairs. He should have known the prissy socialite wouldn't have come to Silver Springs simply because he needed help. She had her own agenda. But if she thought he would give up his daughter, she was sorely mistaken. He stomped down the steps. Tessa was all he had left of Issie—all that had kept him from going crazy these past months.

He couldn't deny he needed help, but he would never allow someone else to raise his daughter. Writing to Ellen had been a huge mistake. He offered a hand and helped her into the wagon, even though a part of him ached to leave her at the depot. For only the second time in his life, he somewhat regretted being a gentleman.

Issie's sister glanced at him with a mix of regret and wariness. Aboard the wagon, she fussed with her skirts while he double-checked the harness. She finally sat when he did with Tessa on his lap, looking as uncomfortable as if she'd flopped down atop a porcupine.

The two sisters were as different as a beautiful indigo bunting and a woodpecker. Issie had been lovely with her golden hair and stunning blue eyes, but it had been her lively personality that had stolen his heart. Her meals might have bordered on the line of barely edible, but she could always make him smile, no matter how hard his day had been. He missed her so much that there'd been times he'd wondered how he'd make it. If not for God and Tessa, he wasn't sure he would have.

Lance slapped the reins against the horses' backs. The wagon rolled forward. He gritted his teeth, thinking again what Ellen had said about Tessa living in St. Louis. In the dark of night, there'd been a time or two when he wondered if Tessa would be better off in St. Louis. There were so many dangers on a ranch, especially for a child. But he couldn't stand the thought of her so far away—that she might forget what he looked like or how much he loved her.

Tessa reached for the reins. "Wait till we clear town, sweetheart."

She looked up and let out a string of jabber. He'd sure be glad when her words made sense. Using his sleeve, he wiped drool from her chin. Tessa leaned back against his stomach, and he bent down, kissing the top of her head. He never knew a man could love a child so much until his little sidekick had come along.

He flicked a glance at Issie's sister. She sat stiff and proper, gazing at the town. Had she honestly thought she could wrangle Tessa from him? Was that her sole purpose in coming to stay at the ranch?

He supposed it was a good thing that he'd learned of her plan early on. Fighting an enemy you knew was much easier than fighting an unseen one. He blew out a sigh as he reined the horses around the corner onto Second Street. Ellen wasn't the enemy. She was concerned for Tessa, but in a different way than him.

"Silver Springs is bigger than I thought."

Lance looked around the town, surprised at Ellen's comment. "I imagined it would look small to you after you've lived in such a large town."

"It is tiny compared to St. Louis, but after what Issie said in her letters, I thought it would be much smaller. She mentioned that there weren't many places to shop, but we've passed several stores already, and we're not even to the end of town."

Lance's heart bucked. Issie had never voiced to him that she thought Silver Springs was inadequate. It was true that she'd had Ellen send her several dresses and a number of fripperies from her former home, but he hadn't thought much about it. Women needed fancy things to make them happy.

He pursed his lips. Ellen hadn't been here fifteen minutes, and he was already doubting his wife's happiness. His memories were all he had left of Issie, and he wasn't about to let her sister muddy them.

He flicked the reins, signaling the horses to pick up their gait as he drove out of town. He needed to get Ellen settled at the ranch then decide how to tell her that he'd changed his mind about her staying. In three days, there was a train headed east, and he meant for his sister-in-law to be on it.

CHAPTER TWO

ELLEN OPENED THE FRONT DOOR OF Lance's house and stared at the big barn that looked almost black against the setting sun. The sky was a riot of orange, pink, and yellow, creating a beautiful scene she seldom got to witness at home with the big houses and buildings blocking her view. She looked at the barn again. She'd been at Lance's home for over three hours now and he'd yet to return. Were he and Tessa still out there, or had he taken his daughter riding? If he had, surely they'd be back by now.

An odd noise to her left made her jump. She slammed the door, and stood there trying to listen over the pounding of the pulse in her ears. Everything here was so foreign to her. She wasn't used to wide, open spaces. In fact, on the ride from town, she had felt oddly exposed with no buildings to block the sun or stop the wind. How had Issie adjusted to such a drastic change? Had love been enough that the rest hadn't mattered?

Lance was certainly handsome—in a rugged manner, but what else had drawn Issie to him? Maybe she could find out while she was here. But then, he hadn't exactly spent any time with her. After dumping her baggage in Tessa's room, he'd mumbled something about her needing to rest after the long train ride, and he'd snatched his daughter off the floor and stormed out of the house. She hadn't seen him since.

If only he hadn't overheard her comment at the depot. The last thing she needed was to start off on the wrong foot if she hoped to get him to see her side of the picture.

She pushed away from the door and walked around the empty house. It felt tiny compared to the large home she'd been raised in, but it wasn't any smaller than most of the ones she had seen in town. She lit another lantern then checked the cornbread she'd made to go along with the pot of stew Lance had left simmering on the stove. Maybe the peach pie she had baked after her short nap would soften his disposition toward her.

She ambled around the parlor, looking at how Issie had made the rustic house a home. She straightened a doily she remembered her sister making when she was fourteen. The blue eight-pointed star design was less than perfect with its puckers and crooked stitches, but all of Issie's creations had been like that. Her sister much preferred finishing a task and moving on to something more fun than perfecting the craft. But now that Issie was gone, Ellen cherished the imperfections that were her sister's signature.

Footsteps sounded on the porch, and Ellen jumped. She rushed back into the kitchen, feeling guilty for being in the house, even though she'd been invited.

The door opened, and Lance stepped in. He paused in the doorway, sniffing the air. Tessa, with one arm wrapped around her father's neck, stared at Ellen. Lance shut the door. "What smells so good?"

"Just a little something I made."

Tessa reached for her father's hat. He tugged it off and placed it on a peg behind the front door. "I guess you found the stew. I hope you didn't wait on us to eat."

Ellen gripped the back of the chair. "Of course I waited. It would have been highly rude of me to have helped myself to your food when you were not here."

He shook his head, as if the subject wasn't worth discussing, then carried Tessa to the table and set her in the highchair. In the corner of the kitchen, he poured fresh water from the pitcher into a bowl then washed his hands and face. After he dried himself, he dipped a corner of the towel into the water, crossed the room, and wiped off Tessa's hands.

She banged on the table. "Ee! Ee!"

Ellen smiled. "It looks like someone is hungry. Shall I dish up some stew for her?"

"Thank you, but I'll do it. You don't know what she likes."

He was right, of course, but she was only trying to help. Wasn't that why he asked her to come? She turned her back on him, grabbed a towel, and removed the cornbread from the oven. When she set it on the table, she saw him glance at it.

His eyebrows lifted as if something about her cornbread surprised him. Did he think she couldn't cook?

She dished up her own bowl of stew then took her seat, waiting for him to get his food and Tessa's. Issie hadn't been much of a cook when she lived in St. Louis, but Ellen thought she had probably improved after getting married. At least she hoped for Lance's sake her sister had. She remembered the last batch of bread Issie had made. It had been shaped like two croquet balls stuck together, and it had been about half the size it should have been after rising.

After baking, the outside had been as hard as sour dough crust, but the inside was gooey. She and Issie had a good laugh over it once her sister had gotten over feeling like a failure. The neighbor's dog hadn't seemed to mind it though.

Lance sat down, staring at her, and she realized she was smiling. He cleared his throat. "I usually offer thanks for the meal."

She nodded and bowed her head. It must feel odd to him that she was sitting at his table instead of Issie.

He mumbled a quick blessing then started smashing the potatoes and carrots in Tessa's bowl with his fork. Tessa squealed, and Lance passed a chunk of cornbread to her. She shoved a big bite into her mouth.

Ellen loved watching her niece. When the little imp grinned, a dimple flashed in her left cheek. Tessa held out a handful of mushy cornbread and mumbled something.

"I think she likes it. Good cornbread." Lance flicked a glance at her for half a second then refocused on his food.

"Um. . . thank you." She wasn't quite sure what to do with the compliment. She certainly hadn't expected it. But then the man had probably been living on his own cooking, although the stew wasn't bad. It could use some seasoning, but the meat was fresh and the vegetables soft.

She wished she knew how to talk to Lance. Being alone with a man without her father's presence felt odd. Her brother-in-law was a stranger to her. All she knew about him was what Issie had gushed in her letters. He was an excellent horseman and shot a gun well—even taught Issie how to handle a gun. Ellen remembered how her cheeks had warmed as she had read Issie's second letter, which talked about how her sister loved cuddling in bed with her husband. Even now, Ellen felt certain her face was red. She hoped in the flickering lantern light that Lance wouldn't notice.

He spooned small bits of carrots and potatoes into Tessa's mouth as soon as she opened it. No wonder he wolfed down his own food so fast. She searched her mind for something to talk about. "I was surprised to see that your house had been repaired already."

He looked at her. "It's been four months since the tornado. Tessa needed a place to live. The barn is no place for a little girl to sleep, and town was too far away to stay there."

"Of course." Ellen stared at her lap. She wished that she and her father hadn't been overseas when Issie had been killed in that dreadful storm. If they'd been home, at least they could have arrived in time to attend Issie's funeral and help with Tessa, but since Father had business to tend to, he'd chosen to continue his journey. It seemed that once Isabelle had gone against his wishes and had run away and married Lance, she no longer mattered to him. That broke Ellen's heart.

She stirred her stew, remembering her surprise at discovering Lance's letters waiting when she and father returned home last week. After reading them, she made arrangements to travel to Silver Springs as soon as she could, but her father made it clear he had no intention of going with her.

Lance cleared his throat. "My neighbors helped with the house. My house took the brunt of the storm, and they all pitched in to get it repaired." He ran his finger along a scratch in the table, as if remembering that awful time. "If Issie had stayed in the storm cellar with Tessa instead of going out to hunt for her dog, she'd still be alive." He shook his head then glanced up with pain-filled eyes. "She was nearly dead when I found her, and all she was worried about was Tessa and that stupid mutt." His shoulders hunched as he exhaled a loud breath. "Issie died about thirty minutes later."

Her sister had left her baby alone during the storm to go look for a dog? Issie had always wanted a puppy, but Father had forbidden it. He didn't want any animals in the house. Still, it was hard to believe she left her baby in a dark cellar alone to chase after a dog. "I'm sorry."

He shrugged. "Nothing to be done about it now."

"What happened to the dog?" She regretted asking as soon as the words left her mouth.

He frowned and pursed his lips together. "I found him

under the front porch—which survived the storm—perfectly fine."

But Issie wasn't. Ellen shifted in her chair, feeling like an unwanted intruder. "I made a peach pie. Would you care for a slice?"

He pushed away from the table, refilled his bowl, then stood at the stove and shoveled the food into his mouth. "Maybe after I get Tessa in bed."

Ellen stifled the sigh that begged for release and carried her bowl and saucer to the counter. "I don't mind putting Tessa to bed, if it's all right with you."

He shook his head. "I'll do it." He set his bowl on the counter with a loud thump, untied the towel that hung around Tessa's neck and wiped off her face and hands. "I moved Tessa's bed to my room, so I can tend her if she wakes during the night."

Ellen thunked the cornbread pan on the counter a bit harder than she should have. Why had the man asked her here if he insisted on doing everything? She rolled her head around, releasing the tension in her shoulders. It shouldn't surprise her that he'd want to care for his daughter after overhearing what she had said. She glanced at the dirty dishes. At least she could wash them while he took care of Tessa.

The situation had completely disarmed her. At home, she was the lady of the house. She planned the meals, oversaw the cooks, and even helped prepare the food because she enjoyed doing so. Here, she didn't know what to do. She and Lance definitely needed to have a talk. She was more than willing to help with Tessa—if he'd give her the chance.

Lance sat in the rocking chair he'd pulled into his bedroom, patting Tessa's back. The poor thing was exhausted from getting a shorter nap than usual on the ride from town and then being hauled around with him all day. He should have left her with Ellen, but after overhearing her plans to snatch his daughter, he didn't dare.

Tessa's body grew heavier as her breathing deepened.

After several minutes of holding her close, he rose and placed her in her bed. Having it and the rocker in here made the room crowded, but he didn't dare go into Tessa's room to tend her in the middle of the night with Issie's sister sleeping there. Tessa let out a screech but didn't try to get up. He patted her back until she relaxed again.

He wished he could crawl in his own bed—that in the morning he'd awaken and find Ellen's visit had only been a bad dream—but she was waiting on him. And she did have pie. His traitorous mouth watered at the thought. Issie had never made a pie that wasn't burnt to a crisp or had some other problem. He doubted her sister's would be any better. After covering Tessa, he quietly left the room, leaving the door partially open.

He took a deep breath then walked back into the kitchen, surprised to find it spotless. Ellen sat on the parlor settee, stitching on a picture. He strode in and dropped onto his chair, which resided next to the fireplace, then his gaze landed on the two slices of pie and cups of coffee on the table in front of the settee. The crust wasn't the least bit burnt, and fat, juicy pieces of peach beckoned him. He sat back, not wanting to look too eager. He hadn't had a piece of pie since right after Issie's funeral when his neighbors loaded him up with food.

Ellen set her sewing aside and looked at him. "I'm terribly sorry you heard what I said to Tessa. While I do believe my niece would have a better life in St. Louis, I want to assure you that I'd never take her anywhere without your permission."

He stared at her, taken off guard by her declaration. "I'm glad to hear that. But I disagree that her life would be better somewhere else."

"Neither of us is likely to budge on our feelings about that, so why don't we avoid discussing it? For now, anyway."

He nodded. "Agreed."

She cupped her hands together for a moment, then scratched her neck and clasped her fingertips. Maybe she wasn't as confident as she appeared. "I truly would like to be of help to you, but in order to do so, you'll have to get comfortable with leaving Tessa with me. What can I do to ease your concerns?"

Lance appreciated her straightforwardness. Issie always flirted and beat around the bush whenever she wanted something. "Your assurance that you won't kidnap my daughter goes a long way in helping with that."

She sucked in a sharp breath. "I'd never do that. Besides, what good would it do? You know where I live, and I have no doubt you'd race there immediately."

She pegged him right. Of course, she could take Tessa somewhere else, but he didn't think she would do that. He bent down, picked up the coffee, and sipped the warm brew. An unusual taste teased his mouth. "What did you put in this?"

Her cheeks darkened. "A pinch of cinnamon and nutmeg. I never could stomach the taste of coffee without it. I must have accidentally mixed up our cups."

"I kind of like it." He took another sip. The spice did ease the bitterness.

"I hope you like the pie. Issie mentioned in her letters that peach was one of your favorites, so when I found a bowl of fresh peaches in the cellar . . ." She shrugged. "I sure hope you don't mind me using most of them."

"Not when you baked a pie. And besides, there's a peach tree out back that's still covered in fruit." Feeling more relaxed than when he first came in, he decided to give it a try. He set the coffee cup down and picked up the plate. As far as he could tell by looking at the fat slice, it was perfect—golden brown crust and juicy insides. He slipped a bite into his mouth, closing his eyes as his senses exploded with delicious flavor. Sweet, tangy, and spicy. He opened his eyes to see a worried expression on Ellen's face. "This is amazing."

She smiled, revealing twin dimples. "I'm so glad you like it. Father never approved of me helping in the kitchen, but I love to cook."

"So you did anyway?"

She nodded.

Kind of like how Issie had run off and married him in spite of her father forbidding it. A small part of him wished she hadn't, because then she'd still be alive. But his life wouldn't have been as rich, even though their time together was short, and he wouldn't have Tessa if she hadn't.

"Could we discuss how I can best help you?"

Baking more pies was the first thought to pop into his mind. He sobered, fighting back a grin. "I have two hired hands who stay out with the cattle most of the time. I work in the barn quite a bit and check on the herd—mend fences, repair things. When I'm in the barn, I put Tessa in a pen I built for that purpose, but she gets fussy after a while. She enjoys riding herd with me, but if I need to tend the livestock, I can't very easily. And then there's the issue of our meals. By the time I get home in the evenings, Tessa thinks she's starving to death, and she's not very patient while I scrounge up something." He inhaled, thinking that was the longest speech he'd made in months.

"So you mainly need me to cook and care for Tessa."

He nodded. "And do some laundry."

Ellen wrinkled her nose. "I learned how to cook, but laundry didn't have the same attraction. I'm afraid I don't have the least idea how to go about that task."

He resisted shaking his head. Wealthy people ought to do better by their children. They think learning French and how to sing or play the piano is more important than learning how to care for a person's belongings. "I can teach you how. Tessa's diapers have to be washed twice a week, so you'll need to learn."

She squeezed her hands together. "All right."

He expected a refusal—not her quiet submissiveness. Issie would have pitched a fit if he'd told her she had to do something she didn't want to do. His wife was spoiled, no doubt about it, but he'd loved her dearly. His throat tightened, and he pushed up. "I should let you get to bed. Morning comes early around here."

She gathered the dirty dishes and placed them in the washbasin. "I imagine you do start earlier than what I'm used to."

"Sunrise."

Her eyes widened. "That early?"

"Yep. Good night." He spun and rushed out of the room before he helped himself to another slice of her delicious pie. He sure hoped her cooking was as good as her baking. Maybe things would work better than he'd first thought.

CHAPTER THREE

ELLEN HUNG THE LAST OF THE clean diapers on the clothesline and stood back to admire her handiwork. They fluttered and snapped in the wind, reminding her of the flags on tall poles in St. Louis. This second washing had gone much better than the first one on Monday. Sweat trickled down her bodice and her neck, and her skirt was damp from when she splashed water out of the big pot. She pressed her fist against the ache in her back, very glad that Lance only had one child wearing diapers. How did women manage with several little ones in diapers?

She turned and walked past the wash and rinse kettles, glad Lance had said he would tend to them. A nap sounded wonderful, but she expected to find Tessa awake when she checked on her. She tiptoed through the house and to the door of Lance's bedroom. She still wasn't comfortable entering his private domain, but there was no way around it. When she found Tessa still napping, she sighed. Maybe she could rest for a few minutes. Until she came here, she hadn't realized how spoiled she was. Servants took away her dirty clothing each evening, and a few days later, the clean items would magically reappear in her wardrobe or dresser drawers.

Ellen stepped on a squeaky board and froze, glancing at Tessa's bed. She held her breath and tiptoed over to the rocking chair and quietly sat. Exhaustion made her limbs feel as limp as damp hair ribbons, and she still had supper to make, laundry to fold and put away, and a baby to watch all afternoon and then bathe before her evening bedtime. Not to mention being around Lance and trying to converse with the quiet man. At times, he seemed to resent her being in his house, but other times, he was extremely grateful.

Leaning her head against the back of the chair, she contemplated what she'd be doing now if she were in St. Louis—probably reading, stitching, or visiting a museum or exhibition with several of her friends. They'd thought her completely irrational for coming to the wilds of Texas to care for her sister's baby. Penelope thought she should hire a nanny for Tessa, while Marilyn insisted she should bring her niece to her home and let the servants care for her. Cecelia said it really was none of Ellen's business since the child's father was responsible for her.

Ellen yawned. They didn't understand the compelling desire she had to help Issie's family. Not just Tessa, but Lance, too. All three of her best friends had been the only child born to their family and were somewhat spoiled. She hadn't thought she fit the same mold until she'd come here and learned what hard work was.

She yawned again, her body relaxing in the comfortable chair. In all truth, she should be starting supper, but she couldn't bring herself to get up. Her eyelids drooped. She was so tired.

Lance finished grooming the gray mare he'd been training and put his tools away. As he exited the barn, he noticed the lines of clean diapers flapping in the warm afternoon breeze. Though the task of washing and rinsing had taken Ellen longer than it should have, she had finished quicker today than the first time. He reached for the wash water to dump it out, when he heard Tessa hollering for him.

Curious, he trod into the house and peeked into his room.

"Papa! Papa!" Tessa stood at the end of her bed and grinned when she saw him. She reached out her arms, and he picked her up, giving her a hug.

Where was Ellen?

Tessa pushed up and leaned over his shoulder. He turned to see what had snagged her attention, surprised to find Ellen asleep in the rocker. She must have been exhausted to not have heard Tessa's cries. He felt a bit guilty for pushing her so hard. He had hoped she'd become overly wrought with the amount of work there was to do on the ranch and would leave, but instead, she had knuckled down and completed each task, albeit some better than others. He certainly couldn't find fault with her cooking skills. Each meal had been tastier than the previous one, and he found himself looking forward to the hearty food.

Ellen's hair had come loose from her bun and rolled down her shoulder, clear to her lap. It wasn't as pretty a color as Issie's but nice in its own right. The sight of a sleeping woman in his bedroom created a longing in his chest. He missed his wife. Issie certainly hadn't been as good at household chores as Ellen. She had frequently flirted and finagled his help with the chores she didn't like, where her sister stoically pressed on by herself. Realizing he was comparing them again, he gritted his teeth and tiptoed from the room. He'd take Tessa to the barn with him so Ellen could rest. She had certainly earned it.

If only Issie and Ellen could be combined into a single woman, she'd have been close to perfect. He grinned and tickled Tessa, eliciting a giggle from her. "You may not know it, Miss Tessa, but I'm certain there's no such thing as a perfect woman." He shook his head and chuckled at the thought. After placing Tessa in the crate he'd made to keep her safe while he worked in the barn, he grabbed a pitchfork and began cleaning out the stalls.

Tessa babbled to herself, and rang the little bell he'd attached to the side of the crate. He accomplished much more when Ellen was watching his daughter, but he'd missed having his little rascal nearby. With the wheelbarrow full, he set aside the pitchfork. He bent down to grab the handles of the wheelbarrow.

"Lance! Lance!" Quick footsteps rushed toward him.

He hurried through the open barn doors, and Ellen nearly collided with him. Concerned, he grabbed hold of her shoulders. Had she had a bad dream? Had someone frightened her? He scanned the front of the house but saw no sign of anyone. "What's wrong, Ellen?"

"I c-can't find T-Tessa. I've looked everywhere. I'm so s-sorry that I fell asleep. She must have climbed out of her bed."

His heart ached that he'd frightened her so badly. He squeezed her arms. "Tessa is with me. She's fine."

She froze for a moment then looked up at him. Her eyes

were blurry with unshed tears, and her nose red. "What?"

He released her and stepped back. "Tessa woke up and was calling for me. I went in to check on her and found you asleep, so I brought her out here with me so you could rest." He stepped back and gestured toward the crate.

Ellen stared past him. Tessa stood and waved. Suddenly, Ellen punched him in the arm. "You scared fifteen years off of me. Couldn't you have left a note? I searched each room in the house. And to think how I dreaded coming out here to tell you that I lost your daughter. Do you know how horrible I felt? Oh!" Her fist connected with his upper arm a second time before she turned and marched out of the barn.

Lance watched her tramp away. He felt bad for scaring her, but he couldn't help smiling. He never dreamed Ellen had so much spunk when she was riled. She actually slugged him. He rubbed his arm and glanced at Tessa. "That aunt of yours sure is upset with me. I'll prob'ly get bread and water for supper." He chuckled as he wheeled the refuse out of the barn. Had Ellen even realized that she'd left Tessa behind?

The next day, Ellen sat beside Lance on the seat of the buckboard as it pulled into Silver Springs. The ride to town had been bumpy and had jostled her against Lance more than three dozen times—she'd stopped counting at thirty-five. Her back ached from holding Tessa. Oh . . . to have a comfortable carriage like her father's to ride in, but such a vehicle would be impractical on a ranch. She should have listened to Lance when he'd suggested laying Tessa down in the bed of the wagon. But what if she woke up and then fell out when they were facing forward?

She kissed her niece and twisted her shoulders to work out the kinks. She glanced at Lance. He'd been quiet on the ride to town. She had half a notion to return home after the way he'd scared her yesterday. She couldn't stop thinking how she felt when she'd awakened and found Tessa gone. All manner of thoughts had rushed through her mind as she searched the house. Had someone kidnapped Tessa? Had she crawled from her crib and wandered off?

Heading out to the barn to tell Lance had been the most difficult thing she had ever had to face. He'd already lost his wife, and she was going to have to tell him that his daughter was missing. She'd nearly bitten off all of her fingernails—and she normally never bit them. And all that time, the big galoot had Tessa in the barn with him.

Well . . . she had learned her lesson. She would never sleep during the day again. No matter how exhausted she was.

She peeked at Lance. He had a handsome profile—straight nose, skin darkened to a pleasing bronze by the sun, and nice lips. His dark brown hair hung down past his collar and a shadow of whiskers gave him a rugged look she found appealing. He was so different from the pale businessmen she knew in St. Louis. In fact, he was close to the opposite of her father—except for the fact he worked hard and loved his child. She turned away before he caught her staring. No wonder Isabelle had fallen so hard for him.

Father told Issie that she couldn't marry Lance, but it hadn't stopped her. Ellen tried to obey her father, but she wasn't sure what she would do if he said she couldn't marry the man she loved. Not that it had ever been a problem, since the few men she socialized with were the sons of Father's business acquaintances or men she knew from church. Boring men, for the most part.

Ellen studied the town as Lance guided the wagon along Main Street. There was no comparing Silver Springs to her hometown, but it had a charm of its own. The shops looked small, although there was a decent variety of them. She was eager to go inside several and see what they had to offer.

Lance pulled the buggy to a halt, set the brake, and climbed down. He patted the horses and talked to them as he passed in front of the buggy, then he stopped beside her. "Why don't you hand Tessa to me, then I can assist you."

She gently passed his daughter to him. "I don't need help."

His lips twitched as he stepped away. Tessa stirred and pushed at Lance's chest until he lifted her so that she could put her arm around his neck, as she liked to do. He stared at Ellen. "Have at it."

She resisted lifting her chin to the rude man who seemed to find pleasure in laughing at her difficulties. She turned away from him, adjusted her skirts, then lowered her foot, searching for the wheel hub. She found it, and slowly backed down. Her free foot tangled in her petticoats, and she struggled to get it loose as she held onto the side of the wagon's seat. Suddenly, her foot on the hub slipped. She screeched as she fell backwards, but instead of hitting the ground, she collided with a hard body. Lance's left arm held her tight against him. Would she never stop embarrassing herself in front of him?

"Easy, there. I've got you."

"I do appreciate that, but could you please release me? People are watching." As he lowered her to the ground, Tessa patted her shoulder. Ellen had no idea how Lance had caught her and still held onto his daughter, but he had. The man was certainly strong.

He stepped away when she turned to face him. "I need to go to the hardware store and order several things. I'll take my shadow with me." He smooched Tessa loudly, eliciting a giggle. "Take your time. If there's anything you need for the kitchen, put it on my tab at the General Store." He tipped his hat, started down the dirt street, then glanced over his shoulder, a twinkle in his eye. "Anything within reason."

Ellen tightened her lips as she nodded. Did he think she was a spendthrift? She turned into the nearest store—a dressmaker's shop. A bell above the door tinkled.

A woman bent over a worktable straightened and smiled. "Good morning. How may I help you?"

"I don't need anything today, but I wanted to see what type of selection you have in case I'm here longer than I first planned."

"I'm Anna May Gibbons. Please take all the time you want to look."

"My name is Ellen Stewart. I'm in town to care for my niece, Tessa Garrett. Her mother died, and her father is in need of assistance."

Miss Gibbons nodded. "It was so sad when Mrs. Garrett died. She often shopped here and was always smiling." She folded a section of fabric and laid it on a shelf with other fabrics of similar color. The whole store was a kaleidoscope of color.

"Issie liked to shop, so that doesn't surprise me. I'm impressed with your selection."

"The ladies in this county like to have a lot to choose from, not merely calico, so I try not to disappoint them."

Ellen paused in front of a shelf of lovely lavender material.

She fingered a fabric with a white background with tiny lilac flowers. It would make such a pretty dress for Tessa. The dresses she had were all getting too short. No doubt Lance had failed to notice. "I wonder . . . do you make clothing for children?"

"Certainly. I love making them. What did you have in mind?"

"My niece is in need of a couple of new dresses."

"Isn't she about a year old? I've seen her with her father when he comes to church."

Ellen wasn't used to life in a small town, where everyone knew each other, but in some ways it must be nice. In most of the stores where she shopped in St. Louis, she was a stranger to the shopkeepers and employees.

"Yes, and she's walking everywhere so we can no longer put her in long gowns during the daytime because she trips on them."

"I understand." She spun around. "I recently acquired some lovely lace that would go wonderfully with that color."

Ellen pulled the fabric from the shelf and laid it on the counter. Tessa would be a little darling in something made from it.

"Here we go." Miss Gibbons laid the lace across the fabric.

"That does look lovely. I believe I would like to have a dress made from it."

"Would it be possible to bring your niece in so I can measure her?"

What would Lance think of her buying his daughter a dress? Surely, he wouldn't be cross with her for buying Tessa a gift. "I don't know if I can bring her since she's with her father, but I'd say she's about two-and-a-half feet tall, and a bit on the pudgy side." She smiled. "Her father is a bit quick to give her a biscuit if she fusses before the meal is ready."

Miss Gibbons returned her smile. "I can fashion the garment without measuring your niece, but keep in mind that I may need to make adjustments later."

"Perfect. It may be several weeks before I get back to town though."

The woman swatted her hand in the air. "That's no problem. I'm used to that. And if for any reason you decide you don't want the dress, I can always sell it."

They talked about the style of the frock for several minutes, and then Ellen smiled at the kind woman. "Thank you so much. I can hardly wait to see the dress on Tessa."

She left the shop and ventured in a shoe store, a milliner's shop, and then she entered the General Store.

Lance looked up from the counter and smiled. He patted his vest. "Got a surprise for you."

Her heart bounced. Had he bought her a gift? Surely not. "What is it?"

He tugged a letter from his vest pocket and held it out. "Surprise!"

"From Father?"

He nodded and handed it to her then paid the clerk. Ellen hurried through the store and plopped down on the bench outside. She tore open the letter and scanned it, half afraid something bad had happened. She sucked in a sharp breath. "No."

Lance stopped beside her with Tessa in one arm and several wrapped packages in the other. "No, what?"

She looked up, certain all the blood had drained from her face. "Father wants me to come home—right away."

CHAPTER FOUR

"BUT . . ." LANCE CLOSED HIS MOUTH, A tornado of thoughts spinning through his mind. Possibly too late, he'd realized how much help Ellen had been the past week and a half. And he was more than a little perturbed that his first thought of her leaving was that he'd have to go back to eating his own cooking. He'd sorely miss her delicious meals, but he couldn't think only of himself. What if something had happened to her father? "Do you think something is wrong with him?"

Ellen stared at the letter for a moment then shook her head. "I don't think so. It basically says that he misses me and wants me to come home. Father must have written this shortly after I left to come here."

"So, he changed his mind about you being here with us. I reckon that shouldn't surprise me considerin' his reaction to my request to marry Issie." What did the man have against him? "What will you do?"

"I certainly can't decide this very minute. Besides, my belongings are at the ranch. Let's go back there—if you're finished with your business."

"I am." He assisted her into the wagon then handed Tessa to her.

"I don't understand why Father would give me permission to come and then change his mind."

Lance gathered the reins, released the brake, and clucked to the horses. The wagon lurched as the horses moved forward. "You know, Ellen, you're a grown woman and well able to make your own choices."

She looked at him, opened her mouth, then shut it and turned away. "You don't understand."

She was right. He'd been on his own since an illness took the lives of both of his parents six years ago. Keeping the ranch had been a struggle at first. He'd worked the ranch alongside his pa for years, but he'd never done the bookwork or managed the finances. Working the ranch and keeping a home without the help and knowledge of his parents had been hard, but it had made a man of him. Now, six years later, pride for his spread and all he'd accomplished made it possible to hold up his head as he walked the streets of Silver Springs.

Life for a woman must be far more difficult since there were few ways for a female to respectably earn an income. Ellen certainly had access to money because of her father's wealth, but still . . . maybe he should offer to pay her. Earning a wage helped raise a person's self-esteem. His thoughts veered back to her quiet comment about him not understanding. "Why don't you explain things so I will understand?"

Ellen leaned down and placed a kiss on Tessa's forehead. His daughter's eyes drooped then bounced open when they hit a rut in the road, only to sag again. As usual, the rocking of the wagon would soon put her to sleep.

"Issie's leaving was terribly hard on Father. He adored her. She was much more like him than I've ever been, and she experienced a closeness to him that I never have. I'm more like my mother—quieter and less vivacious than my sister."

Was that ever an understatement. Isabelle's liveliness was what first caught his attention at a social event a friend had dragged him to while on a business trip to St. Louis. Ellen was . . . calmer. His home now had a peacefulness to it that hadn't been there when Issie was alive.

"I don't think Father ever got over losing my mother. He's lonely and probably realized that the first day he came home from work and it hit him that I wasn't there."

"That may be true, but it's not fair of him to keep you chained to the house for his own benefit. You should be free to do things with your friends and attend events you enjoy—free to find love one day."

She flicked a confusing glance his way. "I am allowed to do things with my friends, mostly during the day when Father is gone."

"But what about in the evening? Don't you attend concerts or social shindigs? I know from my short time in St. Louis that there are scads of events each night."

"I can't say as I've ever attended a *shindig*, but I do attend various events when I can." A soft smile danced on her pretty lips then disappeared. "I'm choosy about the things I do later in the day. Sometimes Father escorts me."

Lance resisted snorting his derision. "Can't you see how he's controlling you? Have you never met a man you thought you might want to marry?"

She shrugged. "Men never noticed me when Issie was around. She was always the center of attention. I usually oversaw the refreshments and made sure everyone was comfortable."

He stared at the flat landscape slowly passing by. This was a glimpse into his deceased wife's life that he didn't like. Not that he was jealous of the other men, but the unfairness of it. Ellen was pretty in her own right, far more skilled at running a household than Issie, and she had a kind, gentle heart. But no man ever noticed because of Issie's beauty and sunny personality—kind of like the pretty Indian Paintbrush blossoms overlooked in a field of blue bonnets. He never thought he would feel bad for Ellen, but he did.

"I suppose Father is merely lonely. I have to admit that I don't know what to do about his letter. You definitely need my help, and I love caring for Tessa. Father doesn't need my help with the house, since the servants tend to everything."

Lance wasn't sure he should voice the thought in his head, but she needed to consider it. "Have you ever thought that your father is simply a controlling man? That kind of personality works well in business and when a man's children are young, but not so much as they grow older. I know one day, I'll have to loosen the reins on Tessa, and it won't be an easy thing to do." He had no idea how he would go about doing that. He hoped he wouldn't shoot the first young man who came calling.

Ellen remained quiet with Tessa sleeping comfortably in her arms. Without his help, the team of horses turned onto the trail leading to his ranch. He loved this time of year. The temperature was warm, but not the stifling heat of summer. White and yellow wildflowers dotted the fresh grass. The lane was shaded with new leaves from the trees overhead, creating a quaint picture, as Issie had said last year. If only he'd known then that she'd be gone so soon.

His gut clenched. He'd done his best to take care of her,

but there was no way he could have known a freak storm would take her life. If only she had stayed in the cellar . . . He glanced at the sky, thankful for the brilliant blue and lack of gray clouds.

What am I going to do if Ellen leaves, Lord? I can't take care of Tessa, fix our meals, and give the ranch the attention it needs.

He wanted to ask God to keep her here, but that wasn't fair. He knew when she agreed to come that her visit would be temporary. He shouldn't have quit his search for someone to watch his daughter. Maybe he should consider remarrying—for Tessa's sake.

Ellen glanced around the small, wooden church as she followed Lance down the aisle. A trio of six-by-three feet tall stained glass windows depicting the life of Jesus illuminated the sanctuary in colorful lighting. When she pulled her gaze away from the windows, she realized she was the focus of attention. In spite of her nervousness, she smiled at several women they passed. Some smiled warmly while several others frowned. Did those women look down on her for staying with her brother-in-law? Or was it because she was overdressed for the small church?

Feeling a bit self-conscious, she slid into the pew Lance indicated, about one-fourth of the way from the back. He sat next to her and placed his daughter on his lap. On the drive to church, he'd mentioned not wanting to sit up front in case Tessa got loud or fussy. Ellen was glad, because she didn't want to have to walk down in front of everyone. Most people had probably heard by now that she was staying with Lance, but surely some had questions, not that it was any of their concern.

The pastor entered from a door at the front of the church, and a plump woman with graying brown hair began pumping the small organ and playing a tune. The congregation rose and sang several hymns in a much livelier manner than she was used to. A few men even clapped their hands in tune with one song. Worship in her church in St. Louis was a solemn affair, and the long-winded minister's message was often boring.

The pastor introduced himself as Reverend Reginald Crowley and welcomed the visitors in the congregation. She was glad he didn't ask for them to stand. The handsome blond-haired man who looked only a few years older than she shared an inspiring message of honoring God by the way one lives life. He spoke of being honest in dealings with others, always telling the truth, and treating strangers with kindness and respect. Ellen wondered what the women who'd frowned at her thought about that.

In slightly over a half hour, the minister had completed his message. Everyone rose and sang the closing hymn. Tessa chose that moment to awaken from her nap. She rubbed her eyes and cried out, "Ee! Ee!"

Lance cupped his hand over her mouth. The couple in front of them turned, smiling. He shifted Tessa to his other arm and tickled her, probably in hopes of distracting her.

The pastor said the closing prayer, then offered everyone a blessing on their upcoming week, and dismissed the congregation. Ellen's head was full of the verses Reverend Crowley had read and his poignant sermon of admonition. She'd never heard such a heart-felt message and eagerly looked forward to next week's service.

Outside the church, people gathered in small groups while their children ran around on the outskirts of the crowd. A few families ambled toward their wagons. Two women headed in Ellen's direction. She glanced at Lance, but he was talking with a man behind her. The women's dresses were pretty and looked fairly new, but they would be considered old-fashioned among her society friends in St. Louis. Ellen felt over-dressed in her midnight blue silk gown.

The women stopped in front of her. The blonde, with sparkling brown eyes, held out her hand. "I'm Stella Dawson. I was a friend of Issie's, God rest her soul."

"A pleasure to meet you. I'm Ellen Stewart, Isabelle's older sister." She shook hands with the woman—not something she normally did as it was frowned on in polite society. She looked at the other young woman with auburn hair and hazel eyes.

"My name is Phoebe Phillips. I met your sister several times, but didn't know her as well as Stella. I'm sorry for your loss."

"Thank you."

Miss Dawson lightly touched Ellen's arm. "My mother and I offered to help care for Tessa, but since it would require her to live at our house here in town for several days at a time, Mr. Garrett declined. I suppose it would have been dreadfully difficult to return home to an empty house each day after having a loving family welcoming him previously."

Miss Phillips shook her head. "I don't know how that man managed before you came to help. I mean, how does a man run a ranch and tend a baby at the same time?"

"I'm sure it was difficult," Miss Dawson replied. "Do you plan to stay long?"

Ellen's first thought was of the telegram she'd sent Father, telling him that she wasn't ready to leave yet. Lance and Tessa needed her. "I honestly don't know."

"We'd love to have you come for tea."

"Thank you for the offer, but I sincerely doubt I could find my way to town, and I surely wouldn't attempt to drive a buggy with Tessa beside me." Not that she'd ever driven a buggy.

The blondpursed her lips. "I hadn't considered that issue."

"Why don't you two come and have tea at the ranch? I'd love to have other adults to converse with."

Miss Phillips covered her mouth and giggled. "I can imagine it must be boring talking with a baby all day—and most men aren't too chatty either."

"Indeed." Ellen glanced over her shoulder, hoping Lance wasn't listening to her conversation, but she found him near the church stairs talking with the minister. Tessa saw her and waved. She smiled and returned the gesture then turned back to the women.

Miss Dawson was staring toward the church. "That Tessa is a darling girl."

"What about Mr. Garrett?" Phoebe Phillips sighed. "He's such a handsome man—and he owns a ranch. I can't tell you how many women our age were so disappointed when he returned from a trip with a wife in tow."

"Phoebe!"

"Well, it's true."

The blonde's cheeks turned rosy. "I realize that, but it's an awful thing to say to Issie's sister."

"Oh." Phoebe blinked several times, as if not comprehending her faux pas. "My apologies, Miss Stewart."

Ellen smiled, hoping to put the pair at ease. "Please, don't be concerned about it. I completely understand." She couldn't tell them that she was also attracted to the handsome rancher. Not that anything would come of it. "As I said before, I'd love to have you come for tea. Would one o'clock on Thursday afternoon be good?"

Miss Dawson glanced at her friend then both women nodded. "That would be perfect."

"Wonderful. I'll put Tessa down for a nap so we'll have time to get to know one another without distraction."

"We'll look forward to it."

As the women walked away, Lance returned to her side. "I see you found someone to talk to." Tessa squealed and leaned toward Ellen.

She lifted her niece into her arms. "One was a friend of Issie's."

Lance stared at the retreating women. "I remember them visiting her."

"I invited them over on Thursday. I hope you don't mind. Maybe I should have asked you first."

"Of course I don't mind. You're probably goin' batty with no one but me and Tessa to talk to."

Ellen smiled as she walked toward the wagon. She hadn't missed the conversation of other women all that much. She'd been far too busy to even think about it, but she would look forward to the ladies' visit.

CHAPTER FIVE

ELLEN WONDERED HOW HER FATHER WOULD receive the telegram. She didn't want to go against his wishes, but neither was she ready to leave. Lance and Tessa needed her. And she liked it here. She felt a sense of accomplishment she'd never felt back home. It was odd that washing diapers and clothing, keeping house, and cooking three meals a day could leave her completely exhausted but quite fulfilled. Or maybe it was caring for her niece that made her feel so good. Whatever it was, she wasn't ready for it to be over.

She closed her eyes, attempting to rest in spite of the jostling from the bumpy road. Tessa would most likely awaken when they got home so this was her only chance. But her mind kept dwelling on Lance. What would he do if she returned to St. Louis?

Later that evening as she was bathing Tessa, her mind was still wrestling with her choices. Tessa squealed and slapped her hands against the water in the basin, splashing Ellen and jolting her out of her thoughts.

"Oh! You little stinker. You got me all wet."

Lance chuckled as he refilled his coffee cup.

Ellen swirled to face him. "You think that's funny?"

He pursed his lips, but amusement danced in his eyes.

"Don't bother denying it." She grabbed Tessa from the water and stalked toward Lance. His eyes widened, and he quickly set his cup on the counter. "Here. You can finish this task. I'm going to change."

As soon as she slammed her bedroom door, she regretted her actions. Tessa splashed most times during her bath, so why did it upset her tonight? She dropped onto the side of the bed, her emotions as tangled as a ball of yarn a whole litter of kittens had played with. She hated disappointing her father, but the truth was, she simply didn't want to leave. In spite of all the work, she enjoyed it here. Caring for Tessa filled a hole in her that she hadn't realized was there. And whether Lance would admit it or not, he needed her.

When was the last time she had been needed?

That was the crux of the issue—Father didn't *need* her. He just *wanted* her home, partly because he didn't like her being with the man who'd stolen his youngest daughter's heart. Did he fear the same would happen to her?

She snorted an unladylike laugh. Not hardly. Lance was still in love with Issie, and even though Ellen was attracted to the handsome man, he could never love her. Tessa was the important thing. Caring for her might be Ellen's only chance at mothering a child. She couldn't—wouldn't—give that up to entertain her father. He wouldn't be happy, but as Lance had said, she was old enough to make her own decisions.

And right now, she needed to apologize. She removed her soggy apron, glad that her dress was barely damp. She wouldn't be wearing it much longer anyway, since bedtime was approaching. Gathering her composure, she walked out of her room. The kitchen was empty, but Lance's door was open. He couldn't have gotten ready for bed yet, so he must be rocking Tessa.

She tiptoed to the doorway and peered in. His head was back against the rocker, and Tessa was hunched up against Lance's chest. One strong hand held her in place. His lips moved as if he were speaking, but she couldn't hear his smooth voice. He must be praying. Was he talking to God about her?

Moving away to give him privacy, she accidentally placed her foot on one of the squeaky boards. Lance's eyes shot open. He lifted a finger to his lips then rose and put his daughter to bed. He patted her back for a few moments then covered her and crept from the room. He motioned toward the parlor, so she headed there.

Lance stopped by the cold fireplace, resting one arm on the mantel. "Did you need something?"

Ellen struggled to find the words to say. She rarely lost her temper so apologizing wasn't something she did all that frequently. "I owe you an apology."

He blinked as if surprised. "For what?"

"I lost my temper when Tessa splashed me. I was deep in thought so her actions took me by surprise. I'm truly sorry for getting upset."

"Don't worry about it. I've done the same thing before when I've been overly tired."

"But I'm not as tired as normal since we went to town. I have no excuse."

He took hold of her shoulders. "I disagree. You have a lot on your mind. Maybe your body isn't as tired as usual, but I reckon your emotions are stretched thin."

She stared into his warm brown eyes. "I didn't know Issie married such a wise man."

His eyes lit up as a smile tilted his lips. "Your temper tantrum was nothing compared to Issie's."

Ellen smiled. "She could pitch a royal conniption fit when she didn't get her way. I remember one time Mother told her she couldn't attend a friend's birthday party because she didn't know how to act like a lady, and Issie stomped around our large parlor throwing every pillow on the floor. Mother said her behavior simply proved she was right."

A soft smile brightened Lance's face. "I can see Issie doing that. She sure had a fiery temper, but that was what fueled her lively personality."

Ellen nodded, wishing deeply that some man would look at her with such affection. She was more than a little aware that his hands remained on her shoulders. "I suppose I should retire. Sunrise will be here before long."

Lance stared at her for a long moment, sending her insides into turmoil. "Don't sell yourself short, Ellen. You have a lot of good qualities. You're a hard worker, especially for a woman who was raised as you were, and you're very patient with Tessa—most of the time." He smiled again. "You just need a bit of self-confidence."

His compliments warmed her, but she didn't dare take hope that they meant anything to him. She shrugged. Too bad the only man to notice her good traits was the one still in love with her sister.

A knock sounded at the front door, pulling Ellen from the novel she'd been reading. She set the book on her bedside table then walked through the house. She still felt a bit guilty taking time away from the many chores to read, but it allowed her to rest and helped revive her for all she had to do the last half of the day. A nap would do more to refresh her, but she wouldn't allow herself to sleep unless Lance was home to watch Tessa, should she awaken from her daily nap.

She patted her hair and pressed down her apron. Reaching for the door latch, she wondered who had come to see Lance. She hoped she wouldn't have to entertain them until he returned from checking the herd. As the door opened, shock ran through every muscle in her body. She would recognize that scent of cologne anywhere. Gripping the edge of the door to keep from falling, she shook off her surprise. "Father! What are you—I mean, how good to see you. How did you find the ranch?"

He stepped aside, revealing a buggy and driver. Father swatted his hand in the air. "You may go now. Remember to return for me by four."

"Yes, sir. I'll be here." The man, one Ellen hadn't met, clucked to the horse, and it started forward.

She longed to call the driver back. How could she entertain her father when she had so much to do? Instead, she called up every bit of hospitality training her mother had instilled in her and smiled. "You're returning to town? Where are you staying?"

He harrumphed. "Can you believe that place they call Silver Springs doesn't have a hotel? I've never stayed in a boardinghouse in my life. It's degrading."

A tiny part of her wished she could invite him to stay with her and Lance, but another part didn't want to have to endure the tension that would surely arise once Lance returned home.

"Well, daughter, are you going to invite me in, or do I have to stand on the porch all day?"

"Oh! Of course. Please come in."

He stepped inside, removed his hat, and scanned the room, which surely looked small to him. His mouth curled up on one side. "You prefer to live here than in our fine house?"

She knew he was upset that she'd refused to return home, but she had never once considered he might come for her. "It isn't this place that keeps me here, it's the people. Or rather, my niece." Her heart jolted as she realized that wasn't completely the truth. She wasn't ready to leave Lance either. He still needed her.

"Would you prefer to sit in the parlor or at the table? I can make tea, if you'd like, and there's gingerbread left from some I made the other day."

His eyes shot to hers. "You've been cooking? Doesn't that man have the decency—or the finances—to hire someone to do that task?"

"I have never talked to Lance about his finances, so I can't answer your question. But yes, I have been cooking, and surprisingly, I enjoy it." She'd never told Father that she had asked Fiona to teach her how to cook and occasionally assisted when the woman prepared the family's meals or did the baking. It helped the hours to pass on the days she didn't leave the house. She realized she was wringing her hands together and dropped them to her side. She was rarely nervous around her father. The last time had been when she had to tell him Issie had run away. "Please, won't you have a seat?"

Grumbling something she couldn't quite hear, he stomped across the room and dropped onto the sofa. He shook his head. "I cannot comprehend how you could be happy living here."

"I'm not *living* here, Father, I'm visiting." She sat in the chair beside the couch and smiled. "Just wait until you meet your granddaughter, then you'll understand."

He stared at her for a long moment. "Perhaps, but I doubt it."

She struggled to find something to say to ease his concern. "You worked hard for what you have, Father, but so has Lance. This was his parents' home—the house he was raised in. They both died suddenly when he was seventeen, and he was left to take care of the place on his own. He works every bit as hard as you do, and he's quite proud of his ranch, so I hope you'll be polite and not say something negative about it. Did you know he owns eight thousand acres and over five hundred head of cattle?" She clenched her hands, hoping her comment wouldn't upset him.

One of his eyebrows lifted. "No, I didn't realize he had anywhere near that much. That's impressive."

"According to him, that's a small ranch in Texas."

"I've heard parts of Texas can be quite dry, so I imagine it takes more land in those places to support a herd of cattle."

She nodded. "Yes. You are correct."

He sat there, looking down while she struggled to find a safe topic to talk about. "Oh, the tea! Please excuse me while I put the kettle on the stove." She hopped up and hurried into the kitchen, glad to be away from his frown. Her hand shook as she reached for the teakettle. Would he insist she return home? Would he berate Lance for keeping her here when it had been her decision to stay longer?

She heard footsteps behind her and turned. Father surveyed the kitchen.

"Don't tell me that he doesn't have a housekeeper either. Surely you haven't been doing menial chores like the laundry and cleaning."

She held onto the oven handle behind her. "It's not so bad. In fact, I've learned to do many things I didn't know how to do. I find it rewarding."

"I work so that you don't have to."

She moved closer to him. "I know that, and I deeply appreciate the life you've given me."

"Then why do you refuse to leave here?"

"They need me. Before I came, Lance would take Tessa to the barn and put her in a crate while he worked for hours. Then, when he rode out to check on the herd, she would go with him, in all manner of weather. It was hard for him to tend the cattle or fences when Tessa was with him."

"Can't he afford to hire help?"

"He has several men who help with the ranch work."

"What about help with the house—and the child?"

"From what little he's said, I think the problem is more that there are no women available to hire than an issue of money."

"Well, he can't have another of my daughters. Just look at what happened to Issie." His expression softened, and he took her hand. "I can't lose you too."

Tears burned Ellen's eyes. This was the closest he'd ever come to expressing his feelings for her. She couldn't remember a time that he'd ever said he loved her. She swallowed the lump in her throat. Tessa yelled, and Ellen stepped back. "That would be your granddaughter. Please excuse me. I need to get her out of her bed and change her diaper."

She didn't wait for his approval but turned and fled the room. This strange awkwardness between them was something she hadn't experienced before. Was it merely because she had said no to him for the first time in her life, or did he truly fear that he might lose her to Lance? She sniffed a sarcastic laugh. That would be the day.

Tessa stood at the end of her bed nearest the door and smiled as Ellen entered. The charming imp stretched out her hands. "Up."

She picked her up and cuddled her, needing the comfort more than Tessa. Then she grabbed a fresh diaper from the stack on the dressing table and placed her on Lance's bed. She quickly changed the wet diaper and put it in the porcelain pot. Washing diapers was her least favorite chore, but it certainly was a necessary one with a youngster in the house. When she turned back to the bed, she noticed Tessa staring at the doorway. Ellen looked over her shoulder to see her father standing there, gazing at his granddaughter for the first time.

Ellen picked up Tessa and carried her to the door. "Father, this is your granddaughter, Tessalyn Elizabeth Garrett—Issie's daughter."

Tessa jabbered something and reached one hand toward her grandfather.

He stared at the little fist for a moment, then took hold of it, and shook it.

"A pleasure to meet you, Little Miss."

Ellen grinned. The teakettle chose that second to screech. She took a deep breath then pushed Tessa toward Father. "Please hold her while I see to the tea."

"No. Wait!" He took her but held her away from his body as Ellen slipped past him. "I don't know what to do with a baby."

Smiling, she hurried to the kitchen and removed the offending noisemaker from the stove. She prepared two cups of tea and set them on the table, then sliced two and a half pieces of gingerbread. Her father stood in the doorway holding Tessa in one arm. The girl reached for the chain of his pocket watch, but he gently moved her hand away.

"What do you think of her?"

He stared down at Tessa. "She looks a bit like Issie did when she was small, except her hair is darker."

"Don't you think she's a pretty girl?"

"Yes, I'd say she is."

Tessa noticed the food on the table and started bouncing.

"Ee!"

Her father's eyes widened. "What does that mean?"

"She's hungry." Ellen retrieved her niece, placed her in her highchair, and then handed her the smaller slice of gingerbread. She turned back to her father, who stood in the same spot, watching Tessa. "Please, Father, won't you sit down?"

He nodded then took the seat farthest away from Tessa, which was probably wise. The little girl still hadn't learned not to toss food.

Ellen busied herself with wiping Tessa's mouth and offering her a drink from a cup. She had little experience in preparing baby bottles so she decided teaching Tessa to drink from a cup would be an easier task. As she wiped the dribbles, she wasn't sure she'd been right. She glanced at her father, who still stared at Tessa. "Is something wrong?"

He blinked. "Uh . . . no. I suppose I've never thought much about being a grandfather, but there's no denying it now. That little girl has your mother's determined chin."

Ellen smiled and studied Tessa's face. "You know, I believe you're right. Mother would be so proud of her granddaughter."

"I am, too, I suppose, although a *grandson* would have been better." He sipped his tea then used the fork to cut off a tiny bite of gingerbread, as if he thought it would be dreadful. His eyebrows shot up. "Why . . . this is delicious. Did you actually prepare it?"

"I did."

"Well, perhaps you'll make another batch once you return home." He cut a larger slice and ate it.

Her heart leapt but then it dropped back into place. He hinted that he'd allow her to cook, but he was still insisting she return home. What was she going to do? Either choice would disappoint someone. Her appetite gone, she pushed her plate toward her father. "You're welcome to my slice. I'm still full from lunch."

"Don't mind if I do."

Ellen rose to prepare another cup of tea when she heard the front door open. She turned to see Lance walk into the room. His gaze immediately latched onto her father then he shot her a frantic look. Did he think her father had come to take her home?

CHAPTER SIX

"MR. STEWART." LANCE NODDED TO ELLEN'S father. "I'm surprised to see you here."

The man rose and locked eyes with him. Lance was a solid two inches taller and with his boots on, Mr. Stewart had to look up—a fact that Lance didn't mind one bit. He wished he could say it was a pleasure to see the man again, but he couldn't. Too many uncertainties rode on his visit—and the last time they'd met, when he asked for Issie's hand in marriage, hadn't exactly been pleasant.

"Papa!" Tessa held out a grubby paw covered in gnawed gingerbread. Lance walked over, gently took hold of her arm to keep her hand at bay, and bent to kiss her head. He straightened and glanced at Ellen. Her lips were pinched, and she wrung her hands like she had the day he picked her up from the depot. Evidently she'd been just as surprised as he at her father's visit. He pointed toward Tessa's plate. "Any more of that gingerbread left?"

Ellen smiled. "Yes. Would you like some?"

"Please. If it's not too much trouble." He pulled out a free chair and sat, then looked straight at Mr. Stewart. "What brings you all the way out here?" As if he didn't know.

The man's eyes narrowed. "I imagine you already know the answer to that."

Lance's heart pounded. What would he do if Ellen left? In the short time she had been there, they'd settled into a routine. He'd come to depend on her. How could he manage all the work he had to do each day and tend to Tessa? For half a second he toyed with the idea of letting Ellen take Tessa with her, but he couldn't do that. He needed his daughter as much as she did him.

Ellen set a cup of coffee in front of him, as well as a thick slice of her scrumptious gingerbread. He sure would miss her cooking. He glanced over his shoulder at her, and she sent him an apologetic look.

Tessa banged her spoon on the table, and Ellen hurried to her. "Are you all done?"

His daughter leaned over the side of her chair and reached toward the floor—a signal she wanted down. Ellen grabbed a washrag from the kitchen counter and wiped off Tessa's face and hands then set her down. She toddled around the table to Lance, and he lifted her onto his lap. She instantly reached for his plate, but he quickly pushed it out of reach.

"She's determined," Mr. Stewart said.

"Father thinks she has my mother's chin, and now that he's pointed it out, I agree with him."

Lance tickled Tessa's jawline. "Well, she sure doesn't have mine, but I reckon that's a good thing."

Tessa giggled and grabbed his fingers. Lance wished someone would say something. Was Ellen leaving today?

"Father doesn't plan to stay here. He has arranged for a man from town to pick him up at four to return him to the boardinghouse." She smiled, as if glad her father would be leaving soon. "Perhaps you'd like to show him some of your ranch operation?"

His gaze shot to Ellen's. The last thing he wanted was to spend time alone with her father. He longed to ask if she was leaving, but he didn't want to give Mr. Stewart the satisfaction of having won. But then again, if the man was staying in town, maybe that meant she wasn't ready to go. He sucked in a steadying breath and looked at Mr. Stewart. "Would you like a short tour of the ranch?"

Mr. Stewart pursed his lips as if it were the last thing he'd like to do, but then he nodded. "I suppose it would help kill some time."

"Do you know how to ride?" Lance held the other man's gaze.

"It's been a while, but I think I can manage to stay in the saddle."

Lance rose, taking Tessa with him. "All right then. We'll leave the house to the ladies for a while." He handed his daughter to Ellen.

She mouthed *sorry.*

He nodded. "See you two later."

He trod to the door and donned his hat then stepped out onto the porch. Mr. Stewart followed.

"My daughter says you have eight thousand acres."

"Actually, it's eight thousand, seven hundred, and fifty."

"That's a lot of land. How do you manage so much?"

"Quite a lot of it is fenced—barbed wire. That reduces the amount of men I need to hire and makes managing such a large spread doable."

"I thought you still had open range down here."

Lance stepped off the porch. "Much of Texas is still open range, but I sense the end is near. As the railroad comes to more of the smaller towns, the cattle drives will end, so fencing won't be as big an issue. Men want to protect what's theirs. By fencing our property, it keeps wild cattle and other critters from grazing our grasslands and protects our cattle from disease mavericks sometimes carry."

Mr. Stewart fell into step beside him. "I suppose that does make good business sense."

"You can take a look at the barn while I saddle a horse for you, if you'd like." Lance stepped through the bars of the corral, removed a coiled rope from a fencepost, and whistled. A trio of horses trotted toward him. He looped the rope over a black and white pinto mare that he knew would be a steady mount for an inexperienced rider then walked her out the gate.

Mr. Stewart leaned on the top rail. "That's amazing that you whistle and they all come running."

Lance slung the end of the rope around a rail. "They're probably hoping for a carrot or slice of an apple."

The man lifted one eyebrow. "You often resort to bribery?"

Lance grinned. "If it makes training them quicker and easier."

Ellen's father chuckled. He walked over and ran his hand down the side of the mare. "Looks like your horses are healthy."

Lance clenched his jaw as he continued into the barn. Did the man think he didn't know how to care for his own stock? He entered the tack room and blew out a loud breath. *Lord, You've gotta help me here. Help me to keep from gettin' angry at that man or sayin' something I'll regret later.* He tossed a bridle over one shoulder and grabbed a saddle and pad.

Twenty minutes later, they had ridden across one of the prettiest sections of his land. A large pond fed a valley filled with wildflowers. He wished he had picked this spot when his friends and neighbors had helped rebuild his home after the tornado, but it didn't make sense to relocate it here, so far from the barn.

"I can see why you like it here." Mr. Stewart's head turned as he took in the countryside. "It sure is peaceful. And the air smells fresher."

"You're right. There are too many people too close together in a big city. I like the freedom of the country—the wide, open spaces." He watched a hawk circling above in the bright blue sky. Not a single cloud could be seen anywhere.

A loud bawl yanked Lance's gaze to the far side of the large pond. He rose up in the saddle then pursed his lips. "Looks like I've got a problem. You might rather stay here."

Ellen's father shook his head. "I'll ride with you."

Lance nudged his horse forward and quickly rounded the pond. A calf stood neck deep in the water, bawling up a storm. Dismounting, Lance unhooked his rope and strode to the bank. The calf jerked and struggled in its effort to get free, then paused, nostrils and sides heaving from the exertion. Its nose dipped into the water, and the calf yanked up its head, the white of its eyes showing.

"How did that happen?" Mr. Stewart stopped beside Lance.

"It must have ventured out too far and got stuck in the mud." He looked around. "What I don't understand is where the mother is. Kind of odd that she's not nearby."

"Are you going in after it?"

Lance shook his head and uncoiled the rope. "No need, but you probably ought'a step back."

Ellen's father did as told, his thick eyebrows dipping downward, but Lance wasn't certain if he was upset at being bossed around or curious. Lance circled the rope overhead then tossed it, landing it around the calf's head on his first try. He tugged the rope gently to tighten it then locked his heels in the dirt and pulled. The calf yanked his head and fought to get loose, but Lance kept the tension tight.

"Looks like you could use some help." Mr. Stewart grabbed the end of the rope and pulled.

Working together, they soon had the quivering calf on the bank. Lance scooped some water from the pond to wash off the worst of the mud. He was thankful he couldn't see any wounds on the bull calf. It had either wandered far from its mother, which wasn't too likely, or something had happened to the cow. He scanned the landscape. Rustlers might have stolen the calf's mother, or it could have been wolves, but wolf attacks were rare in the summer. And it wouldn't make sense if they killed the mother instead of the calf. The only other thing he could think of was that the mother had abandoned it.

"What are you going to do with it?"

"If I can't find its ma, I'll have to take it home and bottle feed it."

"You'd do that? Sure seems like a lot of work."

Lance shrugged. "A calf's too valuable to lose." Especially if he'd already lost the cow.

He eyed his horse, wondering how to get the calf up on the saddle with him. Then he glanced at the man next to him, dressed in an expensive suit. "I don't reckon you could hand him up to me once I'm on my horse?"

Mr. Stewart's brown eyes widened, and he glanced down at his clothes.

"Never mind." Lance whistled, and his horse walked up to him. He hoisted up the calf and slung it over the saddle, ignoring its caterwauling. He mounted and sat behind the saddle—not his favorite way to ride, but it would do in a pinch.

Ellen's father managed to mount his horse. "I don't guess I'm dressed for cattle ranching."

Lance turned his horse toward home. He kept both hands on the calf, knowing his horse would go straight to the barn. He shook his head at Mr. Stewart's comment about his clothing. That was an understatement if he ever heard one.

That evening, Ellen stared out the front door. The brilliant pinks and oranges of the setting sun drew her attention for a moment. "Isn't that pretty?"

Ready for bed, Tessa didn't respond but laid her head on Ellen's shoulder. Lance hadn't come in for the evening, and Ellen hated putting her down without him getting to say goodnight. Was he tied up with the calf he'd rescued or avoiding her for fear she would tell him something he didn't want to hear?

"Let's go find your papa." She crossed the yard, enjoying the beautiful sunset, then walked through the open barn doors. "Anyone in here?"

Lance stood then backed out of the stall he'd been in and secured the gate. "I was about to come in."

At the sound of his voice, Tessa raised her head and held out her arms for him. He glanced down at his shirt then took his daughter.

Ellen leaned on the stall railing and looked at the small calf. "Will it be all right?"

"I think so. He was frightened being here alone, but he settled down once his belly was full."

"Did you find any signs of his mother?"

"I didn't get a chance to search all that far. I wanted to get the calf back here first and make sure he was all right. I'll take him out tomorrow and ride through the pastures where the cattle are. If his mother is there, I'll find her."

"How will you do that?"

"She'll hear his bellowing and respond."

"Why do you suppose she left him in the first place?"

"I suspect something happened to her."

Ellen looked at him. "You mean something killed her?"

He shrugged. "It's possible. But she might have had an accident and got injured or even taken by rustlers. After I check the herd that's closest to the house, I'll bring the little fellow back here if I don't find his mama, and then ride out to the south herd. I need to alert my men who are tending the herds to be extra watchful for a while."

"Where do those men stay? Do they never eat with us?"

"This time of year, they take the longhorns to a fresh pasture to graze and stay in a line shack. It's stocked with everything they need. During the winter, we keep all of the cattle closer to the house. There's a room here in the barn—" he gestured toward a closed door—"with a set of bunks where they bed down, but they usually eat with me."

"I see." She turned to face him. "It looks like Tessa has fallen asleep."

He glanced down and nodded. "Better put her in bed. I'm done here anyway." He turned down the lantern, walked with Ellen outside, and she helped him close the barn doors.

Inside the house, Ellen returned to the kitchen and poured Lance a cup of coffee and cut him a slice of apple pie. She sat down at the table, knowing he had questions. She just wasn't sure she had the answers.

Lance entered the kitchen, sat at the table, and took a long sip from his cup. "You sure do make good coffee."

She smiled. "Father couldn't stop talking about rescuing that calf. I don't believe I've ever seen him so animated."

"If he hadn't been there, I would have had to tie the rope to my horse to get that little fellow free. He was stuck real good."

"So he's all right? No injuries?"

"As far as I can tell, although he may have sore muscles for a few days from all that struggling to get free."

He looked at his pie but didn't take a bite. Instead, he pinned her with a stare. "Are you leavin'?"

She twisted her hands, then realized what she was doing, and dropped them into her lap. "I'm not ready to leave yet, but neither do I want to upset Father. My hope is that he'll grow attached to Tessa and allow me to stay to care for her."

His lips twitched. "As much as I like havin' you here, it's not fair to ask you to stay indefinitely."

"It is if I'm agreeable to the idea."

He stared at her so long, she felt butterflies in her belly. "Are you?"

"I think so. There's nothing all that much for me in St. Louis. Father doesn't need me, he merely *wants* me to be there when he comes home so he doesn't have to eat alone."

Lance stretched out his hand, touching her arm. "I'm sorry. Maybe since he's tasted some of your good cooking, he'll allow you to do more of that—whenever you return home."

She didn't want to think about that or the tingles that charged up her arm at his comforting touch. Why was she having such a reaction to him? This man still loved her sister. "I'm afraid to get hopeful. Father is used to our servants preparing the meals."

While Lance ate his pie, she wrestled with what she would do if Father demanded she return home. Even though she was old enough to make up her own mind, she didn't want to go against his wishes.

Lance rose and carried his empty plate and cup to the counter. "Why don't you go on to bed? I'll wash these. They'll only take a minute."

"Thank you." She stood, although she doubted she'd go to sleep any time soon with her mind in such a tumult. She glanced at Lance's back where he stood in front of the washbasin then headed to her room.

"Ellen."

She paused and looked back at him.

"I want you to know that I tremendously appreciate all that you've done for Tessa and me, but if you feel you need to go home, I'll understand."

Tears stung her eyes. She nodded, then hurried into her room before she started crying. There was no good choice here. Either her father would be terribly disappointed or Lance would.

What bothered her most was that she longed for Lance to ask her to stay—to tell her that he'd come to care for her as she had him.

CHAPTER SEVEN

LANCE RESTED HIS HEAD AGAINST THE cow's side to get a better grip on her udder. Milk streamed into the bucket. His trek this morning to find the orphaned calf's mother had been unsuccessful, and the lonely calf bellowed from his stall, wanting breakfast. The trio of barn cats meowed, drawing his attention. He squirted each one with a spray of milk. Their antics rarely failed to amuse him, but this morning, he could find little humor in anything. He had a feeling Ellen would yield to her father and return home with him. He couldn't see her going against her father's wishes as Issie had done.

He heaved a sigh. What was he going to do if that happened? Too bad none of the local women who lived nearby could help him. They were all busy with their own broods, or else they didn't want their older daughters working in an unmarried man's house. Maybe he should consider getting a mail-order bride? That would solve some problems but create a bunch more. Living with Issie's sister had been hard enough at first. He couldn't imagine what it would be like to wed a stranger. And he had no guarantees such a woman would be kind to Tessa.

"God, I'll be in a real bind again if Ellen goes. Sure could use some help."

The jingle of harness and a faint "Whoa" signaled Ellen's father had arrived. Lance wished he could stay in the barn—or maybe he should ride out to the line shack. If he disappeared, Ellen couldn't leave—unless she did and took Tessa with her.

He rose from the milking stool and patted the cow. As he strode toward the house, he heard raised voices. It sounded as if Mr. Stewart had laid down the law. Ellen would be leaving.

He nearly stumbled as he realized how much he'd miss her quiet ways. She brought order to his home, filled his belly with good food, and cared for his daughter as well as if she were Tessa's mother instead of her aunt. Yep, he was going to miss everything about her. And that surprised him.

He stepped inside, and the voices halted. Mr. Stewart and Ellen stood almost nose-to-nose in the parlor. Tessa sat at their feet, holding a pair of spoons and staring up with brows puckered. When she saw him, she smiled, pushed to her feet, and toddled toward him. He set the bucket on a side table and lifted up his daughter. "What's going on? I could hear you hollering outside."

Mr. Stewart glared at him. "Do you know what they're saying in town about you two?"

People were talking—about him and Ellen? "No, sir, I don't." He glanced at Ellen. Her tear-filled eyes sent a stab of pain into his gut.

"They're saying that it isn't right for you two to be living alone in the same house. My daughter's reputation is being besmirched, and I'll not stand for that." He spun toward Ellen. "Go pack your things. We're leaving today."

"Father—no!"

"Who was gossiping about us?" Lance had a pretty good idea. Probably those trouble-causing biddies—the Elgin sisters—who blathered about everyone.

Mr. Stewart deflated a tad bit. "It was two older women, and they sure weren't bothering to talk softly. Everyone near them could hear their accusations. I know they aren't true, but people in this town don't know my daughter. She's an upstanding woman and would never . . ." His face turned several shades of red. "Never mind. Go on, Ellen."

"I'm not ready to leave, Father. Tessa needs me—she needs a mother."

"*You* are not her mother."

Ellen's expression crumpled. "I know that more than anyone."

Lance curled his hand into a fist. If that man were anyone other than Ellen's father, he'd be flat on his back right now. "I'll go talk to them."

Mr. Stewart shook his head. "There's no talking to people like that. They've already made up their mind. The best solution is for Ellen to leave." He pinned Lance with a serious stare that made him want to step back. "Unless, that is, you're willing to marry my daughter to save her reputation."

"Father!"

For a moment, Lance felt as if a hangman had wrapped a noose around his neck, but then he realized the idea wasn't all that distasteful. Marrying Ellen would solve his problems as well as hers, but it would strap her to a life she'd never planned for and a lifestyle well below what she was used to. Living here had been hard on Issie, but Ellen had adapted far easier. Still, living on a ranch for a few weeks was nothing compared to a lifetime. He glanced at her. What did her frown mean? He focused on her father again. "What if I do agree to marry her? Would you allow it?"

Mr. Stewart's mouth dropped open. Evidently he'd never considered Lance might be willing. "Are you saying you would?"

Ellen stomped her foot. "What about me? Don't I have a say in this matter? It's my reputation, after all."

Lance and her father turned to face her at the same time. The fire in her face withered as they stared at her.

"Uh . . . I mean . . ."

"Sir, I think Ellen and I need some time to talk alone. Would you take Tessa?" Without waiting for an answer, he passed his daughter to her grandpa then grabbed Ellen's hand and tugged her toward the door.

"Hold on! What am I to do with her?" Mr. Stewart hollered.

Lance kept walking, almost dragging Ellen with him. He rounded the barn and didn't stop until they were on the far side of it. Finally, he halted and gazed at her wide-eyed stare. "First thing, let me apologize for the commotion those ladies stirred up. You certainly don't deserve that. I thought by asking a family member to come and help, there would be no problems with propriety." He paused and took a breath, watching various emotions flitter across her face. "This marriage idea is sudden. What do you want to do?"

She ducked her head. "I don't want to leave, but . . . I don't know if I could stand to marry you knowing you're still in love with Issie."

"Ellen," he reached out and claimed her hand. "It's true that Issie still claims a large part of my heart, but I promise I'd be good to you and would do my best to make you happy. You know I can't provide for you in the style you're used to—"

She lifted her head. "That's not important to me."

"I know, and that is one reason I find it so easy to like you. You're a good person, a hard worker, and I know you'd never mistreat Tessa. I can't think of anyone better to be her mother."

Ellen's mouth dropped open. "Do you really mean that?"

Lance nodded. "I do. I've watched you the past few weeks and have been amazed at your fortitude and determination. I think we could have a good marriage," he swallowed the lump building in his throat. He had to be fully honest with her. "You'd be losing the chance to marry for love though, and from what I've heard, that's what most women want."

Ellen walked over to the stall where the orphaned calf lay. When she first came to Texas, she had turned her nose up at the odors of hay, leather, and livestock, but she quickly grew accustomed to them. Now, they reminded her of Lance and his outdoorsy scent. Was marrying him the right choice for her? She'd given up on love a long time ago. Men only seemed to want to spend time with her because she was the daughter of a wealthy businessman. The one time she had almost become engaged, she'd overheard her would-be fiancé bragging on how she was smitten and how he'd be lining his pockets with his marriage to Stewart's ugly daughter. She gripped the rail as the awful memory brought tears to her eyes.

Pushing the disturbing thought away, she considered her options. The easiest thing in many ways would be to return to St. Louis. But if she left now, would she be free to visit Lance and Tessa in the future, or would the gossip begin anew? And how could she leave them? He might not love her, but she feared her heart would never love another man. She could no longer fault Issie for falling head over heels for Lance when *she* had done almost the same thing. He was a wonderful father, a good provider, and protective of his own. Maybe in time, God would heal his heart and allow him to love her a little. The fact that he was willing to marry her to protect her reputation made him even more appealing, but could she be truly happy if he never grew to love her?

And what of Father? She hated to think of him alone for the rest of his life. But in truth, her heart was here. No matter what happened between her and Lance, she could pour out her love on Tessa and see that her niece grew up to become a godly woman. She inhaled a steadying breath. That would be enough. She turned and offered Lance a wobbly smile. "All right. I'll marry you."

The wide grin that broke out on his face was unexpected. He strode forward and took hold of her hand. "I promise to do my best to care for you and make you happy."

Hope soared in her chest as he brushed his thumb back and forth over her hand. "That's all I ask for." She longed to ask about future children, but she didn't have the boldness. Perhaps in time, Lance would be ready for that step. She would hope and pray he would.

He leaned down, kissing her softly on the cheek. "Thank you, Ellen. I know I'm asking a lot of you, but I'm very grateful you're not leaving with your father."

"You do know he will insist we get married right away."

He gave a serious nod. "It's probably wise." He grinned again. "We'll stop those back-stabbing gossipmongers in their tracks, won't we?"

Ellen snickered at his enthusiasm. "We certainly will."

As they walked out of the barn, a buggy pulled up. The two female passengers waved.

Ellen grabbed Lance's sleeve. "I forgot this is Thursday. I invited Issie's friends over. What should I do now?"

"I reckon we should invite them to the wedding."

While Lance and Ellen's father rode to town to arrange the wedding, Stella Dawson and Phoebe Phillips eagerly jumped into action to serve as Ellen's bridesmaids.

"This is all so exciting!" Phoebe clapped her hands. "Just imagine, an impromptu wedding. Have you ever heard of such a thing?" She dropped onto the bed and fell back, her hands clasped over her heart. "How romantic."

Stella rolled her eyes. "Get up, Phoebe, and stop being so dramatic. We need to get to town or Ellen will miss her own wedding."

Phoebe sat up, blinking. "I don't see how that's possible. They can't very well have the marriage ceremony without her."

Ellen bit back a smile and gazed in the mirror. She did look somewhat pretty in the pale lavender gown—one Lance hadn't seen her in. The two women had done her hair up in a pretty style with wispy curls hanging down the front. The dark purple amethyst and diamond necklace her father had given her over three years ago on her twentieth birthday made the perfect accent. There was nothing more to be done. She could only pray Lance would be pleased with their efforts.

"I need to awaken Tessa and change her before we leave."

"I'll do that," Phoebe offered.

Ellen shook her head. "I'd better get her up, or she might be frightened. She can be a bit grumpy when she's not fully awake."

Stella pursed her lips. "Why don't you awaken her but allow one of us to change her. You certainly don't want to attend your wedding smelling unsavory."

Ellen agreed, and thankfully Tessa didn't make a fuss.

Halfway to the church, Stella stopped the buggy beside a field of wildflowers. "You stay there. We'll be right back."

Tessa whined and reached toward the women. Ellen patted her. "Shh . . . they'll only be a minute. We're going to town to find your papa."

"Pa!" Tessa squealed and bounced on her lap.

It suddenly dawned on Ellen—she would soon be Tessa's mother! Just wait until she wrote her St. Louis friends and told them all that had happened. She would certainly be the talk of the social circles for a while. Smiling, she watched her new friends gather up a huge bouquet of yellow daisies, purple coneflowers, and a white variety she didn't recognize.

Stella smiled as she returned to the wagon. "Nothing like fresh flowers for a wedding."

The wagon started rolling, teasing Ellen's senses with a floral aroma. Phoebe turned in the seat. "I read that women started carrying flowers at their weddings because the people back in the early centuries only took an annual bath—usually in June after the weather had warmed." She wrinkled her nose and bent to sniff the bouquet she held. "I can't imagine taking less than one bath a week." She shuddered.

"Phoebe!" Stella glared at the woman beside her. "What a dreadful topic of conversation, especially on Ellen's wedding day."

"Well, it's true. I read it in a book."

Stella shook her head. Ellen bit back a smile. Phoebe was unlike anyone she'd ever met. She certainly spoke whatever came to her mind.

Before Ellen was ready, they drove into town. Several people turned to stare. She glanced to the other side of the street, grateful the pedestrians there continued on their way and didn't gawk. Had word gotten out around town about the wedding? She had often dreamed of inviting her few close friends, but there hadn't been time. She highly doubted they would have journeyed all the way to Texas for the event anyway. At least her father would be walking her down the aisle. If only Issie were there. She blew a breath that lifted Tessa's fluffy hair and cuddled the child in her lap. If Issie were here, *she* wouldn't be getting married. The tumble of emotions rioting through her threatened her composure. She felt a bit like a thief, stealing her sister's husband. In a way, Lance was a hand-me-down husband. Instead of feeling worse, the thought made her smile. She was getting married.

Ellen looked up as Stella halted the buggy in front of the small church. Her heart pounded so hard, she feared it would burst from her chest. Phoebe held Tessa while Stella helped her down. The church door opened, and her father, dressed in a new black suit, stepped outside.

"I'll take Tessa inside." Phoebe smiled then headed for the door, but she paused and glanced at a woman hurrying toward them.

"Oh! Miss Stewart." Anna Mae Gibbons rushed down the boardwalk toward her, holding a small package. She stopped in front of Ellen and handed it to her. "I heard you were marrying Mr. Garrett and thought you might like for Tessa to wear the new dress—if it isn't too late. It's my wedding gift to you."

"That's so thoughtful of you." Ellen leaned forward, hugging the woman. "Would you like to attend our wedding?"

"If you don't mind. I just love them." Miss Gibbons' eyes sparkled as she shot a glance at Ellen's father then back at her. "You look lovely."

"Thank you." Ellen handed the package to Phoebe. "Would you mind changing Tessa?"

"Of course not." Phoebe looped arms with Anna Mae. "Come on. Let's go inside. You can help me since we need to hurry."

"That was a nice surprise." Stella smiled and picked up the flower bouquet from the buggy seat. "I'll wait in back for you so I can do a final straightening and make sure everything is in place before you walk down the aisle."

Tears stung Ellen's eyes. "I can't thank you both enough. You've made this day extra special, and I will always be grateful."

Her friend smiled then turned and entered the church.

Ellen's father stopped in front of her, his brows puckered.

"What's wrong? Is the minister unavailable?"

"No. It's not that." As he looked past her for a long moment, a muscle in his cheek twitched. He cleared his throat. "I fear that I forced you into this wedding. You don't have to go through with it, you know. We could leave now and go home."

She laid a hand on his forearm. "I know. But this is something I want. I'd never know a minute's peace if I left here. I'd worry myself to death over Tessa." And Lance.

His tense expression relaxed. "You're certain this is what you want? To live in this hot, dusty climate in a house that's not as nice as what our servants enjoy?"

"Father, the house is just fine. I feel this is where I belong."

"I'll miss you."

Her eyes misted again. "Perhaps you might consider moving here—or at least visiting often."

"Not if I have to stay in that dreadful boardinghouse."

She smiled. "I can ask Lance if he could build on a room for you."

"Perhaps." He rubbed his chin then cleared his throat. "I was wrong about Lance. He is a good man. Not exactly the kind of man I planned for my daughters to marry, but there's a rare quality about him that I don't often see in the circles I keep."

"It means a lot that you feel that way, Father." That was as close as he'd probably ever come to saying he was wrong to forbid Issie to marry Lance.

His gaze connected with hers as he held out his arm. "Are

you ready to get married, sweetheart?”

She nodded, her throat clogged with emotion, then she looped her arm around his. Ready or not, she was getting married.

EPILOGUE

Garrett Ranch
May 1887

"Keep your eyes closed. No peeking," Lance said.

Ellen smiled at the eagerness in her husband's voice. She tightened her grip on her nine-month-old son, lest the wiggly boy fall. She raked her mind but couldn't for the life of her figure out what Lance's surprise was. Why had he insisted on driving out to one of his pastures? Perhaps he'd planned a picnic for the sunny spring day. At least her father had agreed to keep Tessa. Their three-year-old daughter would probably have climbed out the back of the wagon by now and found a bunny—her favorite animal.

Her shoulder bumped into Lance's solid one as the buckboard hit another rut.

"Almost there, darlin'."

She smiled at the endearment. God surely had worked a miracle for them. On Christmas Eve of their first year together, Lance had confessed his love for her and then had proven it by blessing her with a son. She hoped they'd have a houseful of children, but little James was a handful, so she didn't mind if they waited a year or two for the next youngster. Time would tell.

"Whoa . . . Don't peek yet." Lance climbed down from the buggy, and she heard him stride around to her side. "Give Jimmy to me."

Keeping her eyes shut, she passed him their son.

"Do you think you can get down without looking?"

"Looking at what?"

He blew out a loud breath. "You'd better go ahead and open your eyes. I don't want you gettin' hurt, especially today."

Ellen lifted her eyelids and gasped. Her gaze shot to Lance's.

He grinned. "Surprise!"

"Whose house is that?" She gazed at the beautiful pale green two-story house that sat on a hill with a perfect view of the wide valley and pond they'd picnicked at the first summer they'd married. It was her favorite spot on the ranch.

"It's ours, darlin'."

She looked at him again. "Ours? I don't understand."

He shifted Jimmy to his other arm and held up his hand to her. "Come and have a look while I explain."

She scurried down, hiked her skirt, and all but ran to the large porch, which spanned halfway around the front of the house and curved to encompass half of the left side. A pair of rockers adorned the porch. "It has a turret! How did you know I always dreamed of living in a house with a turret?"

"Your father mentioned it." Lance brushed his hand down her cheek. "I wish I could say this was all my doing, but it's your birthday gift from your father and me." He chuckled. "Just don't expect something so grand next year."

"A woman only turns twenty-five once." She smiled. "If you never gave me anything else, this would be enough—not counting more children, of course."

The smile he gave her warmed his brown eyes and melted her insides. He tugged her close and bent down, giving her a long, slow kiss.

A sudden slap on her cheek pulled her out of the delicious embrace. She grabbed her son's hand before he could smack her again. "I think someone is envious."

Lance's eyes smoldered then he gave her a slow grin. "I'd be jealous too if anyone else kissed you like that."

"No one else ever will, dear." She patted his chest. "Now, as much as I love your kisses, I want to see my new house." She lifted her skirts and scurried up the solid steps, then spun around. "The view is stunning. I can't wait until we can move in."

Lance held the door open for her. "That might take a while. You'll have to order some furniture. There's an account set up at the mercantile—or if you'd rather, maybe we could take a trip to St. Louis to shop."

She rushed through the foyer into a large room, held out her arms and spun around, unable to hold back her excitement. "This large room will make a lovely parlor."

"You can get wallpaper, if you'd like. Decorate it however you want." His eyes gleamed. "It's been so hard to keep this a secret."

She pressed her hands to her cheeks. "I can't believe you did. How long have you been working on this?"

"Over a year."

"A year?"

"Well, your father hired a crew to do most of the work. I helped with the painting and finishing touches when I wasn't tied up with ranch duties. Do you like it?"

She walked over to him, resting her hand against his chest. "I love it. The other house was perfect, but this one gives us room to raise a family."

He kissed her again, as if pleased with her response. "There was another reason to build it."

"Oh?"

He nodded. "Your father has decided to move here and plans to renovate our old house to suit his taste."

"That's wonderful news! Although, it does surprise me. I realize he's gotten the ranching bug, but I never truly thought he'd move to Texas."

Lance took her arm and guided her into another large room. "This should probably be the dining room."

"I love the wainscoting." She ran her hand against the shiny, dark wood.

Twenty minutes later, they finished their tour and returned to the porch. Ellen leaned against the railing staring out at the lovely view. Wildflowers of all colors waved as if welcoming her to her new home.

Lance closed the door then stepped up beside her. He wrapped one arm around her and held their sleeping son in the other one. "Happy?"

"Deliriously. The house is perfect. 'Thank you' hardly seems enough."

"I have an idea how you can show your gratitude." Lance kissed her so thoroughly that she wished they'd left their son with her father. After a few long moments of pure bliss, they stood together, looking out on the valley.

Ellen had never been so happy. God had worked a

multitude of miracles in her life. Never could she have dreamed when she came to Texas, determined to rescue her niece, that God would allow her to win the heart of a cowboy.

The End

You can learn more about Vickie McDonough or sign up for her newsletter on her website:
www.vickiemcdonough.com

MBI